As we got around the corner, Kragar said, "Where to now, Vlad?"

I jumped, cursed, and said, "Back to the office. You can send the muscle home."

"All right."

"Omlo, you can break character now; we're safe."

My captor released me and said, "Yes, my lord." He handed me back my sword belt and I strapped it on.

"See there? You didn't even die."

"When they looked at me, I was sure they could see through my disguise."

"You managed it," I said. "And even if you hadn't, I had a few people there, ready to jump in." There was no reason to tell him that the people were there to keep me alive, and would probably have let him get cut to pieces.

We made it back to the office without incident, and Cawti was waiting there. I suggested everyone sit down.

"Very cute," said Kragar.

"What?"

"The stupid grin on your face when you saw your assassin."

"Her name is Cawti," I said. "And the only reason I don't kill you is that I'm going to let her have the pleasure."

"Sometime," she agreed, "when you aren't expecting it."

"Not until you're married, I hope. I wouldn't want to miss the wedding."

"Oh, of course," she said.

"Goodness, Vlad. She even has your threatening smile."

"It's an Eastern thing."

BOOKS BY STEVEN BRUST

THE DRAGAERAN NOVELS
Brokedown Palace

THE KHAAVREN ROMANCES
The Phoenix Guards
Five Hundred Years After
The Viscount of Adrilankha (which comprises
The Paths of the Dead, *The Lord of Castle Black*,
and *Sethra Lavode*)

THE VLAD TALTOS NOVELS

Jhereg	*Athyra*	*Jhegaala*
Yendi	*Orca*	*Iorich*
Teckla	*Dragon*	*Tiassa*
Taltos	*Issola*	*Hawk*
Phoenix	*Dzur*	*Vallista*

OTHER NOVELS
To Reign in Hell
The Sun, the Moon, and the Stars
Agyar
Cowboy Feng's Space Bar and Grille
Good Guys
The Gypsy (with Megan Lindholm)
Freedom and Necessity (with Emma Bull)
The Incrementalists (with Skyler White)
The Skill of Our Hands (with Skyler White)

STEVEN BRUST

TIASSA

TOR®
fantasy

A TOM DOHERTY ASSOCIATES BOOK • NEW YORK

NOTE: If you purchased this book without a cover, you should be aware that this book is stolen property. It was reported as "unsold and destroyed" to the publisher, and neither the author nor the publisher has received any payment for this "stripped book."

This is a work of fiction. All of the characters, organizations, and events portrayed in this novel are either products of the author's imagination or are used fictitiously.

TIASSA

Copyright © 2011 by Steven Brust

All rights reserved.

Edited by Teresa Nielsen Hayden

A Tor Book
Published by Tom Doherty Associates
175 Fifth Avenue
New York, NY 10010

www.tor-forge.com

Tor® is a registered trademark of Macmillan Publishing Group, LLC.

ISBN 978-0-7653-5058-9

Our books may be purchased in bulk for promotional, educational, or business use. Please contact your local bookseller or the Macmillan Corporate and Premium Sales Department at 1-800-221-7945, extension 5442, or by email at MacmillanSpecialMarkets@macmillan.com.

First Edition: April 2011
First Mass Market Edition: May 2018

Printed in the United States of America

0 9 8 7 6 5 4 3 2 1

For Reesa, with love

CONTENTS

ACKNOWLEDGMENTS

My thanks to Reesa Brown and Neil Gaiman for launching this one, and to Anne Gray for handling so many irritating details so I could work on it. Robert Sloan created much of the background of what became Dragaera, for which I am, as always, grateful. Thank you to Bethani at Twin Peaks, Round Rock, for keeping me supplied with coffee while I worked on this one. I very much appreciate the lessons in tournament poker from Adam "Hatfield13" Stemple and Chris "Pokerfox" Wallace.

Finally, in working on this one, there were three websites that were especially helpful: The Dragaera Timeline by Alexx Kay: www.panix.com/~alexx/drag time.html; and the Dragaera Wiki: http://dragaera .wikia.com/Main_Page.

My sincere thanks to everyone involved in maintaining those sites.

THE CYCLE

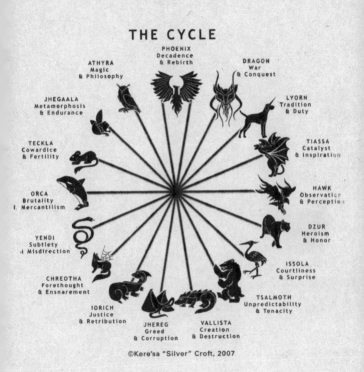

PHOENIX
Decadence
& Rebirth

ATHYRA
Magic
& Philosophy

DRAGON
War
& Conquest

JHEGAALA
Metamorphosis
& Endurance

LYORN
Tradition
& Duty

TECKLA
Cowardice
& Fertility

TIASSA
Catalyst
& Inspiration

ORCA
Brutality
& Mercantilism

HAWK
Observation
& Perception

YENDI
Subtlety
& Misdirection

DZUR
Heroism
& Honor

CHREOTHA
Forethought
& Ensnarement

ISSOLA
Courtliness
& Surprise

IORICH
Justice
& Retribution

TSALMOTH
Unpredictability
& Tenacity

JHEREG
Greed
& Corruption

VALLISTA
Creation
& Destruction

©Kere'sa "Silver" Croft, 2007

Prologue

Sethra greeted me with the words, "There's someone I'd like you to meet, Vlad." I had expected something more like, "What are you doing here?" as I'd shown up at Dzur Mountain without any advance warning. But then, if Sethra Lavode had been accustomed to doing the expected, she wouldn't have been Sethra Lavode.

I had been visiting my friend Morrolan, who had been kind enough to teleport me to Dzur Mountain, and after a long climb up a wide and tiring staircase I had found her in a library, reading a book that looked like it must have weighed ten pounds.

My familiar noticed it as well. *"It's not a book, Boss. It's a weapon. It lands on you, and that's it."*

"I think you're right."

I was torn between curiosity about this person she wanted me to meet, and the business that had brought me. She asked if I wanted wine, and I did, and her servant, a strange, twitchy old guy named Tukko, thumped a bottle and a glass down in front of a chair. I sat and drank and said, "Who?"

"An Easterner."

"From?"

"Far from here."

"All the Eastern kingdoms are—"

"Very far. He doesn't speak any language you've ever heard before."

"But you have?"

"I hadn't either, but I learned."

"How?"

"The Necromancer taught me. Once you've learned a few languages, the others come easy. I'm working on teaching him ours, but it's slow going."

"How'd you meet him?"

"The Necromancer introduced us."

"Well. Now I'm intrigued."

"You were intrigued when I didn't ask what brought you here."

"All right, now I'm more intrigued."

"What did bring you here?"

"Now that I'm out of the army, I thought we could swap war stories."

She smiled and waited.

"Okay," I said. "It's this." I opened my pouch, found the object, and held it out for her to inspect.

"My," she said. "Where did you get it?"

"That's a long story. What is it?"

"I'm not sure. It's interesting, certainly."

"Who goes first?"

"Up to you."

"This guy you want me to meet—what's the deal? He have a job for me?"

"Sort of. Not your usual kind."

"By my usual kind, I assume you refer to my perfectly legitimate herb shop?"

"Yes. Not that."

"What then?"

"He wants you to talk."

"About what?"

"Everything. Everything you do, legal and illegal."

I studied her. She looked serious. "Sethra, if I ever did something illegal—which of course I never have—why would I be so stupid as to talk about it?"

"Reason one: There is a lot of money in it. Reason two: There may, from time to time, be other things in it for you—useful trinkets. Reason three: Because I tell you, on my honor, that nothing you say will ever be heard by anyone who can do anything to you."

"How much money?"

"Five hundred imperials' worth of unminted gold for a few hours of conversation, with the option of doing it again if it works out for all concerned, and maybe several times."

"Five hundred."

"Yes."

"That's a lot. Why me?"

"He wanted me, but I won't. I suggested you instead, because you can give him what he wants."

"What does he want?"

"To understand what life is like here."

"At Dzur Mountain?"

"In the Empire."

"And I can tell him that?"

"I believe you can, yes."

"No one will hear it? On your honor?"

"Yes."

"Okay, I'll meet him, and I'll think about it."

She nodded. "Good." She held her hand out for it, and I gave her the object. She held it up and studied it carefully. It was a really remarkable thing—about the size of my palm, all of silver, except for the eyes, which appeared to be very tiny sapphires. The wings were thin, and filled with a multitude of tiny holes so the light shone through, and there were whiskers around the mouth. After a moment she pulled her eyes from it and looked back at me. "How did you say it came to you?"

"I happened to come across a recently deceased individual, and it was in a pouch at his belt."

She smiled. "No you didn't."

"Why Sethra, whatever do you mean?"

"The idea of you going through the pockets of a random corpse you stumbled over is absurd. You're trying to make me think it was someone you killed. But a Jhereg assassin never robs his victim. It's unprofessional."

"Now, how would you know that?"

"Vlad, I have been around a long, long time. So, tell me the truth. Where did you find the tiassa?"

"Is it important?"

"Yes."

"Why?"

"For reasons full of mystical significance. Now tell."

"I'd rather hear about the mystical significance."

"I'm sure you would."

"All right. You know the old market just above Northpier?"

"Very well."

"That's where I found it."

"Just lying there?"

"Not exactly."

"Well?"

"Now, about that mystical significance."

"Vlad, I was kidding about that."

"No you weren't. You had that look you have when you're telling the truth in a way you hope won't be believed."

That stopped her. "I'm impressed."

"Thank you. Now, what exactly did you mean?"

"Tell me exactly how you found it."

"It came to me in a dream."

"How very tangible it is."

"Okay, it was delivered by someone I only knew from a dream."

She tilted her head and said, "I think it might be straight answer time, don't you?" I opened my mouth, and she said, "Vlad, you know very well you never win these."

That stopped me. "You're right."

"I'm listening."

I started talking.

THE
SILVER
TIASSA

The first time I saw the tiassa was nine Real Years before I was born. Mafenyi was holding it, and it was so pretty! When I saw it again, two hundred Real Years earlier, I had to take it so I did.

I didn't think Mafenyi would mind too much. She hadn't made it to keep. She told me that she made it because she had to, but it shouldn't ever stay with anyone for too long. She used silver that came all the way from Aelma, which is a city on the Chareq River near some mountains called Daeld, which is where the silver was found in the ground.

Mafenyi said she melted the silver in a cauldron made of light, and she cut off her hand and put it in the cauldron, and plucked out one of her eyes and put that in, too, and then shaped it while it was still hotter than hot. She worked on it for years and years, so the ears would be so perfect, and you could see candlelight through the wings; she put tiny sapphires in for the eyes. I asked her how come she still had both hands and both eyes, and she said she was a Goddess and so she grew them back. She said I could be a Goddess if I wanted to be, and I said my grandmother was a Goddess and it didn't seem like much fun.

When we were done talking I went away, but then I came back. I wanted to just look at it some more, but she was sleeping, and that's when I knew I had to have it, so I took it from her shelf.

It wasn't big, but it was so heavy I had to hold it in both hands. I went back home and just held it and looked at it, but I got fingerprints on it so I cleaned it off, and then wrapped it in cloth. I kept it in the cloth after that except when I wanted to look at it.

There was a woman named Chuvin. She was an Athyra, and she was very nice. I thought she should have the tiassa, so I left it in her house, then I went off to see a new world being made, which was very exciting.

When I got back, I went to look at the silver tiassa, but Chuvin didn't have it anymore. She had made some very pretty psiprints, though, and I got to see them. She gave me one of Yevetna Falls that's so good you can almost get wet looking at it. Mommy said that first, but I think it's funny and true, so I'm saying it now. I asked Chuvin what she did with the tiassa, but she said she didn't know, it just got lost somehow.

It wasn't hard to find it, though. When you looked in what the Necromancer calls the other place, it was like a big white light, with two blinking blue thingies. I saw it right away, and followed it because I wanted to know where it was, and really I just wanted to see it again. It isn't hard to follow something in the other place, but it's hard to talk about. It's like painting when you don't have paint, or singing when there's no song, or talking when there are no words. I can't explain. Anyway, I followed it.

It was an old man who had it. He was a Lyorn and his name was Pindua. He made statues from big pieces of marble. I got to hold the tiassa for a little while, but then I left it with him. He made one called "Worill Reclining on Stairway" that they put in the Hall of Monuments in the Imperial Palace.

A little while after he made it he died and they brought him to the Paths of the Dead. He owed a lot of money when he died, and when that happens they sell all your things to try to pay the people you owe money to, so the tiassa was sold to a man named Paarfi who was a Hawk and who wrote books.

I didn't think about it for a long time, but then I remembered it one day a year later, which was almost three hundred Real Years later. I looked for it, and Paarfi still had it. I went to talk to him about it. He talked about what he was writing. He was a nice man.

I told him he should give the tiassa away, and he agreed, but said he wanted to keep it a little longer, until he finished his new book. I said that was okay, and he gave me one of his books and signed it for me. He wrote, "To Devera, a very special little girl." I took it to Grandma's and put it in the chest with my things, next to the seashell that whistles "March to the Kaanas" and the psiprint of Yevetna Falls and the tick-ticker and some other stuff I want to keep.

While I was there, Grandma asked me what I was

doing, and I said I was looking for the silver tiassa and she asked what that was so I explained where it came from. She asked some questions about it, but she had the look she gets when she's being nice and doesn't really care about what you're telling her, so pretty soon I said good-bye and ran off.

I went to a place called Tanvir where it was just spring and there were flowers in all the colors there are. After that, I went to an empty tower in a dead city and a man made of metal played music for me. After a while, I started wanting to see the tiassa again, so I went back to fifty Real Years later, and Paarfi still had it. I thought it was long enough, so I took it but left him a note, then I went to Adrilankha ten Real Years ahead and played with Vlad Norathar. I showed him how to look in the other place, and he showed me how to make a spinnystick with glitters.

Then I was tired from all the jumping around so I put my spinnystick in the chest and took a nap. Mommy says naps are good for you, but I only take them when I'm sleepy. When I woke up again I found Daddy and showed him the tiassa and he said it was very pretty. I asked if he was ever going to come visit me and Mommy and he said he would soon because he wanted his sword back. He looked angry when he said it so I didn't ask about it any more. While I was there Mafenyi came up and said I shouldn't have stolen the tiassa and had to give it back and Daddy told her not to accuse me of stealing but I said I had just borrowed it to give to some people who needed it. They started arguing with each other so I left and took the tiassa with me.

I started to Mommy's but then a while later I looked

in the other place, and saw Mafenyi was coming after me. I hadn't thought she wanted the tiassa that much. I thought about jumping, but then I could never come back to now. I didn't want to go to Grandma's, because then she would fight Mafenyi and I'd feel bad, and if I went to Mommy's I'd have to explain what I did.

So please, Uncle Vlad. She'll be here soon. Can you take it?

TAG

1

I lie sometimes, just so you know. It goes with the job.

Most of what I make comes from running untaxed gambling games of various sorts, owning unlicensed brothels of various qualities, dealing in stolen goods of various types, and offering usurious loans of various amounts. Why, you may ask, do I not pay the taxes, license the brothels, sell legitimate goods, and offer loans at legally acceptable rates? Because of customer demand, that's why. The Empire, which we all naturally love and revere and to which we pledge our undying loyalty, doesn't just tax the runner of the game, but also the customers; and the ones who win prefer not to pay those taxes. The licensing of the brothels requires intrusive observation by Imperial representatives, and customers aren't fond of that. The goods I sell are at the rates people want to pay. The loans I dispense are to those the banks laugh out of their offices.

If it weren't for the demands of the customers, I'd be legitimate; I'd much prefer it that way.

I did say I lie sometimes, didn't I?

Anyway, that's where most of what I live on comes from; most of the rest comes from killing people, which I only do occasionally. And lest you think I'm a terrible person, I assure you that everyone I've ever killed has deserved it—at least according to whoever hired me.

And then there is the in-between stuff, which I don't do much of anymore. I've heard a lot of terms for it: lepip work, enforcement, muscle, convincing—one guy I knew used to say, "I'm a musician, you see. I call myself a repercussionist." Heh. Yeah, there are all sorts of ways to not say that what you're really doing is either hurting someone, or threatening to hurt someone, to get him to do what you want. What you want is for him to go along with agreements he made knowing what was liable to happen if he didn't, so I don't generally have a lot of sympathy for the individual who may become damaged in the process. And they're always Dragaerans, whereas I'm human, so they consider themselves inherently superior to me, so I have even less sympathy than I otherwise might.

I do not consider them superior.

Bigger, stronger, they live longer, and they can do better than us at pretty much everything. I'll concede that. I won't concede superior.

Like I said, I don't do lepip work much anymore, but once in a while something will come up that will make me reconsider. On this occasion, it was a fellow named Byrna, and one named Trotter, and one named Kragar; the order depends on how you look at it.

Let me start with Kragar, who is my executive assistant, or something like that. I need to find him a title. If you ask him, he'll tell you he does all the hard work. Yeah, maybe.

On this day, when I came in to work and was having my first cup of klava (I have it in a cup because glass burns my fingers, okay?), I had a number of things I wanted to talk to him about. I'd recently been through some experiences: I'd fought a losing war against a Jhereg who was tougher than me but I ended up winning in spite of it, I'd been killed, I'd been resurrected, and I'd learned many fascinating things about the internal workings of this great Empire that we love and happily serve. So of course, I was waiting to talk to Kragar about the girl I'd met in the middle of all of it.

He never gave me the chance: he started talking before I even realized he was in the room. No, I wasn't distracted, he just does that.

"You know a guy named Trotter?"

"Sure," I said, pretending I hadn't been startled to suddenly notice him in the chair in front of my desk. "Muscle. Dependable. We've used him a couple of times."

"Yep." Kragar leaned back, stretching his legs out as if he had not a care in the world, and nothing he was about to say mattered; this was a sure sign he was going to give me news that was unfortunate, upsetting, or both, so I prepared myself.

"What is it?"

"We hired him yesterday, to have a talk with The Amazing Elusive Byrna."

Byrna was a young Jhegaala who was into me for a lot of money, and had missed several appointments to discuss his situation; I had told Kragar to find someone dependable to convince him to, if not pay his debts, at least be more reliable in meeting to talk about them. Reliability is one of the great virtues, I've always believed, and I like to encourage it in others when I can.

"Well, and?"

"He's not dead," said Kragar.

I frowned. "Trotter got out of hand? That seems—"

"I meant Trotter," said Kragar, who I have no doubt encouraged the misinterpretation just to increase the shock value. Which worked, by the way.

I sat back. "Okay, talk."

"I don't know a lot. He came stumbling through the streets bleeding from four or five places and passed out from loss of blood. He's with a physicker now."

"How does it look?"

"He'll probably live."

"So we don't know Byrna did it?"

"He was on his way there."

"Byrna isn't a fighter."

"He can hire one."

"What good would that do unless he hired him long-term?"

"Maybe he did that."

"If he could afford to hire a fighter long-term, he could pay me, so he wouldn't need to hire one."

My familiar remarked into my mind, *"Be sure to explain that to him."*

I ignored him. Kragar spread his hands and said, "You know what I know."

"Find out more," I said.

He nodded and left without making any more wisecracks. Good. I didn't need him to make any wisecracks. That's why I have a familiar.

Oh, right; you haven't actually met my familiar. Pardon my rudeness. His name is Loiosh, and he's a Jhereg. If you don't know what a Jhereg is, you're probably better off, but I can at least explain that it is a poisonous reptile with two wings, two eyes, two legs, and one form of wit: irritating. I guess he's a lot like me, except I don't have wings and I'm not a reptile. Well, maybe metaphorically. At this moment, he was sitting on my right shoulder, waiting for me to say something so he could make sarcastic comments about it.

Of course, I obliged him. I said, *"I can't believe he'd hire a free sword."*

"And of course, he can't have any friends."

"Who are good enough to paint the wall with Trotter?"

"I love it when you start theorizing before you know anything, Boss. It fills me with admiration."

I told him some things about him I admired, and he did that head-bobbing thing with his long, snakey neck that means he's laughing. Usually at me.

Of course, the alternative to bantering with my familiar was sitting there and worrying, since I had no intention of charging into anything without knowing what was going on. I'd done that before and come to the conclusion that it was a bad idea.

So I sat there and waited and exchanged more comments with Loiosh; you don't need the details. I didn't, in fact, have to wait all that long.

I have a secretary and bodyguard named Melestav. He poked his head in about an hour after Kragar left and said, "Message for you, Boss."

"From?"

"Don't know. Messenger service, paper message. Showed up, handed it over, left."

"Did you tip him?"

"Of course."

My first thought was contact poison, but that's just because I'm paranoid and had recently gone through an experience with someone who had caused me significant concern for my continued existence. But Melestav was holding it, and he wasn't showing any signs of dropping dead; and contact poison, while it does exist, is rare, tricky, and undependable. Besides, no one wanted to kill me. As far as I knew.

I took the message. The seal was a half circle with a jhegaala sinister facing a flower with three petals, and it meant Byrna. It was addressed to Vladimir of Taltos, House of the Jhereg; which isn't exactly my name, but close enough. There was a very pretty curlicue trailing off from the final symbol; it is always a pleasure to see good calligraphy. I broke the seal.

"My lord the Baronet," it read, "I am anxious to meet with you to resolve the financial matters that lie between us. I have bespoken a private room on the main floor at the Blackdove Inn, where I can be found between noon and dusk every day. I await your convenience.

"I remain, my lord,

"Your servant

"Baron Byrna of Landrok Valley."

Well, wasn't that just the honey in the klava.

"*Gee, Boss. You should head right over. It couldn't possibly be, you know, a trap or anything.*"

"*Heh,*" I said.

Melestav was still standing in my doorway, waiting to see if there was an answer. I said, "See if you can find Shoen and Sticks and have them hang around here until I need them."

"Will do," he said.

He left me alone. Loiosh didn't have anything more to say, and neither did I. I took out a dagger and started flipping it. I thought about Cawti, the girl I'd just gotten engaged to, then realized that wouldn't help the problem. Then realized that until I knew something, it wouldn't do any harm, either, so I continued. Time passed pleasantly.

Eventually some of the more mundane aspects of my job intervened, so I spent the interim saying yes, yes, no, and get me more details until Kragar said, "I've found out a few things, Vlad."

I jumped, scowled, relaxed, and said, "Let's hear it, then."

"He didn't know where the guy came from, but, yeah, Byrna has a protector."

I cursed under my breath and listened.

"Trotter found Byrna at one of his usual hangouts, went after him with a lepip, and the next thing he knew he was full of holes. He didn't get a good description of the guy, except that he wore blue."

I sighed. "All right."

"I imagine," he said, "you'll need me to go find out things I have no way of finding out, right?"

"Naw," I said. "I'll just go meet the guy."

Kragar nodded. "Smart move. I'll send flowers."

"Hmm?"

"I thought that was the Eastern custom."

"Oh, right. It is. Good. I'll be counting on it."

"Vlad—"

"I know what I'm doing, Kragar."

"Sure about that, Boss?"

"Shut up."

Kragar made a grunt, indicating he believed me about as much as Loiosh did. This is a reaction I'm used to from those who know me.

Kragar left, and Loiosh started in. Did I really know what I was doing? Did I care that I was walking into a trap? Did I this? Did I that? Blah blah blah.

"Melestav!"

He poked his head through the door.

"Message to Lord Baron Byrna of Landrok. Begins: 'I will be honored to wait upon you at the fifth hour after noon of this day. I Remain, My Lord, Sincerely' and all that. Ends. Send it to him at the Blackdove Inn."

"Will do."

"Shoen and Sticks?"

"They're both here."

I nodded. I checked the time with the Imperial Orb, and I still had several hours. Good.

I got up from the desk and strapped on my rapier, increasing the number of weapons I was carrying by an insignificant percentage, then put on my cloak, increasing that number by a much larger percentage. Concealing hardware in a big, flowing cloak is pretty easy. The hard part is keeping said hardware from clanking, and arranging it so the cloak looks and feels like it's a reasonable weight. It had taken a lot of trial and error to get there, and it still took a bit of fiddling about before it was adjusted properly on my shoulders. But eventually I got it and I walked out, telling Melestav I'd be back later.

Kragar wasn't in the room. That I noticed. The two guys I'd brought for protection were; I nodded to them, they stood up and followed. Shoen walked like he was one mass of muscle, just waiting to explode as soon as he had a direction to explode in—and that's pretty much what he was. Sticks was tall and lanky and he walked as if he were just out enjoying the ocean scent and wouldn't notice a threat if it was right in front of him. He wasn't really like that.

We went down the stairs, past the little business that gave me a nice legal cover, and out into the street. Sticks kept a couple of steps ahead of me and to the street side, Shoen a bit behind me away from the street. We didn't talk about it, just sort of fell into it. I'd worked with them both before.

The Blackdove Inn is considerably south and just a hair east of my area, in the part of Adrilankha called Baker's Corner for reasons I couldn't guess at. Jhereg operations there are controlled by a fellow named Horin; protocol required me to let him know if I was doing anything major in his area and get his permission if appropriate. But as far as I knew, this would be nothing major. And besides, I didn't like him much.

Just inside Baker's Corner, along Six Horses Way, there's a public house called the Basket that at times has a slab of beef turning on a spit, and periodically they douse it with a mixture of wine and salt and pepper and magobud and whiteseed. You have to get there early, because if you don't it will be either over-cooked or gone. I was there early. The host cut some for me, slapped it unceremoniously on a plate, and nodded toward the basket of rolls. I had some summer ale to go with it and sat down. I also got some for Shoen and Sticks—I figured we were safe here, because Loiosh was watching, so they could eat.

We sat and we ate and it was good.

My philosophy is that if I'm going to do something reckless, I should have a good meal first.

"So, you want to tell us what's up?" said Sticks.

"Don't know," I said. "You heard about Trotter?"

"Yeah. Nasty business. It's like the streets aren't safe anymore."

I nodded. "I'm going to see about it."

"And we're going to make sure you don't get the same treatment while you do?"

"Something like that."

"Any details you feel like sharing?"

"I just know I'm meeting a guy at an inn."

"The guy who did it?"

"Probably, though that's not what was on the invitation."

"All right."

Shoen kept eating. Talkative bastard, that one.

"So, how do we play it?"

I shrugged. "We go in, see what's up, decide. You guys try to keep me alive long enough for me to make a decision."

He ate another bite, chewed it, and swallowed. "It's a good thing you have us to watch out for you, otherwise you'd be helpless." He winked at Loiosh.

"He's as funny as you, Boss."

"Why thank you, Loiosh."

"Point proven. You should probably send one of these guys over an hour early, just to look things over."

"No one is trying to kill me, Loiosh."

"Explain that to Trotter."

We finished up the meal, and they went out the door in front of me to make sure no one was waiting outside to do me harm. No one was; those days were over, at least for a while.

We took our time getting to the Blackdove. I stopped on the way at a candlemaker's and got a candle that stood about four feet high and was scented with lavender, along with a silver holder for it. I figured Cawti might like it. I had them send it to the office, because whatever happened later, walking around with a four-foot-tall candle was unlikely to make it go any better.

"Boss, you know you're going to make those two wonder if you're in control of yourself."

"Feh. Because I bought a candle?"

"No, because you're walking around with a stupid grin on your face."

"You can't even see my face."

"I don't need to see your face."

I got my features back under control, and found we still had an hour or so before the meeting, so we took our time getting there. I looked into shop windows for other stuff to get Cawti, but didn't see anything that felt right.

And then it was time, and we covered the last half mile or so, and I walked into the inn about five minutes early. It was quiet—not the sort of place that's busy between lunch hour and dusk. The hostess looked half asleep behind the bar, and there was one Teckla snoring loudly, his head down on the table in front of him. The other individual was a rather attractive woman who was obviously a Dzur; she wore loose-fitting black clothing and had a whole lot of steel strapped to her side. She was in the back corner, her head against the wall, apparently dozing, but probably watching us through her lashes. I caught Stick's eye, and he caught mine; enough said.

I approached the bar and the hostess opened her eyes, looked at me, looked at me again, hesitated, then said, "My lord?"

A quick glance suggested that she was a Jhegaala, like Byrna, which might or might not be significant. I gave her my name, then his, saying I was to meet him. She nodded and pointed down a dark hallway. "First door on the right, my lord."

I looked back at the Dzur, estimating how long it would take her to get from where she was to the door I was about to go through. The way she was keeping one foot so casually under the chair, I'd say just over three seconds.

Shoen went first, then me, then Sticks. When Shoen reached the door, he looked a question at me; I nodded, he clapped. Someone called to enter, so he did. Sticks and I waited there in the hall. It isn't like we were alert, ready to move and go for weapons at the first sign of excitement; it's just that, well, I guess we were.

Shoen came back out and said, "One guy, sword on the table in front of him."

I nodded and he went back in, then me, then Sticks.

It was a small room, with two chairs and a table, and not a whole lot more space than that—the sort of room for a private card game, maybe, or a meeting of three or four Chreotha who want to pool their resources and start a laundry service. The individual seated behind the table was certainly not Byrna. He wasn't even a Jhegaala; from both his slightly feline features and the blue and white of his clothes, I took him for a Tiassa. A bit younger than middle age—he probably hadn't seen his thousandth year. His hair was light brown and long, his eyes were bright. He was studying me as I was studying him.

"Sit down," he suggested. "Let's talk."

The naked sword lying across the table was slimmer and lighter than usual, though still heavier than mine. His hands were out of sight below the table. If he made a move for the sword while I was sitting in the chair, things were liable to get interesting. The room wasn't big enough for much swordplay, which worked to my advantage, as I was carrying a lot of little things with points on them. I studied him a bit more. He held my eye and waited.

"Sticks. Shoen," I said. "Wait for me. I'll be out presently."

They both left without a word, footsteps echoing as I continued my study. My hard stare failed to intimidate him so I sat down.

"I'm Vlad," I said.

He nodded. "I'm the Blue Fox."

"You aren't really."

"You've heard of me?" He seemed surprised.

"No. No, if I had heard that there was someone going around calling himself the Blue Fox, I'd remember. You don't really, do you?"

"I tried wearing a mask for a while, but it was uncomfortable so I stopped."

"Why?"

"You Easterners have no sense of the theatrical."

"I've heard that said. In any case, I can't think of an Easterner who has ever called himself the Blue Fox, so maybe you're right."

"I've met an Easterner who calls himself the Warlock."

"No, everyone else calls him that."

He shrugged. "In any case, if we're done talking about my name, perhaps we can—"

"What do I call you? Blue? Lord Fox?"

"Blue Fox will do fine. Are you trying to make me angry because you think it will give you an advantage over me?"

"I hadn't actually worked that out," I said. "But probably. If you're going to give me an opening like that—"

"Why don't we talk first, and find out if we even

have anything to quarrel about, before we start trying to get advantages over each other?"

"Oh, we have a quarrel. You sent one of my people to a physicker with a lot of holes in him. It hurt my feelings."

"Sorry," he said. "I didn't know you'd take it personally."

"I guess I'm over-sensitive. I assume the attractive Dzurlord out there is with you?"

"Pretty, isn't she?"

"She is. Certainly prettier than the guys I brought."

"The tall one is kind of cute, in a boyish way."

"I'll tell him you said so."

"Ready to talk business yet?"

"Are you a friend of Byrna?"

"Close enough, I guess. I'm handling the negotiations for him."

"Negotiations," I repeated.

"Do you have a better word?"

"Not just now. Give me some time and I'll come up with one."

"Take as much time as you need. But while you're thinking, we seem to have a problem."

"Yes. Byrna owes me money."

The Tiassa who had introduced himself as the Blue Fox nodded. "That's a problem. He doesn't have it."

"That's another problem," I said.

"He came to me—or, to be precise, his wife came to Ibronka, and—"

"Ibronka? The Dzur?"

He nodded.

"That's an Eastern name," I said.

"And a very pretty one. His wife came to Ibronka, you don't need to know how, and said that you were going to hurt him if he didn't give you money. Seemed like I should step in."

"Did his wife go to her when he needed to borrow the money?"

"No, she should have though. We'd have found it."

"If you find it now, and give it to me, that'll solve the problem."

"Over time, the amount has become rather large."

"Yes, that does happen."

"Hence, I thought I'd negotiate."

"You see, Lord Blue, I'm generally willing to negotiate."

"Generally?"

"Generally. But there's the matter of the holes you put in one of my people. I don't care for that. And then there's the fact that instead of coming to me like a gentleman and explaining that he was having problems, in which case I'd have been willing to work something out with him, he avoided me for several weeks, and then you show up. To be blunt, Lord Blue, I'm just not feeling inclined to negotiate much of anything. So, now what?"

He glanced at the sword on the table. I carefully placed my hands on the table, smiled at him, and waited.

"You're very good," he said at last.

"At what?"

"Fighting. I can tell. You think you can take me. I think I can take you."

I smiled and waited, my hands on the table. The weight of the dagger in my left sleeve was reassuring.

He glanced at Loiosh and said, "You think your friend there will give you an edge."

"Possibly," I told him.

"I don't think it will be enough."

I nodded, my eyes never leaving his. I was pretty sure I could take him even without Loiosh's help. But you never know until you're there.

"But," he said, still maintaining eye contact, "as I told you, I would prefer to negotiate."

"I'm not inclined to negotiate."

"Do you really want to push this?"

"I'm in a bad mood. I told you why."

"You shouldn't lend money at ruinous interest rates, then threaten violence when people can't pay, and then act surprised when they go to extraordinary lengths to protect themselves."

"Have I been acting surprised?"

"Good point."

"I have more good points. Like, he knew the rates when he took the loan. And he would have had no reason to fear violence even when he got behind if he'd come to me and explained his problem. I'm always willing to work with someone, up until the time they bring in a hired sword to mess up my people."

"He didn't handle this very well."

"No."

"He could have gone to the Empire, instead of to me." I didn't say anything to that. After a while he said, "Yes, well, we both know that would have been a mistake."

"Yes," I said.

"So, what do we do now?"

"You're talking, I'm listening."

"What if we give you double the initial amount of the loan and call it even?"

"If I didn't have a guy being patched together by a physicker, I'd probably go for that."

"And I pay for the physicker."

I mulled it over. Evidently, he was serious about wanting to avoid violence. Well, the fact is, I'd like to avoid violence as well. I'm here to make money, not mayhem. But it annoyed me to have a punk like Byrna pull something like this. It annoyed me a lot.

"Boss?"

"Yeah?"

"It's business."

"Yeah."

I said, "All right, I accept the deal. But the money comes through you. I don't want to see Byrna. I don't trust myself."

He nodded. "I'll have the money sent to you. And if you give me the name of the physicker, I'll take care of that, too."

I felt obscurely disappointed, but agreed.

"Good then," he said. "One more thing."

"What's that?"

"You hungry?"

Interesting indeed. What might this be about? Probably nothing it would be smart to get involved in. "Just ate," I told him.

"All right."

But then, we Easterners are curious beasts. "I could stand a drink, though."

"On me."

I stood up and preceded him out the door. He

wasn't a Jhereg, so he might not have appreciated the courtesy.

"Boss? What's this about?"

"No idea. Maybe he wants to show how friendly he can be to Easterners."

"You think?"

"Probably not. But I suspect if we take him up on the drink we'll find out."

We went back into the room, and I could feel the Dzurlord, Ibronka, looking us over carefully. Then she stood up and walked toward Lord Fox. Sticks, who'd been leaning against the bar, walked over to greet me, just coincidentally putting himself between me and Ibronka.

Foxy said, "Lord Taltos, this is Ibronka. Ibronka, Lord Taltos."

I bowed without undue exaggeration and said, "This is Stadol, and this is Shoen. Let's find a table."

We did, except for Shoen and Sticks, who each took a table flanking ours. The guy with the funny name ordered us two bottles of Khaav'n; apparently he was settling in for a while. His hand was under the table; so was Ibronka's. If we were going to be romantic, I wanted Cawti there. If we were going to be violent, I wanted Cawti there for that. I should have thought to invite her, dammit.

They brought the wine, already opened, and Blue poured it for us. We drank some. It was pretty decent, though I'd have served it slightly chilled.

I sat back and studied him some more, and waited. Loiosh shifted a little on my shoulder; he was waiting, too.

"So," said the Blue Fox. "I'm glad we were able to settle things peacefully."

"Uh huh."

He hesitated, then said, "There's a reason, of course."

"I'm sure there is. Want to tell me about it?"

He nodded, hesitated, then said, "I could use your help."

"I wondered about that," I said. "The trouble is, you aren't Sethra Lavode."

2

"No," he said. "In fact I'm not. Um, would you mind explaining that remark?"

"She got away with that once—messing up one of my people as a means of hiring me. I don't think—"

"Oh," he said. "No, that isn't what happened. I agreed to help Byrna, like I said, then I learned something about you, and it occurred to me that if we didn't slaughter one another, we might be able to work together to our mutual advantage."

"Do you believe him, Loiosh?"

"I think so. Maybe."

I drank some wine to give myself time to think, and swallowed wrong and coughed noisily, which gave me lots of time to think but no ability to do so. Embarrassing, too. They pretended not to notice.

When I was recovered, I wiped my eyes and summoned what dignity I could and indicated that I was listening.

"You don't know a lot about me," he said.

No, but more than you think I do, I thought. *And I'll be learning more quickly.* But I only nodded.

"I've been doing what I do for, well, since the end of the Interregnum."

I nodded, waiting; I had no intention of giving him the satisfaction. But then he waited, and then he raised an eyebrow, so I sighed inwardly and said, "All right. What is it you do?"

"I rob people."

"You rob people."

"Yes. I hold my sword at their throats, and require them to give me their money. They oblige, and I send them on their way."

"Is that honest?"

"No one's ever asked me before. I'll think about it and get back to you."

"Thanks. So, how can an honest businessman like me be of service to a dangerous highwayman like yourself?"

"I was told you think you're funny. That's all right, I think I'm funny, too."

"What else were you told?"

"That you have ways of learning things no one can understand, that you practice the Eastern sorcery—"

"Witchcraft."

"Hmm?"

"We call it witchcraft."

"Right. And you also dabble in the more traditional sorcery. And that you've gotten lucky often enough that it probably isn't luck."

I tried to think of who he might have spoken with who would have given him that sort of report, but it was a pointless exercise so I stopped. "All right," I said. "What can someone with my skills do for someone in your profession?"

"You also have influence, and you know a lot of people."

I didn't say yes, or no, or nod, or shake my head. In fact, I had no idea what he was talking about, but if he was operating under some sort of illusion about me, it might work to my advantage.

He glanced at Ibronka, who was leaning back and studying me while, I'm sure, holding his hand under the table; they were probably also talking psychically. He said, "Things have been getting more difficult over the years."

"In what way?" That seemed neutral enough.

"More and more use of sorcery to maintain the safety of the roads, and to learn the identity of those of us who violate it. People with large sums or valuable jewels teleport instead of traveling by road, or if they have to travel, they teleport most of the money, so all we can take is what they have to travel with."

"Sorcery," I said. "Bad stuff." About which I knew fairly little. He was right earlier when he said I dabbled.

"Inconvenient, in any case. And it's getting worse. Now it's becoming difficult to find clients safely."

I laughed. "Clients," I said. "I like that. I like that a lot."

He permitted himself a smirk. "Yeah, me, too."

"I'm missing the part where I can be helpful."

"I usually operate in an area to the east of here."

"Ah. I start to see."

"No, no. Not that far east."

"Oh, all right." My anger receded quickly, because it hadn't had time to work itself up, but I still missed half of his next statement. "Sorry, say that again?"

"I said they're starting to tag the money."

"Tag?"

"That's what they call it. Sorcerously mark it."

"So it can be identified as stolen?"

"Yes."

"Hmm. That doesn't seem fair."

"That's how I feel about it."

"How are they—"

"They've set up places where you can have your money tagged, so if it's stolen, a sorcerer can identify it. I was lucky enough to learn about it before servicing a client who'd done that. Now that we know what to look for, we can tell, but it's getting common enough that we've had to let some prime targets go."

"You have my sympathy," I said. "What happens when the proper owner tries to spend it?"

"The tagging is tied to him, so he just rubs it off."

"What if he forgets?"

"A merchant gets in trouble, I suppose."

"And it's cheap to put on?"

"Very. They do it by volume, so with gold it costs next to nothing."

"Sounds unfortunate."

"Right. So . . . why am I coming to you?"

"I was just getting to that question."

"I'm wondering if maybe there's a way for me to get the money to you, and for you to return me money that hasn't been tampered with. For a fee, of course."

I shook my head. "Can't do it. Not my kind of thing. But I could make a suggestion."

"If your suggestion is the Left Hand, I tried that."

"Oh. You're well informed. Sorry it didn't work. What happened?"

"They were willing to do it. For thirteen orbs for each imperial."

"That's what they wanted?"

"Yes."

I shook my head. "It's like highway robbery."

"That's very funny, Lord Taltos."

"Why thank you, Lord Blue."

Ibronka glared at me a little, then looked away as if I wasn't worth her time.

"I liked it, Boss."

"Thanks, Loiosh."

He said, "So the Left Hand is out of the question. If you don't want to get involved in this, do you have any suggestions for who might?"

"Let me think about that."

"I'd be willing to pay for any idea that—"

"Let's not worry too much about the paying part. Let me just try to think of something. Hey."

"What?"

"Why am I doing the thinking? You're the Tiassa."

He rolled his eyes; I considered myself answered.

Did I know anyone who'd be interested in a deal like that? No one I'd want to give it to, at any rate. But it was an interesting exercise, trying to figure a way around it.

"Boss? Do you care?"

"Let's say I'm intrigued."

"If you say so."

"Any idea who came up with this?"

"Some Imperial sorcerer. There were complaints about the safety of the roads, you know."

"See how it is?" I said. "As soon as you get good at something, they move to cut you off. It's as if they fear anyone being successful. I sympathize."

"Uh huh."

"*The Tiassa isn't doing his job, Loiosh. So if anyone's going to come up with a brilliant idea, I guess it'll have to be you.*"

"*I'll get right on that, Boss.*"

"How does it work, exactly?"

"It's pretty straightforward. It takes a few seconds to do a bagful of coins, and an hour with each one to undo it."

"Sort of cuts into your profits."

"Exactly."

"What if you spend it a long way from where you got it? Every merchant in the Empire isn't checking."

"I've been doing a bit of that. But more of them are starting to. The Empire is offering tax reductions to any merchant willing to check coins. They supply—"

"Oh."

"Hmmm?"

"I heard something about that. Some device, and they'd give me a reduction on my taxes if I—"

"You're a merchant?"

I looked innocent. "I am part owner of a perfectly respectable psychedelic herb shop, thank you very much."

"Oh. I see."

"I thought it was some sort of listening device they were trying to install."

"It might be that, too," he said.

"You don't trust the Empire much, do you?"

"As much as you do. Less, because I probably know it better."

"All right. So it won't work much longer to just use the coins elsewhere. What do they do if you spend it somewhere that doesn't have the means of detecting it?"

"What? I don't understand."

"What if you went to, say, my shop and bought an ounce of dreamgrass. I wouldn't know the coin was tagged. So then I'd spend the coin somewhere, and—"

"Oh, I see. They treat it just like they do a coiner: ask you where you'd gotten the coin, and try to work back from there."

"I was approached by the Empire about six weeks ago. How long has this been going on?"

"About that long, more or less."

I nodded. "A new program. They're always thinking, those Imperial law enforcement types. They never let up. It's an honor to run rings around them."

"That's been my feeling, yes."

"So it sounds like the only choice is to reduce the cost of removing the—what were they called?"

"Tags."

"Right. Reduce the cost of removing the tags."

"That's better than my idea?"

"What was your idea?"

"I was going to write the Empire a letter saying please stop."

"Heh," I said. Then, "Woah. You *are* a Tiassa."

"Meaning?"

"I hadn't thought of that."

"Somehow, I doubt they'd be impressed by the letter."

"I don't think a letter is the best way, but the idea is sound."

"What idea?"

"Convincing the Empire to stop tagging the coins."

"Are you serious?"

"Why not?"

From the look on his face, he thought I was jesting; from the look on mine, I think, he eventually decided I wasn't. His eyes narrowed and he looked even more cat-like, but I declined to scratch him behind the ears. He said, "How would you do that?"

"I've no idea."

"Oh. Thought you might have something."

"I think I might."

"What?"

"The idea you just gave me. Convince the Empire to stop tagging the coins."

"Which you have no idea how to do, and, therefore, no reason to believe it can be done."

"You've stated our position exactly," I said. "I'm proud of you."

Ibronka stirred and said to Bluey, "Mind if I eviscerate him?"

"Just one?" he said. "And an Easterner?"

"I'm not thinking of a fight, more of pest control."

"I'd rather you didn't just yet, love."

"All right." She turned back and smiled sweetly at me.

I decided I liked her. "It must be hard on you," I told her. "Most of the time when dealing with clients, you have the advantage. Has to be hard for a Dzur to take."

She pretended I hadn't spoken.

I spent a few minutes thinking over the problem, and when Loiosh asked again why I was bothering, I pretended he hadn't spoken. I can do that stuff, too.

It wasn't at all the sort of thing I could do, but I had friends—or acquaintances at least—who could do a lot of things I couldn't. Sethra Lavode, Morrolan, Aliera, Kiera—

Kiera.

Kiera had told me once, about . . . how did that work? I remained silent as the idea built a nest and laid some eggs.

Blue-guy might have a stupid name, but he wasn't stupid. He said, "What is it you know that you aren't telling me?"

"Lots of things," I said. "And the reverse is true as well, I've no doubt. Do you want this done, or don't you?"

"Now it sounds like you're in."

"What's the offer?"

"To solve the problem completely? I don't know. That's worth a lot."

"Double what you've already agreed to pay me."

"It's worth more than that."

"You're honest. I'm touched. I know. Is it a deal?"

"Of course."

"Then I'm in." I turned to Shoen and Sticks and said, "Thanks. You're off."

"You sure?" said Sticks. "These characters look all

dangerous and stuff. I wouldn't want to see you un-protected." He was giving Ibronka an amused smirk, I think just to annoy her. She gave no indication of noticing, which meant that her dislike of me was more because I was a Jhereg than because I was an Easterner. Good. Bigotry is such an ugly thing, don't you think?

"I'm sure," I told Sticks. I had turned my head to speak to him, so neither of our new acquaintances could see my face; I silently mouthed, "Follow them."

"You're the boss," he said, and headed out. Shoen, I should add, was already gone.

I turned back to Foxy. "I need to get my hands on some of those coins."

"You have a plan," he said.

"I always have a plan. Ask anyone. 'That Vlad,' they'll say. 'He sure does always have a plan. He—'"

"Why do you work so hard to make yourself dis-liked?" asked Ibronka. "I should think you'd find it happens enough on its own without putting yourself to any extra trouble."

I drank some wine and said, "Yes, I have a plan."

"Tell me about it," said Blue.

"Not just yet."

His face twitched, but I couldn't tell what it meant. "All right," he said. Ibronka looked at him, then shrugged almost imperceptibly; I imagine they'd be talking about that later.

"You need a bag of gold," he said.

"Tagged gold, yes. Or silver. Coins that have been treated so they'll be detectable, and have been sto-len. Which reminds me—can they be traced?"

He frowned. "Probably. Never known it to be

done—they just like to wait until the coins show up in circulation. Paying for a trace is going to cost a big chunk of the total value. But it could happen. Is that a problem?"

"It could be. Can you get the coins?"

"Give me a week. How do I get in touch with you?"

I told him where the office was, and told him to ask the clerk for something Eastern that would last until morning.

He looked amused, which irritated me, but I guess fair is fair. "A week then?"

"Or sooner if you get it sooner."

I stood, bowed, and showed him my back on the way out the door.

"*Well, Boss? Do I get to know what's going to happen?*"

"*Sure. We're going back to the office and find out some stuff, then do some work. Then we wait until he shows up with the coins.*"

"*Which will give you a week to figure out what to do with them. I still don't know why—*"

"*I know what I'm going to do with them, Loiosh.*"

"*Oh? What are you going to do with them?*"

"*Get arrested,*" I said, which shut him up. It was also sort of true, but that was of secondary importance.

First importance (after shutting up Loiosh) was to find out what was going on. If I came up with a clever plan that didn't solve the problem, I'd feel silly. I sort of thought I should figure out what the problem was.

I returned to the office and found Kragar, who

wanted to know what was going on. In answer, I said, "I need to know everything you can find out about someone calling himself the Blue Fox."

"Calling himself the what?"

"You heard me."

"A Jhereg?"

"Tiassa."

"How am I supposed to find that?"

"Use your imagination."

"You mean, make stuff up?"

"He's supposed to be a robber, a highwayman, working somewhere east of here. Ask if anyone's heard of him, then follow it up."

"Do you know how stupid I'm going to sound asking if anyone has heard of the Blue Fox?"

"Yes, I know exactly how stupid you're going to sound."

"The gods will punish you."

"I have no doubt of that at all."

The next order of business was finding Kiera the Thief. I went back out and stopped in a couple of inns, and I dropped the word that I wanted to talk to Kiera. She was waiting for me at a third, a place informally called the Roughhouse, which I'm sure has a story behind it; to all appearances and from all my experience, it's a quiet little place with lots of booths with tall backs, so you imagine you're getting more privacy than you are.

I spotted her—well, okay, Loiosh spotted her—in one of the booths as I was waiting to speak to the host, and we joined her: Kiera the Thief. She was short for a Dragaeran, though some of that was that she tended to slump a little. Her hair was dark, her motions graceful, and her smile full of warmth. I still have no idea why she likes me, but we go back to a day when—no, skip it. She was good to me from the moment we met. As I approached the booth, she gave me a good kiss on the mouth—the only Dragaeran I greet like that, by the way—and a hug to go with it. I sat.

"I was just looking for you," I said.

"I know. That's why I'm here."

I smiled. "I suspected it was all a trick."

"Hmmm?"

"Never mind." She had a small glass with something dark in it; I ordered her another and got myself a light tingling wine. When the drinks arrived, I said, "A long time ago, you mentioned something called, if I remember right, the hamper switch."

"Hamper Load, and you have a good memory, Vlad."

"How do you do it?"

"Are you going into a new line of work?"

"No, but I have a situation where it might be useful. Can you explain it to me? Slowly, as befits the lethargic Eastern brain?"

She snorted. "All right, and you don't have to tell me what this is about, but if you feel like doing so, I'm curious."

"Let me see if I get away with it first. If I do, I'll explain. If I don't I'll try to pretend it never happened."

"Fair enough." She brought her drink to her lips, swallowed, carefully set the glass down. She explained how that particular swindle worked; I listened. When I was done listening, I asked questions and listened some more. Being a good listener is one of the most vital skills in being an effective criminal.

"Good," I said. "I think I have it."

She nodded. "I believe you do. Remember that the Skin needs to be convincing, and to a degree the Runner; the rest just have to go through the motions."

"Understood," I said, and got to my feet.

She smiled at me. "Good luck," she said.

I got back to the office and Sticks was waiting. "They teleported," he said.

"Damn."

"But I have a friend who's a sorcerer, and I thought you might want to know where they teleported to."

"And he got there in time?"

"She. And yeah. Imperial Palace, Dragon Wing."

"I imagine you think you deserve a bonus for that."

"You have a good imagination, Boss."

"Melestav, give him seven. Thanks, Sticks. Good work."

"Always a pleasure," he said.

"*Dragon Wing, Boss?*"

"*It was either there or Whitecrest Manor.*"

"*Why?*"

"*I told you, I recognized him.*"

I spent the rest of the day supplying the wants and needs of the good citizens of Adrilankha.

I saw Cawti that night. She liked the candle a lot, and in the warm afterglow of our first hello, I told her about the Blue Fox, Ibronka, and the difficulty in staying ahead of law enforcement. She listened with her whole attention, as she always did, her dark hair shining on the white pillow, her large black eyes fixed on mine so intently I felt like I could fall into them. It took a while to get the story out, because her eyes kept distracting me.

When I was done, she laughed, which made my stomach do funny things.

"Can I help?"

"Um."

"What?"

"It isn't exactly, I don't know the word. You know, the thing about keeping one's beloved out of danger and all that?"

"Vladimir Taltos, if you aren't kidding I'm going to bite you somewhere painful."

"I thought it was romantic."

"Romantic would be asking for a lock of my hair or something."

"Okay, can I have a lock of your hair? And yes, I'm kidding."

"Then I can help?"

"Sure. As long as you keep saying my name."

"Hmmm?"

"I like it when you say my name."

She smiled. I wondered if she knew just what she could get me to do with that smile.

I returned it, and she sat up suddenly. "All right, then! What's the first step?"

"Hmm?"

"Hey. I'm up here."

"Oh, sorry. The first step. Yes. Wait for the mysterious bag of gold."

"There must be some set-up before that happens."

"Well, yes. There's some information gathering, but I'll get Kragar to do that."

"Why does he get to have all the fun?"

"You think that's fun?"

"Not really, I suppose."

"Okay, then."

"What else?"

"Deciding on the Anvil, and opening the Hamper."

"Oh, perfect! I'm especially trained for those things."

"I thought so. You have no idea what they mean, right?"

"Right. But I wanted you to get full pleasure from being opaque."

"And I did. Thank you, m'lady."

"You're welcome, m'lord. Now, what's the Anvil?"

"That's the person who gets hit by the operation."

"The target?"

"Right. Also called the Bucket, the Lame, and the Narrow."

"I didn't know you knew about those sorts of scams."

"Oh, I've known all about them since yesterday."

"I see. What's the Hamper?"

"In this case, something that will hold a bag of tagged coins."

"Does opening it have some special meaning?"

"That means to set the Anvil up."

"How do we do that?"

"First step is to pick him."

"What are you looking for? Stop kissing me and answer the question. No, skip that, keep kissing me. All right, now answer the question."

"What—?"

"What are you looking for?"

"Love, respect, friendship, loyalty, sensuality, beauty, skill in cutting vegetab—"

"In the Anvil."

"Oh, right. First of all, someone with the authority—or the clout—to stop the evil and immoral practice of sorcerously marking coins."

"How many people like that do you think there are?"

"Well, the Empress."

"Scratch her."

"And Lord Khaavren, but he'd be a bad choice for this. Um, I'd guess about eight or ten."

"Let's make a list."

So we did, and talked about them for the rest of the day, at the end of which time we'd settled on a Dragonlord named Feorae, because he was perfectly placed within the Imperial hierarchy and because I felt he had too many vowels in his name. I closed my eyes, concentrated, and eventually got hold of Kragar. I set him to learning what he could of the poor bastard, in between learning what he could about Blue-guy. He had a lot to say about it, but eventually agreed.

"What else do you need?" Cawti wanted to know.

"First thing we'll need is the Skin, because he has to make contact with the Anvil right away."

"What makes a good Skin?"

Let those who judge goodness or evil in a man note that I let that line pass, and just said, "Charm, warmth, and aristocratic bearing."

"You'd be perfect."

"And being Dragaeran."

"Oh."

"But thank you."

"Do you have anyone in mind?"

"Not yet."

"What about your friend Morrolan?"

"I doubt I could convince him to do anything so disloyal."

"Same with Aliera?"

"She'd probably kill me for asking. What about Norathar—no, forget I mentioned it. Let's forget about true aristocrats and look for someone who can act the part."

"Do you know many actors?"

"A few. I don't think I know any I'd trust, though."

"What about one of your tags?" said Cawti.

I considered. "Yes, that could work. There's certainly acting involved in the job, and some of them play roles for the nums."

"Maybe someone from the Long Carpet, or the Couches? They're fairly high-class."

"How did you—oh, right. I keep forgetting." She'd learned a lot about me, of course, while she and her partner were preparing to kill me. The memory made for an uncomfortable moment, but she squeezed my hand and it passed.

We decided that was enough work, and turned our minds to other things.

The next day I was up early and beat Kragar into the office. I told Melestav to bring me klava and to get hold of a certain Lord Heral-Nocaldi, or H'noc as he was called, who managed the Couches, and let him know I'd be dropping by.

"Should I tell him why?"

"No, let him sweat."

I let him sweat for about an hour before heading over there. Not for any special reason except that I didn't like him—we'd had an unpleasant altercation when I'd first started running the area. It was especially unpleasant for him, so I imagine he didn't like me, either.

I made the walk with no protection this time. Lower Kieron Road was hot and there was an unusual amount of dust. A bird yelled at me as I approached the place, the kind that goes, "kwa-AKA, kwa-AKA." I don't know what kind that is, but Loiosh says they taste good.

The place had been a cheap hotel before the Interregnum, then it was improved superficially: scrollwork added high on the walls, expensive sconces, gold trim, high-quality furnishings in the lobby where one of H'noc's enforcers, a guy named Abror, was standing where he could watch the door. H'noc was also there, sitting and waiting for me. He rose as I entered.

"M'lord, to what do I—"

"Bring me every tag who's not engaged."

He hesitated as, no doubt, a lot of questions came into his mind, but he was smart enough not to ask them. He nodded and went off to follow orders. There were no nums waiting, which was reasonable at this hour on a Farmday. There was a wide fountain, about waist high and of an odd yellowish marble; I leaned against it and waited.

Five minutes later, three boys and five girls were lined up in front of me, in all shapes, colors, attitudes—at least as far as Dragaerans go. "Don't pose," I said. "Just stand there." They relaxed, and they still displayed all shapes, colors, and attitudes. The guy on the left caught my eye, because he was giving me a look of unabashed curiosity. He had an oval face, wide-set eyes, and his general appearance was neutral: I couldn't guess if he'd appeal to a man or a woman, to someone after corrupting innocence, or someone who wanted to be taken along for a new experience. I nodded to him. "What's your name?"

"Omlo, m'lord," he said.

I turned to H'noc. "I need to talk to him. The rest of you can go."

They did. H'noc followed them out. I found a chair and gestured the boy to another.

"You know who I am, Omlo?"

"Yes, m'lord."

"Want to make some extra money? All yours, no juice."

He hesitated. "Why me?" turned out to be his first question.

"You look like you could handle it. It isn't dangerous. I don't think."

At that last, he looked at me quickly, then looked away. "How much money?"

"Fifteen imperials."

"And you don't think it'll be dangerous, m'lord?"

"Shouldn't be."

He nodded. "All right." I could see him spending the money already. "What do I have to do?"

"Do you know where my office is?"

"No, m'lord."

"Number Six Copper Lane sells psychedelic herbs.

Tell the proprietor you want something rare and Eastern that will last until morning. He'll guide you in to see me."

"I'll be there, m'lord."

"Good. That's all. Now go make me some money."

"Yes, m'lord."

I left him there and returned to the office.

Loiosh, who by now had figured out what I was doing, said, "*Boss, even if this works, I don't think the Empire will appreciate the joke.*"

"*Everyone thinks that, Loiosh. But consider how long the Empire has been around. Do you know anyone who could survive that long without a sense of humor?*"

"*I still have no idea why you're bothering.*"

"*Because I recognized him.*"

"*Blue-fellow?*"

"*That isn't his real name, you know.*"

"*I'm shocked, Boss. Where do you know him from?*"

"*Family resemblance. To someone I'd like to have owe me a favor. If I'm wrong, Kragar will let me know.*"

"*Whatever you say, Boss.*"

"Melestav!"

He poked his head in. "Yeah?"

"Find me a map of the city."

He appeared with the map and stood next to me while I studied it. "Looking for something particular?"

"Just trying to remind myself of some of my favorite places."

"To eat?"

"To not get killed."

"Odd," he said, "that I've never gone to the trouble to make a list of those."

I found what I was looking for and gave him the map back, then put the whole thing out of my head. I took care of business until close to noon, when I sent Melestav out to Honlo's to bring back a difowl roasted in wine and stuffed with tartapples, thyme, and garlic. It arrived about the time Omlo did, and I invited everyone in the office to dig in. Kragar almost snatched the gizzard before I could stop him, but I'd been watching for it. My operation, my gizzard; what else would I have gone to the trouble of acquiring the business for?

When we were done and Loiosh was picking over the bones, I went into the office with Omlo and said, "It's time to practice."

He took a chair. "I'm ready, m'lord. What first?"

"Sit," I told him.

"My lord? I'm sitting."

"Sit like someone who's, you know, cocky. Sure of himself. Knows he can get what he wants. More arrogant. Yeah, like that."

He smiled. "Part of the trade, m'lord."

"Good. Now stand up and walk to the door. No, not sexy. Confident. Try again. Better. More like you're going somewhere. Not in a hurry, but—good."

"That wasn't too much?"

"No, perfect. Meanwhile, start walking, talking, and looking as aristocratic as you can."

"I shall, m'lord."

"Got a minute, Vlad?" Kragar's head looked

weirdly disembodied around the edge of the door. "I have something for you to look at."

I excused myself and followed him into his office, where he presented me with a three-page report on the Blue Fox: history, origin, family, and activity. I took a few minutes to read it.

"Good work. How did you find all this?"

"I'm just that good."

"You are, you are."

"I asked a guy who asked a guy and I got his family. And it turns out the Blue Fox is real. Or was, anyway. It's all there."

"You got a bonus coming."

"I am bathed in a warm glow."

"I'll see you when you've dried off."

I went back to work with Omlo; we put in another couple of hours and then called it a day. I told him to return the following day and we'd start work on the hard part—the Load—and then stay with it until we were ready to start the action. He understood; he seemed excited about the whole thing. I liked his attitude; I hoped he wouldn't end up with holes in him.

That night Cawti and I ate at the Blue Flame and talked about the wedding.

"I don't have anyone to make a headdress," said Cawti.

"Noish-pa will find someone," I said, referring to my grandfather.

"You think so?"

"I know so."

She smiled. "All right. Who will stand for you?"

"I'll ask Morrolan. He probably knows some of the customs."

"How is he with rhymes?"

"I don't know. I'll write them for him, if I have to."

She smiled. "Will I get to hear them?"

"Of course not. It's bad luck."

"After the wedding?"

"All right. What rhymes with Aliera?"

"Now, you know I can't help."

"Yeah, yeah. Shall we find a priest of Verra?"

"I'd like that. But then we need a procession. If we do the civil service at the House, and then go to a temple in South Adrilankha, that would be a long walk for everyone."

"So we'll bring the Jhereg clerk to us, then we can make the procession as long as we want."

"Good point," I said. "Or bring the priest to us. Or both."

"Or both."

She leaned her head on my shoulder and my heart flip-flopped. She said, "Oh, thinking about weddings, marriage, and all of that, a small, unimportant question just came to mind. What do you think of children?"

"Um," I said. "Children. I hadn't thought about it. I mean, other than Loiosh."

"You are so going to pay for that."

I felt her laughing. I said, "Seriously, I don't know. It had never crossed my mind. I need to think about it."

She nodded and suggested that, just in case, we should work on the process. She paid the shot and we went back to my flat to put this plan into action.

I worked with Omlo again the next day, and saw

Cawti again in the evening. We didn't talk about children again, but we did get serious about the wedding. I've put less planning into killing people.

When Omlo arrived, I had him run through the entire business, including the Load. "Good," I told him when he'd finished. "But it could stand to be a little smoother."

"Yes, my lord."

"Try it again."

I was still working with him a couple of hours later when Melestav poked his head in and told me someone calling himself the Blue Fox would like to see me, and he had a Dzurlord with him. The expression on Melestav's face as he pronounced the name of my visitor was a precious thing that I will treasure forever. I allowed as to how they could come into my office, and asked him to have Kragar join us.

I rose and sketched a bow. "Blue Fox, Ibronka, this is Omlo, who will be the Skin."

Omlo looked at me, I think to ask whether he should be in character for these two. I shrugged, so he made a fairly obsequious bow, which the Tiassa and Dzur returned in a sort of casual-to-friendly way.

"Your money," said the Fox, depositing a purse on my desk. "This isn't tagged, it's what I agreed to pay you. The extra should be sufficient to cover the physicker."

I nodded and put the purse into my lower right-hand drawer. Then I said, "Feel free to find chairs. I've got things mostly put together. Omlo here is part of it."

As they were finding chairs, Omlo said, "If I may ask, m'lord?"

"Yes?"

"What are their positions in this?"

"He's the Runner, she's the Dog-man, and I'm the Turner, which completes the crew." I smiled. "Now we're ready to get to work."

3

"She's the what?"

"I'm the which?"

"M'lord, what are those things?"

"I'll explain."

"I'd like to hear it, too," said Kragar. "Do I get to do something?"

"Everyone, this is Kragar. He works for me."

I could see them all wondering how long he'd been there.

Fox-boy said, "What was it you said our jobs are?"

"You're going to be the Runner, and the lovely lady by your side will be the Dog-man. If you agree, of course. You're well suited."

"Dog-man," he repeated, glancing at Ibronka. "I'm not sure I like that."

"It's not personal, just the term for that job."

I took a moment to study Blue-boy. I guess, to a Dragaeran, he'd be considered good-looking: his eyes were clear and sharp, his lips thin, hair swept back to show off an unusually distinct noble's point. And he was one of those people who always seemed to be a little amused by everything. I find such people a touch irritating, but that may only be because I'm one myself. I thought over what I'd learned about him, and wished I knew enough to deduce what exactly was going on.

He said, "Where does the term come from?"

"I don't actually know," I said. "But I'm guessing it has something to do with the way a dog will sit somewhere and do nothing and then bark when something happens."

"Ever owned a dog?" he asked.

"No."

"Never mind, then. What are my orders, General?"

"You have the coins?"

He pulled out a medium-sized purse and dropped it on my desk. "Clink," it said.

"I hope," I told him, "you didn't take that from an honest citizen."

"I didn't," he said. "I took it from a merchant."

"And you're sure the gold is tagged?"

"Spend it," he said, "and you'll find out fast enough."

"That's exactly the plan," I told him. "Although it won't be me who spends it. How much is there?"

"A bit more than four imperials, most of it silver. I hope that's enough."

"Plenty. You keep it. You'll be using it."

He picked it up again. "To do what?"

"Get arrested, of course."

"I thought the idea was to avoid that."

"Yes, well, almost get arrested."

"Maybe, if it isn't too much trouble, you could—"

"I will. Just a moment. We're waiting for someone."

He started to ask who, then shrugged. In about two minutes Cawti came in. She bowed to them gravely as I said, "Cawti, this is the Blue Fox, and this is Ibronka. This fellow is called Omlo. Everyone, Cawti."

"A pleasure," said Cawti. "Ibronka, that's an Eastern name."

"So I've been told," she said. From her tone, I'd say she didn't like Cawti a great deal more than she liked me, which in my opinion indicated a flaw in her character. The Fox-guy rose and bowed like he meant it.

I didn't have enough chairs, so Cawti perched on my desk, generally facing the guests. Without turning her pleasant and rather phony smile away from them, she said to me, "Are you about to reveal all, Vladimir?"

"Yeah, I was thinking about going over the plan with our new friends."

She nodded. "Not a bad idea. But then they might see it coming when we betray them to the Empire for the reward."

"That isn't all that funny," said Foxy.

I studied him; the expression on his face was, in spite of his words, amused. I said, "First of all, yes it is. Second, is there a reward for you?"

"Not in this county," he said.

"That would make transportation a problem," I said.

"A big problem," said Ibronka, smiling sweetly the way I smile sweetly.

I said, "How big is the reward? I might need to consider this."

"It's gone up and down a few times," he said, "depending on how busy we've been. Right now, I think it's about twelve hundred imperials."

"I'm impressed," I said. And I was, too: I was impressed that he named the same amount Kragar had found; usually they like to understate if they're scared, or exaggerate if they aren't.

He made a bowing gesture. "I like to think I'm successful in my field."

I nodded. "No question, one takes pride in accomplishment." Ibronka looked carefully blank; Cawti smirked. I said, "For now, we'll skip the whole betrayal-transportation-reward plan, and go with my original idea. Besides, I'd hate to get a reputation for being untrustworthy."

Bluey nodded. "Best not to let that happen."

"I'm going to tell you how this will work. I want Kragar and Cawti here to poke holes in the plan."

"I thought that was my job, Boss."

"If you want to fight a duel with Kragar for the privilege, I won't stop you."

"All right," I said. "It's a simple plan made complicated by the need to not get killed. The idea is to convince the Empire that this method of catching highwaymen is a bad idea. Now—"

"Do you do this sort of thing a lot?"

"What?"

"Convince the Empire to change how it does things."

"Not as often as you'd think."

"All right. Go on."

"We're going to arrange for the Empire to catch us using tagged coins, then make them wish they hadn't."

"Right. I already guessed that part."

"Then here's the rest."

I went over the whole thing, first in general, then more specifically, concentrating on the warning and the false chase. Then I went over it again. Then I said, "Questions?"

Cawti had one. "The first part, the race. What if they pull in help that heads him off before he gets to you?"

I frowned. "Good point. Kragar, get us ten reliable people stationed along the route to get in the way in case the law gets too close."

"How much am I paying them for this?"

"Enough, but not too much."

"Thank you so much."

"You're welcome. Any other questions?"

Fox-fellow had one: "Is this going to work?"

I considered that. "Almost certainly, probably, there's a good chance, perhaps, and I very much hope so, depending on which part of it we're discussing. Your end, almost certainly."

"That's reassuring," he said as if it wasn't.

"And," said Ibronka, "what about your end? By which I mean, the result."

"If everything else works, I'm hopeful about that."

"I'm glad to know your state of mind," she said as if she weren't.

Kragar nodded toward Omlo. "Uh, I don't know you, so no offense, but you don't look like you could pull off the part. Are you an actor?"

"In a way, m'lord."

"He's one of my tags," I said.

"Ah. All right, then."

The Blue one said, "What's a tag?"

"A prostitute," I said. "They have to be able to act, at least a little, and they're usually pretty hungry for money."

He frowned. "I've never heard that expression."

"Years ago," I said, "street prostitutes used to walk around with a tag on their shoulders, listing their price."

"Oh."

Ibronka said, "If we're going to do this, let's do it."

I looked at the two of them. "I take it, then, that you find your parts acceptable."

"Yes."

"Yes."

"Good. The first thing that has to happen is the Skin needs to make contact with the Anvil. Kragar? Find anything?"

"He is exceptionally fond of small sculpted objects, especially jade and silver."

"Silver sculpted objects?"

"Yes."

"Okay, I have something that should work. It's in my flat; I'll send for it. Omlo, in the Dragon Wing there will be an office for Lord Feorae. He is responsible for civic and county investigations. Find somewhere to wait near his office. There's probably a waiting room just outside of it."

"My lord, what do I say if someone asks me what I'm doing there?"

"Give him an evasive answer."

"My lord?"

"You're an aristocrat. Make yourself look like, I don't know, a Hawk." I found a scrap of paper and wrote an address on it, handed it to him. "When we're done, go there and tell them you're from me, and you need to pass for a Hawklord—ears, complexion, and everything."

"I can do that."

"And can you act the part?"

"I believe so, m'lord."

"Look vague and distracted most of the time. If you're asked a question, sniff and look disdainful."

"And if doing so should incite a challenge, my lord?"

"Don't sniff that loudly."

"Yes, my lord."

"If you sniff just loud enough, and hit the disdainful perfectly, you won't have to wait too long to see him. Then, well, lay it out. You have the item and a sudden need for money."

"And if he asks me why?"

"Gambling debts."

He nodded.

"Put the proposition simply. Yes, no, or he'll think about it. Kragar will give you a psiprint and a description of the object. It's a silver tiassa, very small and delicate, with sapphires for eyes. I think Feorae will want to buy it, but we'll see."

"Yes, m'lord."

"If he says yes, you can get it to him as soon as tomorrow."

He nodded. Maybe he'd run out of m'lords.

"Are you clear on what you need to do?"

"Yes, m'lord." Guess he had another.

"As soon as you have the material, head straight over to the Dragon Wing and get started. In the meantime, we'll just wait here. Shouldn't take long."

He nodded, looking a little nervous, like it had just become real to him.

Foxy nodded to Omlo. "Do you like it?"

"My lord?"

"The job. Do you like it?"

"It seems all right so far, m'lord."

"No, not this job, being a pr—, a tag."

"Oh. It's all right."

"What House are you? I can't tell from looking at you."

"Chreotha, m'lord."

"How did you end up in your line of work?"

"My lord? I'm not sure how to answer that. I guess I just fell into it."

"That's it? You fell into it?"

Omlo seemed puzzled. "Yes, my lord." He looked at me.

"My lord the Fox wants to hear a hard luck story," I told him.

Omlo frowned. "There wasn't anything else I wanted to do, or was any good at. And the money is all right."

"Do you have a pimp?"

"No, m'lord. What I earn is all mine after I split with the house."

"Earn," he said.

Omlo looked puzzled.

"I just don't know much about it," said Blue. "I'm curious. That's a whole world I've never come in contact with, and it makes me curious. What it's like working in a house, sex with someone you've never even met—"

"Or," I told Omlo, "he might be considering switching careers."

Ibronka reached out a hand and touched his arm. "Maybe you should drop it," she said. I couldn't tell who she was addressing, but if it was me I was willing.

Sometime during the conversation Kragar had returned; I know because it was about then he said, "It's ready."

I nodded to Omlo, who rose, bowed, and set off to begin the operation, Kragar leading the way.

"What now?" asked Fox.

"Nothing until we get a solid draw on Feorae."

"You're that sure we will?"

"If not, it'll take longer, or we'll find a different Anvil. Is there an especial hurry?"

"Not as long as my money holds out."

"If you need a loan, I have some names for you."

"Thanks."

"Where do you stay in town?"

"With friends. Why?"

"If you tell me how to reach these friends, I'll let you know when we're ready to start."

He looked at Ibronka, who stared back at him; I suppose there was a fair bit of conversation I couldn't hear, but then he said, "Ironstone Manor, home of the Lady Lewchin, House of the Issola."

"I can get a message there."

"We'll be waiting."

He and Ibronka gave us each a bow. I called Melestav to escort them out of the office, then went back to my flat, found the tiassa still wrapped in its cloth, and brought it back.

Kragar, having finished guiding Omlo, had returned. I gave it to him with instructions to write up a description and have a psiprint done. He said, "It's a pretty thing, Vlad. Sure you're willing to lose it?"

"It's in a good cause," I said. "Get the material to Omlo, then send him on his way."

"Right."

"You know what to do with the case?"

"Yep."

"Good, then."

"By the way, Vlad, I didn't want to contradict you in front of the civilians, but the tags weren't worn on the shoulders. Around the wrist like a bracelet."

I stared at him. "You mean, I was right about where the term comes from? I was just making it up."

"I know," he said. "So am I."

"Be funny if we were right."

"Not that funny."

"If you were in town after a successful robbery, where would you go to spark the dark?"

"Somewhere not in town."

"Right. Failing that?"

"I don't know. Someplace not too low, not too high. Big enough for a party, but—"

"Not in general. Name the place."

"What do I win if I guess it?"

"Loiosh won't eat you."

"*I don't think you can guarantee—*"

"Can't pass that up." He shrugged. "The Flagpole?"

I nodded. "Yeah, that should work. Good call."

He glanced at Loiosh through narrowed eyes. "You heard that, right?"

"*Tell him I think he's really cute when he acts tough.*"

"*I think I won't.*"

Kragar left me alone. I laid out a map of the city, and drew circles over the two significant places, then a line connecting them. I studied the various paths until I had one that would work, then went back out onto the streets, heading for Malak Circle, feeling pretty happy about things. I knew what everyone was supposed to do, and we had even gotten started. The only things that were a little hazy were the consequences, and I've never especially concerned myself with those.

I took my time walking across town until I reached the Flagpole, a public house that overcharged for everything. I went in, received scowls because I was human or Jhereg or both, and studied the place.

First of all, yes, it felt right: if I had to bet on some particular place checking for tagged coins, I'd be willing to lay good odds on this one. From the look of things, its fortunes had changed a few times over the centuries. The main room was a big square, with a large bar forming a circle, with an island in the middle full of glasses and bottles. There were a lot of windows, all of them big and with the look as if they'd once had glass. The tables were of varying sizes and quality; same with the chairs. The floor was cracked and chipped marble, and the place smelled of ales and pilsners. There were nine patrons at six tables, Teckla except for a pair of Chreotha. All of them were old. It seemed about right for the middle of the day in a place that didn't serve food.

There were two hosts—no doubt there would be more when the place was busier. One of them was kind enough to pour me a cup of stout. I found a table, sat, and pretended to drink the awful stuff while I looked around.

Yes, there were decent escape routes. The Phoenix Guards would come in the main door. They might have one covering the back, but that wouldn't matter; it would take too many of them to secure all the windows, and even if they tried, the Dog-man would see it in plenty of time. If we had bad luck, and there were already guards in the place, it would be even easier, because the door would be available. Good.

It took me about a minute to learn everything I had to, but I stayed for a while because not to would have attracted attention. There were no convenient floor plants to dump the stout into, so I forced myself to drink half of it. I should have asked for more money for this job.

I left the Flagpole and headed back to my office, thinking about Cawti.

I need to tell you about the place they jumped me. Right about where Garshos connects with North Garshos there is an area where, because of some strange confusion or dispute among the lords of the city, a stretch of some sixty or seventy feet is not actually part of any district. The only effect of this is that the row of three apartment buildings there— three, three, and four stories, respectively—has no effective garbage pickup. The garbage builds up in one corner, just off Garshos, until, usually once or twice a week, they burn it. The rest of the time, it stinks. When they're burning it, it stinks, too. Not my favorite part of town.

It was stinking pretty bad that day, because the pile was ten or eleven feet high. There were two Jhereg toughs hidden behind it. Across the street from the trash heap, there was a grocer's with an open front; the other two Jhereg were inspecting vegetables, with their backs to me about ten feet away. For a job that had to have been done with minimal planning, it wasn't a bad set-up.

The two of them turned around; presumably they had a lookout giving them timing, but I never saw him. I did see the first pair of Jhereg tough guys start turning toward me, and then things happened fast.

"Two behind you, Boss. I'm on 'em."

I took a step toward them, because stepping into an attack always throws off the other guy's timing and distance. I had time to notice that they were carrying lepips, which meant they wanted to beat me, not kill me. I would have been relieved if I'd had time.

I pulled a knife from each boot and tossed them underhanded at the two in front of me—one missed, the other poked a guy in the side; both of them flinched. I drew my blade and slashed at the nearest, ruining his pretty face, which gave me time to skewer the other in the middle of his body. He dropped his lepip and doubled over; must have gotten a good spot. I slashed at the first again, but missed when he fell backward.

I took the opportunity to turn around, which was just as well; one of them had gotten past Loiosh and was coming at me. I didn't like the idea of his heavy lepip against my little rapier, so I pulled three shuriken from inside my cloak and sent them in his direction. One shuriken scratched his forehead, one missed, and the last almost clipped Loiosh's wing where he was tagging around the other one's head.

"Boss. . . ."

"Sorry."

The scratch on the forehead was enough to disorient the guy a little. It got worse for him when I raised my rapier like I was going to bring it down on his head, and even worse when I let a dagger fall into my left hand and then put it into his stomach. He indicated that he was no longer interested in the contest, though he didn't say it in so many words.

I turned toward the one who'd fallen over. He was just starting to get up. I raised my weapon and said, "Don't." He looked at me, then relaxed again. That left the one Loiosh was dancing with. I turned my attention to that one, but he was running away as fast as he could.

I took a couple of steps forward and stood over the one lying on his back. I don't think I'd have known him even if his face weren't bleeding, not to mention contorted; he didn't look very happy. I put the point of my rapier at his left eye and said, "Feel like telling me who gave the orders?"

He was vehement in the expression of his feelings; no, he didn't feel like telling me anything. The others wouldn't either; it was a waste of time to ask them, so I cleaned my blade on his cloak, patted his shoulder, and walked away.

"Who, Boss?"

"I'm wondering that myself."

I checked my clothing as well as I could; it had come out of it more or less intact, but I stopped at the fountain near Boiden Square Market and splashed some water on my face. I wasn't shaking too bad, and after standing in the market for half an hour or so the shaking was gone completely.

"Any idea how to figure it out, Boss?"

"Not yet."

I went back to the office and nodded to Melestav, who nodded back. I guess there were no visible signs of what I'd just been through or he'd have raised his eyebrow or something. I sat behind my desk, told myself I was fine, and spent a few hours dealing with business and trying not to worry too much about how Omlo was doing with Feorae or who had just wanted to inflict harm on me, and why. I did spend some time thinking about how I was going to play it with Foxy after it went down, but I couldn't come to any hard conclusions; some things you just can't plan until you get there. And there were still too many things I didn't know.

Omlo returned early in the evening. He came sauntering into my office like a Dzurlord into a parlor. He had the dark complexion, narrow eyes, and wore the black clothing of a Hawklord. He looked good. "Ah, Lord Taltos," he said, before I could open my mouth. "I suppose you'd like to hear the results of my little venture." He pulled a chair up close to my desk, sat in it, and put his feet up. It would have annoyed me if it weren't so funny, especially when he yawned.

I kept my face straight and said, "If you'd be good enough to tell me, m'lord."

He blushed and dropped character and said, "He went for it, my lord. It went almost perfectly."

"Almost?"

"He met my price too easily; I should have asked for more money."

I chuckled. "Good work. Take a moment to relax, and we'll go over your next part—it's the tricky one."

"Yes, m'lord."

I stuck my head out of the office and had Melestav send word to Ironstone Manor for the rest of the crew to be here in the morning; then I returned to Omlo and said, "So, how was it?"

He smiled bashfully. "I may change careers, m'lord."

I grinned. "You like being a confidence artist?"

"An actor."

"Ah. A bit of a drop in money and prestige, but I suspect you'll do well. I can probably give you some help with that, in fact."

"My lord? Are you serious?"

"Are you?"

He hesitated, then nodded.

"Then so am I," I told him.

"My lord," he said, "I'd be very grateful."

"It's nothing. No trouble for me. Meantime, let's work up the next part. We have a day to get ready, so let's be at it. The timing is tricky, but it shouldn't be *too* tricky."

He nodded. "I'm ready, m'lord."

"All right, we'll start with the transfer. Here's how it's going to work. . . ."

In an hour he had it. In two, he was good at it. So we kept at it for about six, with a break for some food. During the break, Omlo said hesitantly, "My lord?"

"Hmm?"

"Did you mean it? About helping me?"

"With an acting career? Sure. There are two companies that operate in this area, and they both like the idea of me being well disposed toward them."

He made grateful sounding mutters for a while.

I said, "But you know, the theater isn't the same as just putting on a role like you did today, or like you've been doing. Having a big audience is different."

"I know, my lord. It's something I've wanted to do for a long time, though. Ever since my paener used to take me to the Marketday Players on Settler."

I nodded. "What House are you, Omlo? I mean, when you aren't pretending?"

"Chreotha, my lord."

"I'm surprised."

"My lord?"

"You said that before, in front of the civilians. I just assumed you were lying."

"My lord? Why?"

I shrugged. "So, what do your people do?"

"My father does ceramics, my mother works with pewter."

"And you ended up in one of my brothels."

"My lord?"

"It's just a curious thing, that's all. What do you think our friends are up to?"

"My lord?"

"Blue-boy and Ibronka. What do you think their game is?" He looked blank, so I said, "Don't worry,

I don't expect you to know; I'm mostly thinking aloud. Wondering what they really want."

"You think they lied to you, m'lord?"

"I know they lied about some things, so that makes me think they're lying about more."

"My lord, what did they lie to you about?"

I started to answer, but stopped before the words were out of my mouth. "What did he lie to you about?"

"My lord?"

"You didn't ask what he lied about, you asked what he lied *to me* about. I want to know what he lied to you about."

"Oh. He said he didn't know anything about the life, my lord."

"He was lying? You've seen him?"

"The two of them, in the house, the Couches."

"Why didn't you tell me this before?"

The question seemed to surprise him. "My lord, we never publicly recognize a num unless the num invites us to. That's just, that's how it works."

"Hmm. All right. But you did see them?"

"A few times in passing. I never entertained them."

"When were they there?"

He squinted. "The first time, maybe half a year ago. Then two or three times after that. The last time was last month. Not since then."

"Who entertained them?"

"Neritha. She was good with threesomes."

"What can you tell me about her?"

"I think she's a Tsalmoth. She started there three years ago, just after I did."

"What's she like?"

He rubbed his chin. "Nice enough, but kind of

hard. Not the kind who was making a career of it, but more like she wanted to get a score together and go somewhere."

"She's still there?"

"No, my lord. I haven't seen her in, I think, about three months. She was just gone one day. I heard she was caught stealing from nums."

"I'll bet H'noc loved that. Any word on what he might have done to her?"

"No, my lord."

"She have a pimp?"

"I don't think so."

"Addicted to anything?"

He shook his head.

I nodded. "So, that answers some questions. And asks some more. I'll total them up later and see which is higher. Just a minute."

I left him there while I found Kragar, to whom I said, "I don't think you have enough to do."

He rolled his eyes. "Vlad, you've already got me—"

"This one is easy. Get the story of a tag named Neritha, at the Couches, who was probably caught stealing from nums. That's all."

"Any reason I can't just ask H'noc?"

"No. Yes. Try to find out some other way."

"Now?"

"Now."

I went back and worked with Omlo for another hour or two then let him go, confident that he had his part down. I hung around for about an hour after that, until Kragar showed up.

He said, "The most surprising thing is that it really was simple. She was caught stealing, and—"

"How?"

"Num complained, H'noc checked it."

"Heh. Good for him. What did he do?"

"Broke her arms, broke her legs, gave her a case of the drips, and kicked her."

"The drips. Nasty. When did this happen?"

"Nine weeks ago. I'm sure she's fine by now. Do you need me to find her?"

"Set someone on it in case, but don't put a lot into it. I'm guessing there's no need."

"All right. Anything else?"

"Yes. Touch Omlo and let him know I need him here early tomorrow. Real early. Seventh hour."

"Care to grab some food after I do that?"

"Why not? Nothing else to do. You paying, what with all the bonuses I just gave you?"

"Keep dreaming, Vlad."

I didn't see Cawti that night; she was spending time with her ex-partner, Norathar, who—no, skip it, it's too long a story. So without her there, I passed a bitter night alone with my guilt for all the evil I've done. Okay, not really; I had two glasses of Fenarian brandy (because Dragaeran brandy tastes like the stuff you use to clean the klava press), read a chapter of Devin's *Trial of the Bell Ringer*, and went to sleep. But I did miss her.

I got to the office very early the next day, but Omlo was there before I'd finished my second cup of klava. I had extra klava brought in for him.

"Run through it all," I told him. "Just words. Talk it."

He nodded, sipped his klava, and spoke in a slow,

measured stream. When he was finished, I said, "Good. That's good. You have it."

He bobbed his head.

I had some more klava and said, "You want to make some extra money?"

He looked suspicious; it was like he was getting to know me or something.

I said, "I'll lay it out for you. You don't have to do this, but if you decide to, we have to go over it fast, because you need to be solid with it before the rest of the crew shows up."

"Is it dangerous, my lord?"

I took a moment to decide how to answer; but as the Shereba players say, *if you're going to hesitate that long, pass.* "Yes," I said.

"How dangerous?"

"I don't know yet."

"M'lord, may I wait until you know before deciding?"

I chuckled. "That's only fair, I suppose. The trouble is, we don't have that kind of time. Foxy and Ibronka will be here in a couple of hours, and if you're going to do this, you need to be solid on it by then. I don't think the heat will go to you, and if it does, I think I can protect you. But I can't promise. Tiassa are almost as unpredictable as Tsalmoth, and Dzur are as bad-tempered as Dragons. Do you understand?"

"Yes, m'lord."

"So take all the time you need to decide, up to five minutes. The job pays one hundred imperials."

His eyes widened at the amount, but greed did not

instantly overcome him, the way it would have a Jhereg, or an Orca. He sat and thought about it. After about four minutes, he nodded.

"Good," I said. "Now, let me run it down."

When he had it, I still had a little time, so I had him wait while I spoke to Kragar about the rest of it. He listened quietly as he always does. When I'd finished, he didn't say anything. After a bit, I said, "Well?"

"I'm just trying to remember if I've ever heard of anything stupider. I think I have. I'm pretty sure I have. I just want to see if I can—"

"Okay, okay. What would you suggest instead?"

"You want me to—"

"Cut it out. Come up with a better suggestion, help me fill the holes in this one, or at least tell me what they are, all right?"

"I didn't mean to say you shouldn't do it, just that it's stupid."

"Not as stupid as getting married to the girl who killed you."

"Well, yeah, that would be . . . wait. Are you serious? You mean that girl who—"

"Yeah."

"You want to marry her?"

"She asked me. I said yes."

"Vlad, have you lost it completely?"

"Pretty much."

He was quiet for a long two minutes. Then he cleared his throat and said, "Uh, congratulations, I guess."

"Thanks, I think."

"Feel like telling me about it?"

"Not really. I'd rather we go back to talking about

the other stupid idea. You're saying we should go with it?"

It took him a moment to recall what we'd been talking about, but then he said, "I can't come up with anything better."

"All right, then."

"Who do you want me to grab for this?"

"We'll need a sorcerer who specializes in light extraction from candlebud, a smith who can fabricate a four-foot surgical-quality needle, an acrobat who can do both wide-spar and high-rope, a swimmer who is fluent in Serioli, a—"

"You can stop now, Vlad. I saw that play, too."

"Good. I couldn't remember the other two."

"Who do you need?"

"You. Me. Omlo. Enough muscle to keep me alive during the fun part if things go wrong. Sticks, Shoen, and two others who are reliable."

"If we add a couple more, can we keep me alive, too?"

"We could, but I don't want to spend that much. Get on it. I have guests arriving soon."

4

They all arrived on time—a small miracle—and took seats.

"How are things so far?" asked Foxy.

"Good. Today we do the swap."

He looked at Omlo. "Is he ready?"

"Omlo, are you?"

"I think so."

"So, what do we do next?" asked Kragar.

We all looked at him. I cleared my throat and said, "Three of them are practicing their parts. You're going to run out and bring us back some breakfast. Steamed sweet rolls stuffed with kethna. Make sure they're hot."

"I should have seen that coming," he said.

"Don't forget one for Loiosh."

He shook his head and walked out.

"Boss, you're the best."

"Don't ever forget it."

I went over things with them, then did so again,

by which time Kragar was back with breakfast. Everyone enjoyed the food—Blue-guy exceptionally so. I liked that; it's always a pleasure to introduce someone to a delicacy he hadn't been aware of.

We ate, went over things once more, then I said, "All right. Unless there are questions, the Runner and the Dog-man might as well get started."

"No questions here," said Ibronka.

I studied her. "Sorry," I said.

"About what?"

"The lack of action for you."

"Sorry? I assumed you'd done it just to annoy me."

"I probably would have, if I'd thought of it."

She made a sound somewhere between a sniff and a snort.

I told Omlo, "You should get into position as well. Good luck."

"Yes, m'lord. Thank you, m'lord."

They set off. Kragar ate another roll, wiped his fingers, and said, "You know, Vlad, the biggest hole with the plan is that it isn't a plan, it's about six."

"Four. Depending on how it plays out."

"That's all right, then."

"You have about half an hour to round everyone up and get them in position."

"Oh, good. I was afraid you were going to rush me."

I led the way to the Cups, about three-quarters of a mile south and east of my office. It was as I remembered it—cramped and crowded on the inside, spacious on the outside. The street it faced was narrow and curved; there was a wide market area just out of sight to the north, or right as you faced the street.

Directly across the street was a three-story stone-work house—the sort of place that held families of Teckla who for some reason worked in the city. On the wall facing me, someone had created quasi-abstract art in which I could, possibly, make out male genitalia, the face of the Empress, and various obscenities.

It was early evening, and the inside of the Cups was full of Teckla and a few merchants; the outdoor area, mostly taken up with Lyorn and Hawklords, had plenty of empty tables. I took one, and eventually got someone to bring me a pitcher of iced wine.

And now, for a while, I can only give you a combination of speculation and what I was told or deduced afterward: I was drinking iced wine when all the fun stuff was happening, and since I didn't get to see it, neither do you. Sorry.

So, while I was sitting at the Cups, a host at the Flagpole checked one of the coins he'd been given, and, whether by bell, vibration, changing color, or some other way, he learned that the coin had been tagged.

Maybe he found a kitchen boy to run an errand. Maybe he had a bell that rang sympathetically in the headquarters of the Phoenix Guards. Or they may have had some other means of communication that hasn't occurred to me. It doesn't matter; what matters is that the constabulary were called and told that tagged coins had been passed, which, in the lingo of the trade, kicked the first log. We were moving now, and things would happen in regular sequence—or not. Of course, at the time I didn't know just what was happening, or exactly when.

The Phoenix Guards showed up—two of them, I later learned. Ibronka spotted them easily, warned Blue, and he was through a window and gone.

I wish I'd been able to see the race. From what I heard, Foxy started out with a good lead, and had to slow down a bit to avoid losing them completely.

I was told none of the guys I'd set up to interfere with the chase were needed. Wasted money, unless you believe that if I hadn't hired them I'd have needed them. I sort of believe that.

Blue found me at the Cups and sat down across from me.

"Any problems?" I said.

"None so far." He set the bag of coins on the table.

"Good," I said, as Omlo arrived from behind me, scooped up the bag, and walked away; never saying a word or even acknowledging our presence—just like a damned Hawklord. Blue-boy walked off in the other direction. So far as I could tell, no one had noticed anything.

I remained at the table and had some more wine.

I was only there for a couple of minutes after Omlo left when Ibronka showed up. She sat down across from me and said, "Well?"

"As far as I know. I imagine my lord the Fox will be a while yet. Meantime, we wait. What shall we chat about?"

"We could discuss what your corpse will look like after it has been left to rot on the beach for a month or two."

"I'm going to assume that means you'd rather not engage in small talk while we wait."

Around the time we were having that conversation,

Bluey had let himself be caught. If he'd been a Jhereg, it wouldn't have mattered as much that he didn't have tagged coins on him—they'd have either planted something on him or beaten him. But he was a Tiassa, so eventually they let him go.

Not fair, if you ask me.

Just to remind you, I didn't know about any of this at the time. I knew what was supposed to happen, and I learned later what actually did happen, and since at this point they were the same, that's what I'm telling you, all right? Turn that thing off for a minute, I need some water.

Where was I? Right. Fox-boy was taken and, after an hour or so of questions, released. Meanwhile, Omlo proceeded to his meeting, now carrying several imperials' worth of tagged gold. The meeting was set for Feorae's office in the Dragon Wing of the Palace—a bit that pleased me. It's always worth a little extra to have one on a Dragonlord, even if you can't let anyone know.

Omlo made it to Feorae's office pretty close to when he said he would—close enough for a Hawklord, anyway. Omlo pulled out a case, opened it, and carefully removed a lovely silver tiassa with sapphires for eyes. Feorae studied it and tried not to show how excited he was. Omlo accepted six hundred and forty imperials in gold and pushed the case toward Feorae, leaving a little present in it as he did so. He rose, bowed, and left. The good lord Feorae studied his new prize for a few minutes; then, being a conscientious administrator, he put the tiassa back in its case, put the case on a shelf of the room where he kept his treasures, then went back to doing the work the Empire paid him to do.

And he continued doing it until the Phoenix Guards came to see him.

The first I knew of any of this was when Blue arrived at the table. He and Ibronka kissed while I signaled for more wine and another cup. I poured for each of them out of the pitcher.

"Good stuff," said Fox when he tasted it. "I like the fruit."

"An Eastern drink," I said. "Wine, fruit, and fizzy water. Good for hot days."

"It isn't all that hot anymore."

"No, but I imagine it will be before we're done talking." He cocked an eyebrow. I asked him how it went.

"Like you said," he told me. "They said I'd been detected with coins that had been used in a robbery. I was offended. They asked if they could search me. I said they couldn't. They insisted, and brought in some friends in case I chose to resist. I protested, but gave in to overwhelming numbers—" He chuckled here and exchanged a grin with Ibronka. "—and let them."

"Of course, they didn't find any coins."

"Of course not."

"Must have made them suspicious, what with you running and all."

He nodded. "I had the impression they didn't believe me. I was offended."

"Did you challenge them to a duel?"

"I thought about it. They asked me where I had gotten the coins. I said that if there had been any coins, which I wasn't admitting, I'd received them from Lord Feorae, who kept them in a small case that also held a silver tiassa. I had no idea why he kept money there, and I did not choose to tell them what I was being paid for."

"Perfect."

"What happens now?"

"If everything goes right, Omlo should come strutting in like an Amro bull and announce that everything worked."

Blueboy chuckled. "I can't imagine the boy strutting."

"Playing the part. He's good at it."

Out on the street, people walked by, mostly Teckla on their way home from menial jobs.

"What did you mean," said Fox, "about it getting hot. That sounded, uh, what's the word, love?"

"Ominous," said Ibronka.

"Right. Ominous."

"Didn't mean to be ominous. I was aiming for dire, but with this wind, sometimes my distance shots go wide."

Omlo appeared just then, still acting the part of the Hawklord, giving Ibronka a bow, Blue-boy a nod, and me a glance; then he sat down without any invitation, stretched, and put his hands behind his neck. I called for another cup and poured him some wine.

"Told you," I said.

"You were right," said Blue.

"Care to tell us about it, Lord—uh, I don't know what name you gave yourself."

Omlo became himself again. "Chypan, m'lord. It went as you said it would."

"So he has the tiassa."

"And the case."

I nodded. "And by now, the Phoenix Guards have Feorae, and are wondering what to do with him."

Blue nodded. "Hard to arrest for tagged coins the man in charge of carrying out arrests for possession of tagged coins."

Omlo said, "Is there any chance—"

"No," I said. "You're safe. Though I'd run off and change clothes pretty fast. You wouldn't want to be recognized by any of our fine law enforcement officers."

"Yes, m'lord. I'll be right back."

"And so," Foxy said when he'd left, "now we just wait for the results? They get so embarrassed that they stop tagging coins?"

"Something like that," I said.

"You're being evasive, Lord Taltos," said Ibronka. The Blue Fox frowned at her, then looked at me.

"Pretty," I said, "and smart, too. You're a lucky guy." His eyes narrowed. "What haven't you told us?"

"What haven't you told me?"

"No, you answer our question," said Ibronka.

"Why?"

"Because if you don't I'll eviscerate you."

"All right. I just wanted to be sure you had a good reason."

She leaned forward and started to say something, but Bluey put a hand on her shoulder, and she sat back, still looking at me. I decided I would really prefer it if she didn't decide to kill me.

"Right. It's pretty simple. The whole thing you came to me with was nonsense to begin with."

"What do you mean?" asked the guy with the funny name.

"The idea of the Empire trying to stop robbery by sorcerously marking coins is reasonable, but you being worried about it isn't. In a year or two there will be so many tagged coins floating around that they'd go nuts trying to separate the innocent from the guilty."

"Then why did they do it?"

"They don't worry about there being a bit of robbery on the highways, they just have to make it look like they're worried about robbery on the highways, so the merchant Houses don't raise too much of a fuss. They're always coming up with ways to try to make the roads safe. Remember when they had teleporting squads of Phoenix Guards? How long did that last? A year? And before that, they tried using ravens to watch the roads. And Phoenix Guards dressed up as merchants. All sorts of crazy things. So I asked myself, why would you even be worrying about it when it will go away by itself?"

Ibronka was staring hard. I ignored her. "So, I wondered what you were really after. I thought it over, and did a little checking. I was wrong about you. I thought you'd made up the part about being a highwayman; but it turns out that you actually were one, a few hundred years ago. I was surprised."

"So you know who I am," he said.

"I knew who you were when we met. You're the Viscount of Adrilankha. That's why I agreed to do the job in the first place: I thought it would be useful to have your mother owe me a favor. Your father, too, for that matter."

"I see." He didn't look very happy. "Well, I wouldn't think anyone would owe you a favor if that escapade we just pulled off didn't do anything. And you've just explained why there was no need to convince the Empire to stop tagging coins. So—just what is it that we did?"

I shook my head. "That part's easy. What bothered me was: Why?"

All expression was gone from his face. He said, "Did you find out?"

"Nothing more than theories."

"And you think I'm going to tell you."

"Probably."

"*Careful, Boss. She looks like she's ready to move.*"

"*I've noticed. Think she's a sorcerer, too, Loiosh?*"

"*Don't know. She's a Dzur, so probably.*"

I felt the weight of Spellbreaker around my left wrist, but left it there.

"The first time we met," I said, "you were trying to make me attack you."

"Yeah? Why didn't you?"

"Because I figured out you wanted me to. I'm just contrary that way."

"So what does your contrariness want now?"

"There's an ancient Eastern sport called fox hunting. The best hunters, I'm told, used to have a remarkable collection of tails."

"Perhaps," he said, "now isn't the best time to turn my bait."

"Yeah, all right."

"You were saying something about why you think we did whatever you think we did."

"I know," I said, choosing my words carefully so

that it wouldn't sound like I was choosing my words carefully, "that people do stupid things. I've done stupid things. It happens."

"What's your point, Jhereg?"

"Nothing is more stupid than falling in love with a tag."

His hand jerked toward his blade, but stopped and he sat back. He glared. It was a good glare; I was impressed. I took another chance: "I'm sorry," I said. "I didn't mean to call your lover stupid. These things happen."

He remained motionless, still glaring.

"Tags don't fall in love," I said.

He snorted. "Right. Their profession means they aren't human."

I ignored the potential confusion over what "human" meant and said, "My mistake. Tags do fall in love. But they don't fall in love with nums."

"Nums?"

"Numbers. Clients. It doesn't happen. That means it's all one-way."

"If you're giving me advice on—"

"Foxy, shut up before you say something stupid. You went out for some fun, and you or your lover or both of you fell for the tag. It happens. But it doesn't go the other way. Maybe she likes you two, but that's as far as it goes. That's as far as it can go. If you don't figure that out, you'll both end up more miserable than you already are."

Ibronka stood up; her hand was shaking. She really wanted to kill me. "Stop it," I told her. "You're only upset because you know I'm right. I don't like you any more than you like me, but I'm telling you the truth. Tags don't fall for nums. You know that."

Fox-boy, still glaring, one hand on Ibronka's arm, said, "If I already know it, why are you saying it?"

"I'm trying to figure out why you're coming after me."

"Because you had her beaten, and cursed."

"Actually, H'noc did, as you know."

"He works for you."

"True enough." I shrugged. "She worked for me, too. And she stole from nums. That's what happens when you do that. And there are healers, you know. By now—"

"Not the point," he said.

"No," I said. "I suppose it isn't." I sighed. "You understand, I hope, that you're an idiot."

Oddly, that did nothing to reduce the glare he was still sending at me. Fortunately, I'm used to being glared at, and it no longer gives me the night sweats.

I leaned back. "You went through all that work because a tag who stole from a num got slapped around a little. What was my man supposed to do, give her a bonus? So you arrange to have me beaten—nice move, by the way, two for one, and then—what—you wanted to get me arrested? You know what happens if I go down for possession of tagged coins? A fine, a few lashes, maybe a little time. Then I'm right back here. What's your point, anyway?"

"I've heard all I want to," he said.

"If you'd talked me into attacking you the first time we met, you weren't even planning to kill me, were you? Just cut me up a bit." I shook my head. "Like I said, you're an idiot."

"If you want to pay in full," said Ibronka, "it isn't too late."

"Yes, it is," said Blue-boy. "He wouldn't be talking like this if he didn't have his people all around us. They'll cut us down before we have time to draw, love." He looked at me. "Right?"

I looked back at him and nodded once.

Ibronka said, "It might be worth the attempt."

The Viscount shook his head.

"Stay alert. If it happens, it'll be fast."

"I was about to tell you that, Boss. I'm on the Dzur."

I signaled for another pitcher. No one had spoken by the time it arrived, but after I'd poured us each another cup, Ibronka sat down. Fox-guy said, "So, what do we do about this?"

"I don't know. The wine is good. We can just enjoy one another's company. Talk a little. Exchange thoughts. Do you think any of the new foot-tax will actually end up helping the poor? And just who counts as the 'poor' anyway? Or we could talk about the new Botanical Garden they're building near the Tsalmoth Wing. I'd like to see a section of roses. What would you like?"

Ibronka said, "I think I have a good chance of taking your head off before your people drop me."

"Okay, then, you pick the topic."

"Or maybe instead of taking it off, I'll split it down the middle. Like a melon, you know? If I do it just right, both halves will sort of tilt away from each other. It's the cutest thing."

"I'd be sad to miss it."

"There's something I'm not getting," said the guy in the blue cloak. "You've set up this meeting. You don't want to kill us, or you wouldn't do it this way, but you can certainly protect yourself. Or you at least think you can, which is the same thing."

"Philosophically, that's—"

"So, why are we here?"

"We really *are* getting philosophical, aren't we?"

"You enjoy banter as much as I do, but you've just been . . ." He cocked his head, then straightened up suddenly. "You're waiting for something." He stood. "Let's go, love."

"Too late," I observed, gesturing over Foxy's left shoulder at the gentleman who was approaching. He wore the black and silver of the House of the Dragon, and had the high cheekbones and characteristic bridged nose. His eyes were dark, and he didn't look altogether pleased.

As he approached, I rose and bowed. "Lord Feorae, I presume."

"You presume wrong," he said coldly. "My name is Donnel, and I have the honor to serve the Lord High Investigator of Adrilankha."

I nodded to Blue-boy. "The Lord High Investigator is Feorae. This guy works for him."

"I picked up on that."

"Of course you did." I turned back to Donnel. "I am Vl—"

"I know who you are," he said. His voice hadn't warmed up. "That was a nice move you made. My lord the Lord High Investigator is at present entangled with the Phoenix Guards. It will take some time

to get that straightened out. In the meantime, you,
Jhereg, may come along with me now, or wait until
the Phoenix Guards appear to escort you. But I assure you, if you wait for them, it will be more unpleasant for you."

I felt my eyebrows climb. "Me? What did I do?"

"You didn't think we could trace the coins?"

I sighed. "I had hoped not."

Foxy chuckled. "Not what you were hoping for,
perhaps? The wrong person getting arrested?"

I shrugged. "You take your best shot. I'll live."

Donnel turned to the Fox. "And as for you, sir,
I have nothing to say. This is between you and your
father."

Blue-boy stared off into space. "My father will understand. My mother will be disappointed, however." Then he turned to me. "Have a pleasant time
with the magistrates, Lord Taltos."

I stood and unbuckled my sword belt, passing the
rapier over to the constable. To Foxy I said, "Can I
expect you to be at the flogging, at least? It will help
to look into your smiling face."

"Sorry," he said, "public punishments aren't my
thing."

"I'll be there," said Ibronka. "If they give you more
than fifty. Otherwise it isn't worth my time."

I smiled. "When I'm done with this, maybe we'll
finish our conversation."

"Maybe we will," said Foxy.

"*Loiosh, take off; it'll save trouble.*"

"*Whatever you say, Boss.*" He launched himself
from my shoulder and flew in a high circle before
heading back toward my part of the city.

Donnel took hold of my arm above the elbow. I wanted to glance back at the Blue Fox and Ibronka, but I resisted the temptation.

Donnel led me away.

5

As we got around the corner, Kragar said, "Where to now, Vlad?"

I jumped, cursed, and said, "Back to the office. You can send the muscle home."

"All right."

"Omlo, you can break character now; we're safe."

My captor released me and said, "Yes, my lord." He handed me back my sword belt and I strapped it on.

"See there? You didn't even die."

"When they looked at me, I was sure they could see through my disguise."

"You managed it," I said. "And even if you hadn't, I had a few people there, ready to jump in." There was no reason to tell him that the people were there to keep me alive, and would probably have let him get cut to pieces.

We made it back to the office without incident,

and Cawti was waiting there. I suggested everyone sit down.

"Very cute," said Kragar.

"What?"

"The stupid grin on your face when you saw your assassin."

"Her name is Cawti," I said. "And the only reason I don't kill you is that I'm going to let her have the pleasure."

"Sometime," she agreed, "when you aren't expecting it."

"Not until you're married, I hope. I wouldn't want to miss the wedding."

"Oh, of course," she said.

"Goodness, Vlad. She even has your threatening smile."

"It's an Eastern thing."

I sat down behind my desk.

Omlo said, "My lord? Is it over?"

I nodded. "Yes. All finished. At least for a while."

"A while?" said Kragar.

"Until Foxy and his little friend figure out that I haven't been arrested and won't be fined and flogged. Then they might come back for me. Or maybe not. And you," I added, addressing Omlo, "should expect a visit from the Phoenix Guards."

"I—"

"Don't worry. You delivered some gold from the Viscount of Adrilankha to a Hawklord named, uh, whatever you called yourself. You received three copper pieces for this service. That's all you know. They won't spend much time with you."

"My lord," said Omlo, "can you explain?"

"Explain what?"

"Why we just did, ah, whatever it was we did."

"Oh. Our friend the Fox wanted me arrested and flogged and such because I owned the brothel where Neritha was beaten. They had an attachment to her. So we just convinced them that I've been arrested."

"But then, if it was all a fake, why did we go through all of that with Lord Feorae?"

"In the second place, to make it look good. In the third, just because it's fun to mess with the Phoenix Guards. In the first, because when Feorae sorts everything out, they'll do a trace, and the trail will lead back to you, and then to His Excellency the Viscount of Adrilankha, also known as the Blue Fox."

"But you—"

"I never touched the bag of gold," I said.

"*Boss, you're really irritating when you're smug.*"

"*Shut up.*"

Omlo considered this. "What happens then?"

"To him? Nothing. But word will get back to his mother and father, and now they owe me, because they'll know I could have made things uncomfortable and embarrassing for all of them, and I didn't."

"When," said Kragar, "did you figure out they didn't really want to hire you about the tagged coins?"

"It didn't make sense from the beginning," I said. "What's the point of working to beat a system that will collapse on its own? He had to be setting me up for something. I suppose I wasn't absolutely sure about it until I saw your report on him, and learned he hadn't been a highwayman for a long time."

"And how does this fit in with Byrna?"

"My guess is they went looking for someone who was in trouble with me. It shouldn't be too hard to find if you're willing to be friendly, spend money, and listen a lot in the right places."

Cawti said, "You know, Vlad, we really need to be aware that, once they realize what you pulled, they will come after us again."

I very much liked that "we" and "us." I said, "Maybe. But I have a theory that getting me in hot water was secondary. The main thing they wanted was something else, and they'll get that."

Kragar knew what his job was: "What's that?" he asked.

"The next order of business. Omlo, unless you have more questions, I won't need you for this part. It's just as well you don't know about it."

He stood and bowed. "You have my thanks, my lord."

"I'll see you on the stage," I said.

He smiled and backed out, still bowing—like you do for royalty. Nice touch, I thought.

When he'd gone, Kragar said, "Well?"

"The last bit is firing H'noc."

"For what?"

"For trying to have me beaten."

Cawti nodded. Kragar frowned. "When did he do that?"

"A few days ago. I didn't mention it because it didn't work out for him."

"How do you know it was him?"

"Because nothing else makes sense. Who else has a reason to attack me?"

"Everyone who knows you, Vlad. But what reason does he have?"

"Fox-boy got him to do it. I don't know, a bribe or a threat. I'll confirm it before I actually fire him."

"Why would he do that?"

"He was the one who actually beat Neritha, so Fox-boy and Ibronka are going to want him to pay. What better way to make him pay than to have me do it for them?"

"Oh," said Kragar. "And he could be that sure you'd figure it out?"

"Yeah. He studied me enough to know I'm not an idiot."

"I guess I should study you more."

"Heh."

Cawti said, "Can I help with the firing?"

"Sure. You and Kragar can escort me there, and then hang around outside and make sure I'm not interrupted."

"When are we doing this?" asked Kragar.

"Now," I said, and stood up.

On the way over, Kragar said, "When you fire H'noc, who are you going to get to run the place?"

"You want it?"

"No."

"Think Melestav will want it?"

"I doubt it."

"Maybe Tessie."

"He'd be good. Experienced."

"Yeah."

We reached the Couches and I walked in like I owned the place, partly on account of I did. The muscle at the door was someone I didn't recognize, but he evidently recognized me. He bowed and said, "My lord, how may I—"

"H'noc," I said. "Here. Now." There were a couple of nums hanging around, drinking and waiting to pick out their tags. They looked at me. I didn't much care.

He went off to get H'noc. I told the two nums that the business was closed for now, but they were welcome back tomorrow. I suggested that they leave right away. The Dragonlord looked like he might want to make an issue of it, but then he just shrugged and left. When they were gone, I moved to the back of the room and leaned against the wall, looking tough. H'noc arrived at once, flanked by the tough guy who'd been at the door, and another, taller and broader and equally dangerous-looking. I said, "You two: Go."

They looked at H'noc for instructions. I said, "Don't look at him, look at me. I'm saying to go away. Do it now."

They hesitated. Then first one and then the other turned and walked away. H'noc said, "My lord, if I have somehow—"

"Let's take a walk," I said.

Cawti and Kragar were behind us as I led him around to an alley behind the Couches; then they pulled back out of sight. H'noc didn't look altogether happy.

I drew and placed the point of my weapon under his chin. "You," I said, "are fired. Depending on how you answer my question, you might also be dead. Do you want to be dead? I think you don't want to be dead. If I'm wrong, tell me. Do you want to be dead?"

Ask someone a question with an obvious answer, and then insist he answer you. It's kind of humiliating, because it drums home to the guy just what position he's in. I know a few tricks like that, and I keep learning more.

H'noc said, "Ask your question."

"How did he talk you into it?"

He looked even less happy than he had, but he glared instead of cowering. Good decision: if neither is going to do any good, you might as well take your best shot at not being laughed at.

I pressed a little with my rapier. His head went back and a bead of blood appeared and ran down his neck. I said, "I know you wouldn't do it for money, not from a civilian. So what was it?"

"If I tell you, I get to live?"

"Yes."

"All right. He said if I didn't he'd shut me down."

"Now, just how was he going to do that?"

"His mother is the Countess of Whitecrest."

"He used his family influence? That's cheating. Why didn't you think to come to me with this problem?"

"My place, my problem."

"My place," I said. "Though right now I agree it's your problem, too."

He made a point of glancing down the length of my blade, then back up to meet my eyes. "Seems like," he said.

"All right," I said. "That's all I need to know."

"He said you wouldn't find out. Ooops, I guess."

"I guess."

I'd told him that if he answered my question, he'd get to live. But, like I said, I lie sometimes.

WHITECREST

Chapter One
KHAAVREN

The Captain of the Phoenix Guard received a summons at the ninth hour of the morning on Midweek. The Empress, it seemed, wanted a private audience with him in her breakfast room. Such a meeting at such a time was not unprecedented, but neither was it usual, so when Khaavren found the message waiting, he knew something was up.

He took the long walk to Her Majesty's apartments without speculating, or even wondering. He nodded to the guards on duty, and exchanged good-mornings with various acquaintances on the way, until he finally presented himself, and was admitted.

The Empress Zerika was dressed simply in her gold morning gown, which anyone but Khaavren would have at least admitted to himself was fetching, and she sat at her table nibbling at fruit and drinking tea. She nodded to Khaavren and gestured him to one of two chairs that had been set across from her. Khaavren knew that the Empress customarily breakfasted alone.

"Good morning, Captain. Tea?"

"Klava, if you have it."

The Empress nodded to a servant, and the klava was presently brought. Khaavren drank it as poured, with a napkin wrapped about it to protect his fingers, and waited for Zerika to speak.

She ate another bite of fruit, sipped her tea, and carefully set the cup down. It was, Khaavren noticed, a tiny little cup, thin and fragile-looking, decorated with red and blue wavy lines. She said, "Forgive me, Captain, but we're waiting for someone. I'd prefer not to have to repeat this."

"Of course, Majesty." He smiled. "I have klava."

"Have some fruit as well, if you wish. And there's some cheese and rolls."

"I'm fine, Majesty."

She nodded, and there was no further conversation for some minutes, until a servant announced the arrival of Kosadr. Khaavren kept his surprise to himself, nodded a greeting to the Court Wizard, and waited patiently while Kosadr accepted tea, cheese, and bread. The wizard ate slowly, carefully; Khaavren wanted very much to kick him. Studying Her Majesty, he had a suspicion that the Empress felt the same way.

Kosadr was lanky, dark, and not as young as he looked. He eventually seemed to realize he was holding things up, and said, "Please, Your Majesty, proceed."

Zerika smiled briefly. "Good wizard, you're the one who needs to speak. Please explain to me and to Khaavren what you began to tell me earlier."

Kosadr wiped his lips with a napkin and said, "Oh. Sorry." He cleared his throat. "Two days ago, we began to observe fluctuations in the yellow spectrum of the Esswora monitor rods. We immediately began localizing the surge and measuring the distension. As far as we can tell—"

"Excuse me," said Khaavren. "If I am supposed to understand any of that, I don't."

"Oh. Right. We are looking at a breakthrough."

"A breakthrough? Who breaking through what to where?"

"Into our world. The Jenoine."

"The Jenoine!"

"Please, Captain," said the Empress. "Sit down."

"Sorry." Khaavren sat down while a servant hurried to clean up the klava and replace it. "When? How many?"

"It's hard to say when. Our guess is that we have sixty hours, but not more than eighty. That assumes the inflow remains constant. Call it a bit less than three days. We can't be sure—precision isn't possible in something like this. And we don't know how many, but from the size of the fluctuations, it looks to be a major incursion."

"The first thing," said the Empress, "is to station troops nearby, as well as sorcerous defenses."

"I can't do anything about those," said Khaavren.

"I know. Please, Captain. Remain calm."

Khaavren nodded, took a deep breath, and exhaled slowly, berating himself. Losing his head would be of no help to anyone. But still, Jenoine!

"Are you back with us, Captain?"

"Yes, Majesty."

"I," said Kosadr, "will ask for assistance from Sethra Lavode."

The Empress nodded. "Good, but, Kosadr, you must also look for other means. For this purpose, the Orb will be at your disposal for fact-checking and research. I would have preferred to have more warning, but we work with what we have."

She turned to Khaavren. "From what we know, troops will be of no use. To the extent we want to test this, I'll speak with the Warlord. You're here for something else."

Khaavren nodded. "I'd wondered why you sent for me instead of Aliera."

"Because we have time to organize troops, and we have time to prepare arcane defenses and attacks. What do we not have time for, Captain?"

"The people."

"Exactly. Once we begin preparations, we'll not be able to keep this a secret. We cannot afford a panic. The Phoenix Guards and the troops can do little enough against the Jenoine, but are all we have against unrest."

"I understand, Majesty."

"Good, then. You each have your tasks; be about them."

The wizard and the captain rose, bowed to Her Majesty, and took their leave.

Their paths, as it happened, ran together for a considerable part of the long walk through the Imperial Wing. As they walked, Kosadr said, "Captain, may I make a confession?"

"I'm not a Discreet, but feel free."

"I have to admit, I'm looking forward to this."

Khaavren looked at him.

"I know, I know. It's terrible. But the fact is, I've held this post for twenty years, and I've spent my time re-wrapping spells before they unwind, and supervising interrogations. This is what I've trained for, you know what I mean?"

"I guess I do. But if you don't mind a word of advice—"

"Not at all."

"Don't let it go beyond me. I don't think Her Majesty would be pleased."

"Yeah, you're right."

Kosadr went off toward his chambers while Khaavren continued on to the Dragon Wing. Once there, he asked if the Warlord was in, and, upon being told that she was at her residence in Castle Black, asked that a message be sent requesting a meeting with her. He then dispatched another messenger to inform his staff where he was, and he settled in to wait. Being an old campaigner, he waited by, if not sleeping, then let's say dozing heavily.

He woke up, fully alert, nearly an hour later when he heard the words, "The Warlord will see you now."

He rose, bowed to the messenger—a young Dragonlord with light brown hair done into a tail that went halfway down his back—and entered the Warlord's chamber.

"Lady Aliera," he said. "Thank you for seeing me."

"Lord Khaavren. Always a pleasure."

"We are expecting an attack by Jenoine."

Aliera stared up at him, then slowly sat behind her desk. "Sit," she said.

Khaavren did so, noticing that Aliera's eyes were

turning from green to blue, which he had never seen before; he wondered if she did so sorcerously, or if it was natural. She was, he reflected, not only a Dragonlord, but e'Kieron; anything was possible.

"Give me the details," said Aliera.

"Kosadr will have more, but it seems there are signs of a buildup for a breakthrough. Magical signs. Something about the Esswora rods, or fluctuations. I don't know. But from what he said, it seems strong, and imminent. He said we probably have a bit over two days or—"

"I'll speak with the Necromancer," she said. "It may be possible to block it. I'll coordinate with Kosadr, of course."

"Her Majesty wants troops available as well."

"Why? To die gloriously? What else does she imagine—?"

"I don't know, Warlord. I'm passing on what Her Majesty said. No doubt if you speak to her—"

"Oh, I'll speak to her!"

Khaavren nodded. "If you can spare some for helping me control the city, and to help with evacuation, I'll appreciate it."

"Evacuation?"

"Probably. Anyone who remembers the Interregnum—"

"Of course."

Aliera obviously didn't care for her troops being used that way, but finally she grunted a sort of agreement.

"Thanks," said Khaavren. "Then that's all I have." He stood and bowed. "Thank you for seeing me, Warlord."

"Most welcome, Captain," said Aliera. Then she scowled. "Jenoine," she muttered.

"Indeed," said Khaavren, and took his leave, returning to his own quarters in the Dragon Wing. Once there, he pulled out his maps of the city, and lists of guard detachments, and began to work. Throughout the day he received reports of the state of the city, and was pleased that, although people were already starting to leave, there was as yet no sign of panic.

It was fully dark in the city when he finally finished. He stood, stretched, and called for his retainers to see that his orders—an impressive stack of paper— went to the right places.

Although entitled by his rank to transport provided by the Empire, Khaavren usually preferred a cab, because the chatter of the cabbie relaxed him. This time, however, it didn't relax him at all. The cabbie kept hinting that he wanted Khaavren to tell him what was going on in the city; that something was stirring, and people were nervous. Khaavren answered in grunts and monosyllables, and after a long time, the cabbie shut up. Khaavren undertipped him, then walked into the Manor feeling bad about it.

Upon entering, he handed his cloak to Cyl without a word, after which he at once went to his den, where, in due time, Orile arrived with wine and to help Khaavren off with his boots.

Khaavren sighed, wriggled his toes, tossed off half the glass of wine, and leaned his head back and closed his eyes.

"A difficult day, my lord?"

Hearing his wife's voice, he smiled, but didn't open his eyes. "You know me too well, Countess."

She pulled up a chair and sat down in front of him. "I've had dinner held. Do you want to talk about it?" As she spoke, she took one of his feet and began rubbing it.

"We could talk about how adorable you are," said Khaavren.

"Or about the shoulder-rub I'll be getting later," she said, smiling.

"Or that."

"Or about what's bothering you, if it is something you're permitted to discuss."

"No reason why not. Rumors are already circulating, you may as well hear the truth."

"What is it?"

"Signs the Jenoine are going to attempt a breakthrough."

"The gods!"

"Yes. And this time, it isn't by either sea, it's right here, just outside the city."

"They're going after the Orb?"

"It's possible."

The Countess exhaled loudly. "There was an attack only a year ago."

"Yes, by the Lesser Sea. Sethra Lavode herself dealt with that one, along with Aliera. This looks to be stronger. We don't know how many there will be."

"What are you doing?"

"Stationing guards to handle panic in the city and assisting evacuation. There will be a detachment around the Manor."

"I don't need more—"

Khaavren opened his eyes. "Countess!"

"My lord, we have twenty good soldiers here at all times. If necessary, I can call up thrice the number again. That is more than sufficient to protect our home against civil disturbance."

"But—"

"My lord! Just how frail do you imagine I am that you need to weaken the Empire itself just to see to it a glass window isn't broken? In another minute, I'll take insult."

Khaavren sighed. "Very well. It will be as you wish."

She gently set his foot down, put the other in her lap, and began rubbing it. "There, that wasn't so hard, was it? I'm told I'm very charming when people do what I want."

"You're always charming. And that feels wonderful."

"Hungry?"

"If I say yes, will it make you stop?"

"Fifteen minutes on your feet, then time to clean up. Dinner in an hour. Capons in plum sauce, vinegar beef round with juniper berries and mustard seed."

"An hour, then. That will do very well."

The next morning Khaavren rose early, dressed, and called for his horse to be saddled. This was not a day on which he wanted to depend on either Imperial or public transport.

He kissed the Countess, and set off for the palace, his eyes never resting as he watched the faces of the people he passed, and studied how and where they gathered.

Upon arriving, he went first to his office to write out a few supplementary orders, then to the First Antechamber, to have the Empress told that he wished to speak with her at Her Majesty's convenience.

Her Majesty's convenience came quickly; he was once more ushered into her breakfast room. This time, she didn't ask: at a sign from the Empress he was given a glass of klava.

"Good morning, Captain," said Zerika.

"Good morning, Majesty. I'm sorry to have kept you waiting."

"It is nothing. What have you to report?"

"I've made what arrangements I can, and we'll need them. The city is frightened, Majesty."

She nodded. "Aliera has agreed to turn the Songbird River Division over to you for the duration."

Khaavren nodded. "That will help. I think I know the division. The commander is Garsery, e'Terics line."

"Aliera says they're stationed just past Oldgate. The lead elements should be here before noon."

"Good."

"Now," said Zerika. "Kosadr was telling me about some new information. Wizard?"

"Your Majesty," he said. "I have heard rumors of a device, of divine origin, which may have the power to prevent the Jenoine from manifesting."

"What device?" said Khaavren.

"It is called the silver tiassa, and was supposedly made by Mafenyi."

"I've never heard of it," said Zerika. There was a

pause, and the Orb briefly flickered white and yellow. "Nor has the Orb."

Khaavren said, "Where did you hear of it? It seems oddly convenient to appear just now."

"The first thing I did was put out word to anyone who knew anything that might help. I heard of this from a cousin, who said a bard told a story about it. I'm looking for the bard."

"Have you asked Sethra?" asked the Empress.

"She'll be arriving later this morning," said the wizard. "I'll ask her then. And the Necromancer."

"Good," said Zerika.

"Other than that," said Kosadr, "we are doing well in gathering what weapons we have that may be effective. We have asked the Lord Morrolan to make himself available."

"Very well, then. Anything else from either of you? Then that is all for now. Stay in touch; do not hesitate to bespeak me directly through the Orb if it seems called for. I'll do the same."

Khaavren took a last sip of his klava as he rose; then he saluted the Empress and followed Kosadr out the door.

The day passed in something of a fury; he checked the arrangement of his forces, dispatched some to take up positions, received messages about the state of the city, met with General Garsery and her staff, met with Aliera twice, and seemed never to have a moment to breathe.

In the middle of the afternoon, Khaavren was once more called to meet with Her Majesty, Kosadr, and Aliera, this time in the alcove, as it was called—an intimate area adjoining the throne room. Also present on this occasion was Sethra Lavode—the Enchantress of Dzur Mountain—who openly carried Iceflame at her hip. She gave Khaavren a nod as to an acquaintance, which he gravely returned. He couldn't help feeling a certain thrill at being acknowledged by Sethra Lavode; but he could at least keep the reaction from showing.

Zerika began with Aliera, who gave a concise report about the divisions now moving toward Adrilankha, when they would arrive, and how useless she expected they would be.

When she had finished, the Empress turned to Khaavren for his report. He explained what he had done, what he had prepared, and what he proposed. When no one had questions or suggestions, Her Majesty expressed her approval.

Kosadr spoke next, describing at length the measures he had taken, the spells prepared, the sorcerers who remained on alert.

"What of the Necromancer?" said Zerika.

"She will be ready to assist," said Sethra.

"Good. And what of this device, the silver tiassa?"

"I have spoken of it with Sethra Lavode," said Kosadr. "She has heard of the artifact, but had no knowledge that it had such properties. The Necromancer has never heard of it, but said that such a thing is possible."

"But," asked the Empress, "can it be found?"

"Perhaps. There's a rumor."

"What sort of rumor?"

"That it is in the possession of a certain Easterner, an Imperial Count named—"

"Szurke," said the Empress.

"Yes, that's the name."

"Vlad Taltos."

"Yes, Majesty. A Jhereg. We're attempting to locate him now. It is difficult; he appears not to want to be found."

"We don't have a lot of time," said the Empress. "The question is: Is this the best use of yours?"

"I don't know," he said. "If we find it, and it works, it makes everything else unnecessary."

"What of the gods?"

"I've attempted invocations of Barlen, Trout, Verra, and Ordwynac. Nothing."

"That's odd; the Orb tells me that they are eager to speak with us when the Jenoine threaten."

"Yes, Majesty. It is not impossible that the Jenoine have, somehow, interfered with our ability to reach them."

"All right. See what you can learn. That's all for now."

Khaavren threw himself into his work again, forgetting everything else. Eventually, he realized that it was well into the evening, and so he closed up his office, dismissed his staff, and had his horse saddled and brought to the door.

The city was unusually quiet, which puzzled Khaavren until he recalled that he, himself, had earlier declared a curfew, and put the city under the control of the military. He made the rest of the journey quickly, reflecting that he didn't much like the city this way: quiet and empty. It seemed somehow eerie, almost threatening. *I suppose that's appropriate,* he decided.

He had his horse stabled, and, as usual, handed his cloak to Cyl, this time giving the Teckla a friendly nod. "Where is the Countess?"

"In her sitting room, my lord."

Khaavren nodded and took himself there, politely clapping outside the door, then entered at her word. She was seated, reading. She looked up and gifted him with a smile. "My lord," she said. "Another late day, as I had expected. I had Cook prepare a summer stew."

"You're adorable, Countess. I'll eat in a bit; right now I just want to sit down and brush your hair."

Daro smiled. "Because it relaxes you?"

"Exactly."

"Then I suppose I'll permit it."

He found the rosewood brush she always kept in her sitting room, pulled a chair up behind her, and began to brush.

"A difficult day, my lord?" she said.

"A busy and unpleasant one."

"I know you've closed down the city."

"Yes. I didn't care for that."

"Was there another choice?"

"No."

"Well then?"

"I know. It's just—we've survived one catastrophe. I fear a second. It is one thing to be on a campaign, to face battle. It is another when our home is threatened."

"Yes it is, isn't it? I'd be lying if I said it didn't frighten me, too."

Khaavren continued brushing her hair. "Maybe it won't happen," he said.

"We can always hope."

"No, I mean specifically. There's talk about a device that can prevent them coming through."

"Really? That would be perfect!"

"Aliera doesn't think so; she wants to fight them. But I'm with you."

"What sort of device is it?"

"From the gods. A silver tiassa, of all things. Fills me with House pride, and all." He chuckled.

"A silver tiassa?"

"So I'm told. They're looking for it now. It is supposed to be in the possession of an Easterner."

"Let us hope they find it," said Daro. "Do you think you could eat now?"

"Another hundred strokes."

"All right. After the stew, there are Imperial strawberries."

"Fifty strokes."

The next morning, Khaavren was back at the Palace by the seventh hour. During the night, he had received several reports about the state of the city. He spent the first half hour reading them, and coming to the conclusion that things weren't as bad as they could be; the citizens of Adrilankha seemed to have settled into an attitude of alert patience.

His mind thus relieved, he went about checking on the dispositions, which required two brief trips outside of the Palace, and several visits with Kosadr and the Warlord. Kosadr, for his part, seemed optimistic about finding the silver tiassa. "I'm certain this Szurke has it," he said.

"But can you find Szurke?"

"Not so far," he said. "I believe he has acquired

Phoenix Stone from somewhere, so no usual sorcerous trace will work."

"Could he be trying to keep the artifact out of our hands?"

"It's possible. But that doesn't matter; the Orb can always find him."

Khaavren nodded and went about his business.

CHAPTER TWO
DARO

The Countess of Whitecrest was at breakfast when Noli said, "Forgive me, my lady, but is something wrong?"

She brought her mind back to the present and said, "What do you mean?"

"Your Ladyship seems distressed. I thought perhaps there was something with the food."

"Oh. No, nothing like that, Noli. Distracted, not distressed. I have a lot on my mind."

"Yes, my lady. I'm sorry to have—"

"No, no. It's all right. In fact, you could do something for me. Have a message sent to the Viscount, saying I wish to see him, today. He can come here, or I will go to him, as he prefers."

"I will see to it at once, my lady."

Daro finished a breakfast that she didn't taste, then went to the front room. She signed the declaration turning county military control over to the Empire and called for a messenger to bring it to the Palace, thinking wryly that, as the Empire had already taken that control, she might as well make it legal. She had received scores of complaints about it. Most of these she could pass on to her staff, but a few she had to answer directly, so she at once set in to doing so.

Next, she met with the Captain of the Whitecrest Guard. Yesterday, she had explained to him the necessity of a central command structure during the crisis, and he grudgingly agreed. Today, he had discovered that this would put him directly under the command of Lord Khaavren, rather than under the command of some nameless colonel under some general who reported to the Warlord. Serving under Khaavren, whom he knew and trusted, took away the sting of losing his own command, albeit temporarily. Daro said she understood, and he returned to his duty.

After some hesitation, she opened up the county books and made some notes about matters to discuss with her staff next week; she knew perfectly well that there might not be a next week, but she may as well act as if there would be.

She was still doing this when Cyl came in to inform her that the Viscount of Adrilankha had arrived, and been shown into the East Room. Daro smiled, closed the books, and stood. "I'll meet him there."

When she arrived, he was still standing. "Viscount!" she said. "Thank you for coming!"

"It is always a pleasure, madam."

Daro hugged her son and said, "Where is Ibronka?"

"At the Palace, hoping to find a way to be useful."

"Ah, yes. Of course. Cyl, bring us some wine. Sit, Viscount. How are the city preparations?"

"In truth, madam, the Lord Mayor is handling everything. I've offered her my services, but she seems to have everything in hand. I'm feeling useless; but I admit my life has not prepared me to be useful in this kind of crisis."

"Then perhaps you can be useful in another way."

"Really? That would please me very much. How can I help?"

"Something your father said triggered a memory of something you told me about several years ago. Do you recall something about a silver tiassa?"

Piro's eyes widened a little. "Why, yes. You have a good memory."

"Viscount, are you blushing?"

"I may well be, madam."

"I'd like to know what makes you blush."

"No, you wouldn't."

"Really? Well, all right. What of the silver tiassa?"

"I'm familiar with it. I've seen it. Why?"

Daro shook her head and frowned. "Something odd. Something feels wrong."

"What does?"

"Viscount, who has the silver tiassa?"

"So far as I know, Lord Feorae still has it."

"Feorae? County investigations?"

"And city. He works for us both and collects a double salary. You know him?"

"We've met."

"He is the last one I know to have had it."

"All right. How did he acquire it?"

"Through the machinations of a Jhereg. His name is Taltos, and he's an Easterner."

"Yes. I recall him."

"You recall him, madam?"

Daro smiled a little. "You must not underestimate the concern or curiosity of a mother. This Taltos prevented you from facing criminal charges, Viscount."

Piro stared at his mother. "He—"

"We need not speak of that. Where is this Easterner, in case I need to talk to him?"

"He has left town."

"Oh. That makes it harder. You don't know where?"

"No, but he had a lover."

"That was several years ago, Viscount; you know how changeable Easterners are."

"That's true."

"Still, it's worth checking. What was her name?"

"Cawti."

"South Adrilankha?"

"No, the City. Lower Kieron area, near Malak Circle."

"All right. Thank you."

"Madam, can you tell me what this is about?"

"I don't know, Viscount. It's bothering me."

"Is it related to the expected attack?"

"Related? In some way it must be, because that's how I heard about it. But it might be tangential. It's probably tangential. Perhaps I'm only concerning myself with it because there is so little I can do about the real problem."

"That doesn't sound like you."

She smiled. "You're right."

"It is more likely that you have the feeling this is important, even though you don't know why."

"You know me well, Viscount."

"What are you going to do?"

"Look into it."

"Can I help?"

"You've already helped, Viscount."

"I could accompany you."

"No, thank you. It may be that your presence would impede my inquiries."

"I understand. If there is anything else I can do, madam, you know I am ready."

"Well, if you don't mind being demoted to messenger—"

"I don't."

"Run to the Palace, then, and tell Feorae that I'm about to call on him."

Piro bowed. "I'm on my way. You will give the Count my warmest greetings?"

"Of course."

Daro considered for a few minutes after her son had left, then said, "Cyl, have a horse saddled for me."

"Yes, Countess."

"And have Noli prepare a valise with cosmetics and my winter walking outfit."

"Yes, Countess."

When she was ready, she left from the north door. Cyl handed her valise to the groom, who tied it to the saddle, after which he assisted Daro to mount.

Cyl said, "Any instructions while you are away?"

"No. I'll be back by this evening."

"Yes, Countess."

She set off, riding with the easy seat of the accomplished horseman, to the Palace.

Feorae was expecting her, and she was admitted at once. He rose as she entered and bowed, then gestured to a chair. Daro nodded to him. She remained standing, though she set her valise down. She said, "Some years ago, you purchased a silver tiassa."

His eyes widened. "Yes, my lady. Though I don't know how you could know—"

"Please get it. I want to see it."

Feorae hesitated, then said, "Yes, my lady. It is with my collection, in my chambers. I'll be back at once."

Two minutes later he was back, looking distressed. In his hand was an open case. He turned it around to show that it was empty. He said, "I don't—"

"Yes," said Daro. "I hadn't thought it would be that easy." She sat down. "When did you see it last?"

Feorae sat down behind his desk. "I spend a day with my collection every month. The last time would have been, let me think, a week ago yesterday."

"Send for one of your sorcerers."

He nodded. "I was just about to do that."

Daro didn't recognize the small, frail-looking woman who arrived ten minutes later, but she recognized the arms of Whitecrest (party per bend sinister ship and tiassa counter-charged argent and azure) on the collar of the shirt she wore, and at once identified the slightly flattened features, the dark complexion, and the colors of her clothing. *An Athyra, it would seem,* thought Daro. *I should really learn more of the names of those who work for me.* "Greetings," she said. "I am Daro."

"I recognize you, Countess. I am Lyndra, at my lady's service." She bowed to Feorae and said, "My lord?"

"This box," he said, handing it over. "The contents were stolen. What can you tell me?"

Lyndra took it, and gave the inside and the outside a careful examination, after which she ran her fingers over it, her brow furrowed and her eyes almost closed.

Eventually she opened her eyes and said, "The thief was careful, and calm. There is a slight trace here, in the center, no doubt where the thief touched the box while removing the object."

"What can you tell us?"

"There's a hint of personality. Cold, distant, nothing to rely on. A professional. Male, I think. And—odd."

"Odd?"

"I mean, there's something odd here. I can't—I think this may have been an Easterner."

"Ah," said Daro.

Feorae frowned. "Could it be—"

"Feorae."

"My lady?"

"I'll handle this."

"My lady, the tiassa—"

"I'm sorry about your loss, Feorae, but this is bigger than you. If possible, I'll see to it you're compensated, but whatever happens, I do not expect you to see the object again."

"Will there be anything else?" said Lyndra.

"No, that is all. And unless you hear from the Empire, do not speak of this."

"Yes, my lady."

When she had gone, Feorae said, "I don't understand, my lady."

"Nor do I," said Daro. "But I will."

"And what am I to do?"

"The same as Lyndra; nothing. Speak of this to no one, unless there is an official inquiry from the Empire. Do you understand?"

"Yes, my lady."

"Now, wait here while I use your chambers. I must change my dress a little for the next part of my errand."

Daro picked up her valise and, without waiting for a reply, entered Feorae's private chambers. She quickly changed her dress, and, with a few quick strokes of the appropriate color to her eyebrows and lips, and a slight darkening of her complexion, became, to all appearances, a Lyorn of some minor family. Daro generally favored the Lyorn red for her dress; she had learned that with only a little work it could become an effective disguise. She returned to Feorae, reminded him again to say nothing, and called for her horse.

An hour later, Daro was in Malak Circle, where a contingent of tired-looking Phoenix Guards was gathered. Other than the guards, the streets were nearly deserted, and those who did have business seemed furtive, keeping their eyes too straight ahead, walking too fast. Daro dismounted and approached the guards. They turned with friendly expressions— according her the respect a Lyorn is given, no matter the Lyorn's station in life.

The one with the corporal's badge said, "I beg your pardon, m'lady, but the streets are to be kept clear."

Daro nodded. "I will be off the street soon, I just need . . ."

"Do you require assistance, m'lady?"

Daro gave him a friendly smile. "I don't require it, exactly. I was simply wondering if you could recommend a good place to eat."

"I'm sorry, my lady, but everything is closed. The crisis, you know. That's why no one is permitted on the streets, save on urgent business."

"Crisis? Oh, yes. The Jenoine silliness. I don't believe they're really going to come. Do you?"

"Well, my lady—"

"I've been meaning to visit this district for so long, and today I can because county archives are closed, and everything is closed here, too. I guess I should have known."

The other guards were carefully looking off into space. The corporal smiled indulgently.

"Think nothing of it, m'lady. Come back again after this is all over, there are many fine places to eat in this neighborhood."

"I should think so! All sorts of different kinds of people live here."

"That is true, m'lady. Teckla, nobles, Jhereg, craftsmen."

"There must be lots of stories."

He laughed. "Oh, yes. After my term, I should write my memoirs."

"Everything but Serioli and Easterners."

"Oh, we have an Easterner."

"Here? I thought they were all in South Adril-ankha."

"Most of them are, but a few live other places in the city."

"My goodness! I've never met an Easterner socially. What are they like?"

"This one—that is, these two—are pretty rough characters. Jhereg. One of them ran all the illegal operations in this area until the Jhereg got tired of an Easterner putting on airs, you know, and drove him out."

"It sounds terrible."

The corporal shrugged. "No more than he deserved."

"And what of the other?"

"His wife. She still lives here, I believe. At least, I saw her not more than a year ago, walking around like she owned the place."

"Really! I would like to meet her. What is her name?"

The corporal frowned. "I don't know. I'm not sure I'd advise meeting her, my lady. She's a desperate character, from what I hear."

"Well, but surely you could protect me."

"Yes, my lady. But our orders are to remain here, to keep an eye out for any disturbances."

"You couldn't spare a couple of men for a few minutes?"

"Well . . . I suppose. I'll send for a couple more while they're with you."

One of the guardsmen, a dark Dragonlord with curly hair and a hooked nose, turned to the corporal and said, "I know the Easterner, m'lord." He then bowed to Daro. "Her name is Cawti."

The right one, at least, she thought. *And married, are they?*

The corporal nodded. "All right. Take Wyder with you."

Another Dragonlord stepped out, and the two of them set off down Copper Lane. Daro led her horse instead of re-mounting so as not to out-pace them. The horse, named Breeze, seemed to resent the restraint. Daro patted her neck and apologized.

She fell in next to the curly-haired Dragonlord and said, very softly, "Thank you."

"My lady?"

Daro smiled at him. He let a slight smile pass his lips and said, just as softly, "You're welcome, Countess. I assume you don't wish your husband the captain to hear of this excursion?"

"He would want to protect me, and that would be inconvenient."

"I understand, my lady. I trust you'll protect me from him if he hears?"

"I'll do my best."

In her normal voice, she said, "Where are we going?"

"They live just ahead there, upper flat. That is, she lives there; he used to."

"All right."

"If you don't mind, my lady, I'd prefer to go up first."

"You think she's a threat?"

"I've been told she's an assassin. And it is all but certain that her husband is."

Daro felt her mouth curl up in distaste. "What a family," she said. "Very well."

"She can't be that bad," said the other. "She used to run around with Princess Norathar."

"Not anymore; not since the Princess's matters were put right."

"Doesn't matter; let's do this."

She and the one called Wyder waited for five minutes, then ten, then twenty. She noticed Wyder becoming more and more disturbed, his fingers tapping against the hilt of his sword. She said, "What did this Cawti and Norathar do together?"

"It's said they killed people. For money."

Daro nodded. "I did hear something about that; gossip during her coronation."

"I've heard the same, don't know if it's true. Dammit, where is he?"

"If you wish," she said, "I'm sure I'll be fine here."

"No, my lady. We must—there he is."

"Sorry for the delay. It seems she's moved, and it took some work to find out where."

"But you found out?" said Daro.

"South Adrilankha. I have the directions."

"We'll have to clear it," said Wyder. "And get horses."

"Oh, would you?"

"I'll ask."

"That would be splendid."

"Yes, my lady."

An hour later they were in South Adrilankha. *This part of the city is part of my county,* she reminded herself as she worked to keep the distaste off her face.

As they turned onto Elm, she said, "This neighborhood isn't all that bad, really."

The long-haired Dragonlord, whose name Daro discovered was Sahomi, said, "I was stationed in South Adrilankha for a couple of years. This is one of the better parts. Clean. They pick up after themselves, at least sometimes. The streets aren't always full of—"

"Sahomi!" said Wyder.

Sahomi coughed. "Sorry, m'lady."

"I thought it was the horse," she said.

"Beg pardon?"

"Never mind," she said, keeping her smile to herself.

"This is the house," said Wyder. "If my lady will be willing to wait a moment—"

"No," she said, studying the house. "I'll do this myself. Wait here."

"My lady—"

"Sahomi, explain who I am. You are under my orders. You'll wait here. If things go wrong, and I die and this destroys your careers, you have my apologies."

"Yes, my lady," said Sahomi.

"Amazing you can speak so clearly with your teeth clenched like that," said Daro as she dismounted.

She strode up to the little house, noting clear signs of a child's presence in the holes dug in the yard and the toys scattered around it. She stood in front of the wooden door and clapped. She heard movement through the door, but it didn't open. She clapped again.

She heard approaching footsteps and the door opened. A small, dark-haired Eastern woman stood before her, frowning and looking wary.

"You are Cawti?" said Daro.

She watched the Easterner's eyes focus behind her, on the two Phoenix Guards who remained mounted in the street. "Who are you?" she said.

"I am called Daro, Countess of Whitecrest."

The Easterner took a step back, as if startled. "Are you indeed! Yes, I am Cawti." She hesitated, then took another step back. "Please, come in."

Then Daro in turn hesitated, but from what she could see, it looked clean, so she took a step forward.

"Sit, if you wish. May I get you something? Wine? Klava?"

"I'm fine." The room *looked* clean, but still.

A small boy came into the room; Daro had no idea about what the age would be in an Easterner, but he was just over knee-high, and able to walk well enough on his own. Cawti picked him up, gave him a hug, and set him down again. "Go play outside, hun. In the back yard."

"Why in back?"

"I'll tell you later."

"Why can't you tell me now?"

"Because it would be impolite to say in front of our guest."

"Why?"

"Vlad, make your bow and go to the back yard."

"Yes, Mama."

When the boy had left, Cawti said, "What does my lady wish?"

Daro wasn't certain, but she thought she heard a certain emphasis on "my lady." She said, "He calls you Mama."

Cawti tilted her head, as if to say, "I can't imagine you'd say such a thing."

"I'm sorry," said Daro, feeling herself blushing. "My son addresses me more formally, and I suddenly found myself wishing—never mind. I believe I will sit after all. Klava would be lovely."

"Of course."

Daro seated herself on a stuffed chair while Cawti went through an archway into what was presumably the kitchen. The room was small, and tastefully sparse save for a surprising number of books on two floor-to-ceiling bookshelves. Daro resisted the temptation to inspect them.

Cawti returned with only one glass. *It's going to be like that, is it?* thought Daro.

Cawti seated herself at one end of a plain brown couch and said, "Now, to what do I owe the honor?"

The stress on the word "honor" was just barely there. Daro felt a flash of anger, but sipped her klava until it had passed. It was good klava. She said, "You are married to a certain Vladimir Taltos, are you not?"

Cawti stared at her until it was almost rude, then looked away. "We are separated."

"I'm sorry. I should have realized; I heard that he has left town. Do you know where he is?"

The Easterner's surprise at the question seemed genuine. "My lady, do you think that, if I knew, I would simply tell you?"

Daro frowned. "He is in hiding?"

"Yes, he certainly is."

"I didn't know. Who is he hiding from?"

"The Jhereg, my lady. For years now. They want him very badly."

"Why?"

Cawti looked away. "You would have to ask them, Countess."

"I see. Then perhaps you could tell me something else. Are you familiar with an artifact, supposed to be of divine origin, called the silver tiassa?"

"I imagine," said Cawti, "that you already know I'm familiar with it. I hadn't been aware that it was of divine origin."

"Perhaps it isn't. It is being sought by the Empire. I come to you because it is rumored to be in the possession of Lord Taltos, and because—" She hesitated. "And because there is something about this that feels wrong."

The Easterner's features remained impassive. "My lady, is there a reason you would expect me to help you?"

"You must have heard of the threat to the city."

"I've heard of it, yes."

"There is a story that this artifact can help. In fact, can stop it."

"I see."

"I assume whatever your resentment of me in particular, or the aristocracy in general, or the Empire in total, or whatever it is you resent, you are not anxious for the Jenoine to replace the Empire, or kill us all, whichever they'll do?"

"Let me think about that while you recover your breath," she said.

"Take your time."

"I hadn't realized it showed."

"Your resentment?"

"I'm not sure that's the right word, but yes."

"Whatever the word is, yes, it shows."

"No, I wouldn't care for a Jenoine victory."

"So, will you help?"

"My lady, you said you heard a story. How reliable is it?"

"I've no idea. Why?"

"Yes, I'm familiar with the item. Or, at least, with a small tiassa made out of silver that could be what you're referring to. But I had no idea there was anything to it other than a nice piece of silver-work. It seems unlikely."

Daro nodded. "It seems unlikely to me, too."

"It does? Then why are you here?"

"Because there's something going on that I don't understand, and it intrigues me, and worries me."

Cawti sat back on her couch. "I see," she said.

"You're going to have to trust me," said Daro.

"Which is why you came to my home, rather than summoning me?"

Daro nodded.

"But you brought a pair of Phoenix Guards with you."

Daro nodded again.

"In fact," said the Easterner, "I don't trust you. But I was a Jhereg once—I'm used to working with people I don't trust."

"What do you have in mind?"

"I don't know. Give me the details. I'm no Tiassa, but I've been known to have an idea now and then."

Daro let it pass. "All right, here's what I know: There is an artifact called the silver tiassa that is reputed to be able to stop the Jenoine from manifesting. At one time, it was supposedly in the hands of your husband, then it was given to a certain Lord Feorae, and then passed again to your husband. That, at any rate, is the story. Hence the desire to find him."

"So, who is attempting to locate him?"

"I don't know. Presumably Kosadr."

"Who?"

"The Court Wizard."

"Oh. He cannot be found with sorcery."

"He cannot?"

"He has protection. Phoenix Stone."

"What is Phoenix Stone?"

Cawti laughed a little. "I was hoping you could tell me. But I know sorcery can't find him, nor witchcraft, nor—"

"Witchcraft?"

"The Eastern magical arts."

"Are those real?"

"Some think so. But for finding Vladimir, they may as well not be. Those with psychic skills won't find him either."

"I see. What of the Orb?"

"The Orb?"

"Yes. What if Her Majesty should use the Orb to locate him?"

"Can she do that? I know little of the Orb, of what it can do."

"I am no expert. But it should be possible. It must be, because there are laws regarding under what circumstances she may or may not do so."

Cawti nodded. "It makes sense, then." The Easterner appeared to be speaking to herself.

"What does?" said Daro.

"I believe I know what is going on, Countess. And you were right to be suspicious."

"What is it?"

Cawti closed her eyes for a moment, then opened them and said, "I beg a boon, Countess."

"A boon? That can't have been easy for you to say."

"It wasn't."

"What is this boon?"

"You can reach the Empress at any time, can you not?"

"Anyone can."

"You're the Countess of Whitecrest. You can do so without running the danger of having your mind burned out if the Empress is in a bad mood."

"All right. What do you wish?"

"Ask her to delay finding Vladimir."

"To delay? She may be doing it now."

"Then Your Ladyship must hurry."

"And in exchange for this delay?"

"I called it a boon, my lady. Not a trade."

"Then you'd best explain why you want it."

"Because I know who is doing what, and why."

"My l—that is, Cawti, I think you ought to explain that to me."

"You asked if I trusted you. Will you trust me?"

Daro took a deep breath and let it out slowly. "Is this a test?"

The Easterner seemed to consider for a moment. "No."

"You are a friend of the Princess Norathar, are you not?"

"You've checked on me."

"Only a little."

"Yes, we're friends. Why does it matter?"

"I'm looking for a reason to trust you."

The Easterner pressed her lips together. "I see."

"I understand," said Daro, "that it isn't flattering. But you're asking me to ask the Empress to delay finding an artifact that might prevent the Jenoine from invading the city. I am to do that merely on your word?"

"And on your own instincts, which have told you that all is not as it seems."

"That is still not much on which to risk the safety of the city."

"It isn't much of a risk. I just want a little time to find out if my guess is right."

"And you won't tell me what this guess is?"

"It would be wrong for me to say anything until I'm sure."

"And when you're sure?"

"It won't matter to you or the Empire."

"You just want it delayed? Not stopped? I am to simply ask Her Majesty to wait before locating your husband?"

"Estranged husband. Yes."

"And if she asks for how long?"

"Be vague."

"And if she asks why?"

"Be evasive."

"And if she doesn't agree?"

"Be convincing."

"You aren't giving me much."

"My word is good. Ask Norathar, if you must."

Daro spoke slowly. "Your hus—that is, Lord Taltos once did a significant service for my son. I have felt that I should repay that service, if I ever had the chance. Can you speak for him? And is this the service?"

Cawti laughed, but didn't explain what she found amusing. "Yes, to the first, and most definitely yes to the second."

"All right. I agree."

"Let me know when you've spoken with her."

"And not what she says?"

"If you have any sense, you'll tell me she agrees whether she does or not. I won't even be able to tell if you really spoke with her, will I?"

"You said you don't trust me."

"I don't trust you. But I have no choice. Let me know when you've spoken with her."

Daro nodded, focused, and reached the Empress, who was, fortunately, not especially busy.

"*Majesty, it is Whitecrest.*"

"*Yes, Daro?*"

"*You have been asked to find this Easterner?*"

"*Count Szurke, yes.*"

"*Majesty, might I beg you to wait before doing so?*"

"*Why?*"

"*I have reason to believe that—*"

"*What is it?*"

"*Majesty, I have suspicions I do not even wish to hint at until I have verified them.*"

"*This sounds serious, Countess.*"

"*Majesty, it is.*"

"*You know we only have a day or two?*"

"*This will only take a few hours.*"

"*Perhaps you should come and see me in person, Daro.*"

"*I will do so at once, Majesty. Until then?*"

"*I won't locate Szurke before then.*"

"*Thank you, Majesty.*"

She opened her eyes and said, "Her Majesty agrees."

"I am grateful. I will do my best to see to it you don't regret trusting me."

Daro stood. "I appreciate the sentiment. And now, I am off to the Palace."

"The Palace, my lady?"

"Her Majesty wants to see me."

"I see. May I accompany you?"

Daro frowned. "Why?" Then she felt herself blushing. "If you don't mind my asking."

"There is someone there I want to see, and I'd enjoy the company."

You're lying, Jhereg, thought Daro. "All right," she said. "Let's go."

"Countess," said Cawti, rising to her feet. "If you would be good enough to wait outside, I will join you shortly. I must arrange for the care of my son."

"Of course. Take as much time as you need."

The Easterner was gone for some few minutes. She returned and said, "A moment more, please, and I'll be ready." Cawti vanished into the cottage's other room, pulling a drape across the door. It seemed to Daro that the drape wasn't used very often. There was the sound of rustling, and of heavy objects moving; when Cawti emerged, she wore a cloak of Jhereg gray, and a wide leather belt with a sheathed dagger at each hip.

"Thank you for waiting, my lady. I'm ready now."

Daro rose. "I see that you are."

"I'll need a horse. There is a livery a quarter of a mile west."

"All right."

They walked out of the cottage. Daro gave the guards a sign to dismount, and so the four of them walked to the stable. The Easterner's face was set, determined. But determined to do what?

"If I may ask," said Daro as they walked, "why are you accompanying me?"

Cawti smiled. "Perhaps I want my share of the credit."

The aristocrat laughed. "Not likely."

"No, I suppose not. I have a friend at the House of the Dragon."

"And you just decided that now was a good time to visit?"

"Perhaps there is more to it than that."

They reached the livery and Cawti picked out a tall gelding. Daro offered to pay for it, but the Easterner declined with a smile that tried to be polite.

When they set off from the stable, one guard rode ahead, the other behind.

The Countess didn't speak for a while; then she said, "I don't expect you to trust me. And I shan't attempt to compel you to tell me. But if whatever you're doing has an effect on my mission, it may be to your advantage to tell me of it."

After another quarter of a mile, Cawti said, "Why?"

"It feels like the right thing to do."

"Do you generally rely on your feelings, my lady?"

"Yes. Don't you?"

"No."

"Perhaps Easterners are different; I haven't known many."

"You mean you haven't known any, my lady?"

"Yes."

"We scare you a little, don't we?"

Daro looked over at her, then returned her eyes to the road.

"Yes," said Cawti. "I'm impertinent."

Daro nodded. "You are that."

They reached the Stone Bridge and started across. Daro watched the river, and inhaled its scent—so different from the ocean. The swells pushed their way toward the ocean as if they were solid objects. On the upriver side, a barge was being worked into a berth by bargemen and dockside sorcerers.

"The river," she said, "is so peaceful. I mean, compared to the ocean-sea."

"You live on the cliffs, don't you?"

"Yes. In the mornings when the weather is fine, my lord the captain and I breakfast on the terrace so we can watch it."

"That must be very pleasant."

"You and your husband, did you have such customs?"

"My lady the Countess, are you attempting to find common ground with me?"

She laughed a little. "Yes, I suppose I am."

"And of all the things we might have in common, all you can find is marriage?"

"It was just my first try; we still have a long ride before us."

"Your first try wasn't about me, but about who

I'm married to. Is who you're married to the most important thing in your life?"

"I'd never thought about it. Would that be so horrid?"

"Just odd. Seems like a strange way to live."

The horses of the Dragaerans were shod with iron; Cawti's was shod with an iron and copper alloy, producing a higher-pitched sound. The combination was oddly musical.

"Out of curiosity," said Daro, "do you hate me because I'm human, or because I'm a Tiassa?"

"I don't hate you, my lady."

"No?"

"Hate is personal. I don't know you."

"I see."

"I doubt that is true, my lady."

"Perhaps you're right."

They reached the Palace without further conversation. When they were before the Imperial Wing, Cawti said, "I thank you for the company, my lady."

"You are most welcome."

Daro dismounted and turned her horse over to the care of a groom, while Cawti continued on toward the House of the Dragon. Daro entered the Palace and followed the familiar path to the Last Antechamber, where she gave her name and asked to speak with Her Majesty. She was admitted in less than two minutes, and at once walked up to the Empress, making the proper obeisance.

"What is it, Countess?"

"Your Majesty, may we speak privately?"

Zerika frowned. "Very well." She rose, as did everyone else in the room. She nodded to the nearest guard and announced, "I will be in the Blue Room for a few minutes."

Daro followed her out the east door and down a very wide stairway that had, in Daro's opinion, far too much gold filigree. The second door on the right was the Blue Room, named not for the walls, which were an inoffensive beige, but for the furnishings—a long couch and three comfortable chairs. There was also a table, upon which a servant deposited an open bottle of wine and two glasses. Neither Daro nor the Empress so much as glanced at the wine.

Her Majesty sat in one of the chairs and nodded to Daro, who sat at the end of the couch.

"What is it, Countess?" The Orb, slowly circling her head, was a pale green.

The Easterner left the Tiassa who dressed like a Lyorn and spoke like an Issola. Then she continued on to the House of the Dragon, where she put her horse into the hands of a groom, with instructions to return him to the livery stable in South Adrilankha. The groom bowed, and Cawti tipped him, thanked him, and approached the House itself.

The doors stood open; she walked past the guards who flanked it, ignoring the way they ignored her. They'd seen her before, and had learned not to interfere with her, but they didn't have to like it. She walked through the Grand Hall and took the White Stairway up three floors and so to the private chambers of the Heir. A single guard stood beside the pale yellow door with the e'Lanya symbol embossed in silver. This guard, too, recognized Cawti, and pulled the rope hanging next to the door.

Presently the door opened to reveal Her Highness Norathar. "Cawti! Come in!"

Cawti smiled and entered. "Greetings, Princess. Ouch!"

"I told you I'd smack you if you called me that again. Sit. What are you drinking?"

"Nothing. I need a clear head. You aren't drinking either, sister."

"Sounds serious."

"Don't play stupid; you see how I'm dressed."

Norathar nodded. "Either something is up in South Adrilankha, or it's about Vlad."

"Nothing is up in South Adrilankha."

"Start at the beginning."

"The beginning would be when Her Ladyship the Countess of Whitecrest came to my door."

Norathar sat back. "Really! She came to your house? That's priceless!"

"Isn't it just?"

"What did she say?"

Cawti described the conversation; Norathar appeared to enjoy it; especially the negotiation.

"So," said the Dragon Heir. "We have a Jenoine invasion—"

"The *threat* of a Jenoine invasion."

"Right. And an artifact that can help that is supposedly in Vlad's possession, and an Empress agreeing to use the Orb to locate him."

"Yes."

"So you've drawn the obvious conclusion."

"I'm glad it's obvious to you, too, or I'd have to wonder if paranoia were contagious."

"It's obvious. Any idea how they're going to do it?"

"Not yet."

"What is this silver tiassa?"

"I don't know anything about its history or properties, if that's what you're asking. It's something Vlad used in a caper a few years ago. Before we were married, in fact. So far as I know, it doesn't actually do anything. I wouldn't mind seeing it again."

"Why?"

"I don't know. It was pretty."

"And it reminds you of Vlad."

"This is a lovely room. Is the still-life new?"

"Cawti—"

She sighed. "I'm not the Countess of Whitecrest."

"I beg your pardon?"

"Everything I do does not, in fact, revolve around the guy I used to live with."

Norathar stared at her. "Where would you get the idea that I thought it did?"

"All right. It was a strange conversation with the Countess. I mean, while we were riding over. Nothing significant, just strange."

"It must have been."

"Have you met László?"

"The Empress's . . . I mean, the Easterner?"

"Yes."

"Sure, we've met."

"He's one of the finest masters of witchcraft the world has ever seen. Ever. He has two familiars, which as far as I know has never . . . he has extended his life for hundreds of years. You can't do that with witchcraft. He—"

"What's your point?"

"He's the Empress's lover."

"Just because everyone sees him—"

"No, no. That's how he thinks of himself. That's the most important thing there is to him."

"That's very odd."

"Yeah. And from some of the things the Countess said, it sounds like she's another. Maybe. I don't know, I could be wrong. But it sounds like what matters to her is that she's married to the captain. And then you said—"

"Oh. I see."

"You know about my work, even if we don't talk about it."

"Yes."

"Whatever you think about it, that matters."

"I know it matters to you."

"No, it—all right, we won't get into that. My point is—"

"I'm way ahead of you, sister. I'm sorry."

"But you know why Vlad is on the run."

"I know."

"I hate it that he threw everything away to save me."

"I know."

"I hate it that he saved me."

"I know."

"I hate it that I have to feel grateful to him."

"I know."

"And now—"

"Yes. I understand."

"Are you in, Norathar?"

"Is that a stupid question, or a formality?"

"A formality."

"I'm in."

Cawti smiled. "Thank you."

"Do you have a plan?"

"Of course."

"All right. This is your score. What's the first step?"

"A visit to the Empress. You can get me in?"

"Of course. I'm a princess."

"Hey, it's got to be good for something."

"Are we in a hurry?"

"I don't know. Best to assume we are."

"Give me a moment."

"Of course."

Norathar vanished into her dressing room, and emerged five minutes later wearing a cloak of Jhereg gray over her clothing, which was the black and silver of the House of the Dragon. She wore a sword belt; she took her sword from where it hung on the wall and slid it into the scabbard.

"Ready," she said.

"Like the bad old days," said Cawti.

"For me, they were good."

"They were that, too. Let's go. I'll fill you in as we walk."

It was only a couple hundred yards from the House of the Dragon to the entrance to the Imperial Wing.

As they passed through on their way to the throne room, Cawti said, "You saw the looks?"

"The tall one tried to keep his face blank. I think he may have sustained a permanent injury."

"I may have sustained a permanent injury trying not to laugh at him."

"The Dragon Heir and an Easterner, both wearing Jhereg cloaks. I don't think I blame them."

"Nor do I. But I am tempted to go out the Liscom Door, circle around, and do it again."

"Aren't we in a hurry?"

"I suppose so."

They had no trouble until they reached the Last Antechamber, where the pair of guardsmen seemed to have some trouble admitting Cawti. Norathar was about to demand to see the captain when the door opened from within and Lord Summer announced that the Empress wished to see the Princess Norathar and her guest. Summer guided them through the throne room and out the Orb Door and conducted them just a few steps down a wide hallway, where their guide opened a pale blue door and stepped aside for them.

Cawti felt a quick thump from her heart, and silently cursed herself for it.

They entered. Her Majesty was standing next to a chair of the same shade of blue as the door; the Orb, circling her head, was a light shade of green. Facing Her Majesty was the Countess of Whitecrest. Cawti and Norathar bowed.

"Please sit," said Her Majesty. They all did so.

Old eyes in a young face, thought Cawti.

"Lady Taltos, Princess Norathar." She smiled without warmth. "Let's hear it."

She didn't offer us refreshment. I think I won't correct her about my name.

"May I ask Your Majesty a question?"

"Princess, if this concerns the threat from the Jenoine, ceremony is a waste of time. If it doesn't, this whole conversation is a waste of time. Ask your question."

"In the matter of finding the silver tiassa, have you had an offer of assistance from a Jhereg?"

The Empress briefly appeared startled, started to speak, stopped, and said, "Not assistance; a request to observe the process."

"On what basis?"

"A legal one."

"Your Majesty?"

"Using the Orb to locate a citizen is illegal except for 'pressing Imperial reasons,' which means whatever the Emperor wants it to. So legally, any House that wishes may send a witness."

"So," said Norathar. "The Jhereg wants a witness. No one else?"

"The Athyra, but they always do. Locating someone via the Orb is unusual, and they like to send someone to study the spell."

"Always," repeated the Princess. "How many times has this been done?"

The Empress hesitated, presumably consulting the Orb, then said, "This will be the thirtieth."

Cawti looked at Norathar, who was looking back at her. They nodded to each other.

"Well?" said the Empress. "What is it?"

"I'm afraid," said Norathar, "that Your Majesty has been duped."

The Orb darkened. "I was beginning to get that feeling. Daro?"

"As I told Your Majesty, it was a request from Cawti. I trust her."

"You do?"

"Conditionally."

The Empress looked at Norathar. "Is it about the silver tiassa?"

"No, it is about the individual who doesn't have it."

The Imperial eyes turned to Cawti. "Your husband."

Cawti nodded.

"We learn of a Jenoine invasion, we suddenly learn of an artifact that can help, then we learn that it is in the possession of your husband."

"Yes."

"Is it possible," said the Empress slowly, "that this entire threat is false?"

"Possible, yes," said Norathar. "But it's more likely the Jhereg learned of it and decided to exploit it for their own purposes."

"The Jhereg?" said the Empress.

Cawti cleared her throat.

"Speak up."

Cawti forced herself to ignore the irritation she felt and said, "It would be more accurate to say elements within the Jhereg."

"I will find them and destroy them."

"Your Majesty—"

"But until we know, we must assume the threat is real."

The Countess said, "Was that the royal we, Majesty, or did you mean the four of us?"

The Empress chuckled, and the Orb briefly flickered white. "I meant the four of us."

"What would you like us to do?"

"I'm not the one with the plan," she said. "They are. True, Your Highness?"

"True, Your Majesty."

"Let's hear it, then."

"Your Majesty," said Norathar. "We want to test

this theory by asking you to feign locating Count Szurke, and then give a false location. If we are wrong, Your Majesty can always give the true location later."

"And this false location will be?"

"A place Cawti and I will choose."

"What will happen at this false location?"

"We will see who arrives there."

"And report back to me?"

"Of course," said the Dragon Heir, staring at a place on the wall over Her Majesty's shoulders.

Zerika stared at her, frowning.

"All right," said the Empress at last. "I'm willing to do that much. But I want to know what's behind this."

"After it's over?" said Norathar.

"Very well. When do you want to begin?"

Cawti caught her friend's eye, and nodded. "We're ready now," said Norathar.

The Orb flickered again, and Her Majesty said, "Very well; the wizard will be in the throne room shortly. Have you selected a place?"

Norathar looked at Cawti. "Do you have something in mind? It should be far enough from the city to be believable."

"Remember that little hamlet just east of Candletown?"

Norathar smiled. "It would be hard to forget. Bevinger's House."

"Yes."

The Princess bowed to the Empress. "Your Majesty may take the location from me. I'm thinking of it now."

"I have it. Go. I'll return to the throne room and make sure everyone knows what I'm doing. Tell me when you're ready."

"Yes, Majesty."

Norathar led the way out, taking a long detour around the throne room. The Countess walked with them.

"I am concerned for the Empire," she said.

"As am I," said Norathar.

"I'm not," said Cawti. The Countess gave her a look, but Norathar just smiled.

"Not," added the Countess, "that I have any special concern for what happens to the Jhereg."

"There we all agree," said Norathar.

"But the last thing the Empire needs is warfare within the Empire. The Interregnum did not end so long ago. A battle among Houses, and the slaughter of Imperial personnel, would not be good just now."

"I don't think the Jhereg would have much of a chance," said Norathar. "But still, you're right."

"So, what do we do about it?"

"What I'm going to do about it is deal with the immediate threat."

"The threat to—?"

"You don't need to know that, Countess," said Norathar.

Whitecrest started to speak, but then stopped and nodded. "Very well. If I am there when Her Majesty does the location spell—"

"Yes?"

"Perhaps I can discover who will be taking the information."

"How?"

"Her Majesty might tell me, if I ask nicely." She smiled.

"Then what?" said Norathar.

"Then I'll tell you."

Norathar nodded. "I'll expect to hear from you, then."

"Good luck."

"And to you."

The Countess left; Cawti and Norathar continued out of the Palace.

"Are you comfortable doing the teleport?" asked Cawti.

Norathar nodded. "I'm fine with it."

They left the Palace through the Hearthfire Door, and took the path toward the Athyra Wing, stopping in Songbird Circle. "This is good," said Norathar.

"I'm ready," said Cawti.

Norathar concentrated, and, just to be safe, gestured. Cawti felt the world spinning, and the ground seemed to move. She closed her eyes and knelt down.

"It's been a while," she said. "I'd forgotten how much I hate teleporting."

"Take your time."

Cawti nodded and regretted it; then just waited for it to pass. When it did, she stood up and opened her eyes.

"It hasn't changed," said Norathar.

They had appeared behind the inn, between a pair of oak trees near the stable, blocked from view of the back door by an old well.

"This is the spot you gave the Empress?"

"Not exactly. Closer to the well."

"Good. A triangle, then."

"Yes. Do we give him a chance?"

"Can't afford the time; it's liable to be someone good."

Norathar nodded.

Cawti said, "Testing me, sister?"

"Yes. It's been a while. I need to be sure—"

"Now you're sure."

Norathar nodded.

Cawti looked around, moved to a place two feet in front of the stable, and drew her daggers. Norathar walked to a place equidistant from Cawti and the well, and drew her sword.

Cawti felt her shoulders relax. The daggers felt cool in her hands, forefingers at the balance points, middle fingers for leverage, palms up just above her hips, pointing just a little bit toward each other. For knife-fighting, she would be using different weapons, holding them with the points inward and the edges out—but this wasn't for fighting, this was for killing.

"Ready, sister?" said Norathar.

"Just like the old days," said Cawti softly.

"Just like. I'm telling Her Majesty to go ahead."

Cawti nodded. Her eyes unfocused, and she felt her breath coming evenly and slowly. "Good," she said, a little surprised to hear the soft, distant monotone of her own voice. "Let's get it done."

Then there was the wait.

There was always the wait.

If nothing else had brought it all back, that would have—the familiar easy tension, the hint of excitement, the trace of anticipation.

Gods! Do I miss this?

Across from her was Norathar, sword relaxed in both hands, point slightly off to the side, face like stone, eyes like ice.

She isn't missing this.

One endless moment from when she took her position to the appearance of—may as well say it—the targets. More, stretching from the first target, a cleaner's assistant who couldn't keep his hands off the stock. All the way from him, and twenty-eight others. Twenty-nine, counting Vlad. In, then out, then back in. Like stepping in and out of a different world; the colors were duller but the edges sharper, and nothing and everything mattered and didn't matter. All moments were one moment of waiting for the targets that were all the targets, with her sister, Norathar, silent and steady and ready and dire, like two walls that could never fall over because they were leaning on each other.

Then she was moving forward, and knew that Norathar was moving as well, and it was an instant later that she was aware that they had arrived.

Barlen's balls. Five of them.

One of the parts of her mind that had nothing to do with action found the time to be pleased that they were obviously so afraid of him.

But *five*!

By the time this thought had completed itself, she had already left one of her daggers in one of them: her favorite strike, coming up under the chin, through the throat into the brain. With her left hand, she threw her other dagger in the general direction of a pair of startled eyes.

She pulled a pair of fighting knives from the sheaths behind her back and then rolled as she felt something swing in her direction.

Of course, it does make sense. One for Vlad, one for Loiosh, one for Rocza, and two for backup.

She came easily to her feet and turned to see what was going on; she was aware that Norathar had neatly decapitated one of them. Three left. She didn't notice unimportant details like their appearance. What mattered was that they were all carrying swords and daggers, none had completely recovered from the surprise of being attacked, and they looked to be hired muscle, rather than assassins; this could be good or bad. If one of those still standing was a sorcerer, things could get very ugly. She sensed the presence of a Morganti weapon, but couldn't tell who had it.

Norathar was dueling with one of them, so Cawti looked at the other two; one was cautious, the other aggressive. Good.

The aggressive one came at her just like he should. Cawti hesitated, then moved in quickly to throw his timing off, and—left to deflect the sword, right to guard against the dagger, another half step in, and left again. She stepped out quickly before the other one could flank her—the aggressive one dropped his weapons and put his hands over his throat. Futile; he was already dead.

There was a grunt and a cry, and Cawti knew she didn't have to worry about the one Norathar was fighting; not that she ever had.

The remaining one looked from her to Norathar, sword out, knife ready. If he was frightened—and he almost certainly was—he didn't let it show.

Norathar worked her way around him; he backed up to the well. Cawti said, "As far as I'm concerned, you can walk away. Can you walk away?"

His eyes flicked between the two of them. "Yes," he said.

"Go, then," said Norathar.

He hesitated, then turned his back on them, sheathed his weapons, and walked. Apparently he had the Morganti weapon, as its presence diminished as he left.

Cawti looked around. Three of the enemy were dead, and the other was probably dying.

"He might have recognized me," said Norathar.

"And if he did?"

"Good point. All right, then. Now what?"

"We're not done."

"I know. Back to the Palace, then?"

"We need to find who's responsible."

"We could have asked our friend."

"You're funny, sister."

Norathar grinned. Cawti couldn't remember having seen her grin in years. She grinned back.

"Suggestions?" Norathar asked.

"Know anyone who can do a mind-probe?"

"No one I can ask. You?"

"The Empress."

"Well, yes. But the consequences?"

"For her, Cawti? You care?"

"For the Empire, and no, but you do."

Norathar nodded. "She'll go after the Jhereg with everything she has."

"They deserve it."

"Whoever came up with this idea deserves it."

"And whoever approved it. Think it had to go through the Council?"

"No. I think it had to, but didn't. I can't see the Council approving something like this."

"I suppose you're right," said Cawti. "So the question is, is it our responsib—we're attracting attention."

"I'll bring us back to the Palace."

Cawti took a deep breath, then nodded. "Go ahead."

Then the churning, the twisting, the flopping around; and once more she knelt with her eyes closed, waiting for it to pass.

"Ugh," she said.

"You'd think there'd be a way to prevent those effects," said Norathar.

"There is; I just haven't gotten around to it. I haven't needed to teleport in years." She stood up. "I'm all right now."

Norathar shook her head. "Five of them. Can you believe it?"

"We did all right."

"Yes, we—you're bleeding!"

"Am I? Where? Oh. Just a scratch. I can't think of how it happened."

"Here, wrap this around it. I'll tie it."

"It's really nothing."

"The longer you wait, the more blood you'll have to get out of that blouse."

"All right."

"Too tight?"

"No, it's fine. Thanks."

"I should have learned a few healing spells."

"We're attracting attention again."

"I suppose it comes with being in Jhereg outfits outside the Imperial Wing, and one of us being an Easterner and bleeding, and the other waving around a big honking sword."

Norathar sheathed her weapon. "Other than that, why would we be attracting attention?"

"Let's leave off exchanging witticisms until we're somewhere more private."

"Back to my rooms?"

"Maybe."

"What are you thinking?"

"I'm wondering if you know a Jhereg from the old days, someone who owes you a favor."

"Enough of a favor to finger whoever tried to shine Vlad? No."

"How about someone you can threaten?"

"The only one we could threaten is the guy who did it."

"Or," said Cawti, "whoever paid for it."

"What could we threaten him with? Even if we knew, we couldn't prove it."

"We don't have to prove it, sister. It's enough if the Empire believes it."

"Oh," said Norathar. Then, "Not bad."

"Can you find out who paid for it?"

"I can get enough information to make a good guess."

"So, where to?"

"Nowhere. Right here. Let them look. I just need to ask a few people."

Cawti nodded to a bench a few feet away. "I'm going to sit down. I haven't enjoyed standing as much as I did before the Boulder."

"You don't still call him that, do you?"

"I haven't. But if he keeps growing so fast and still wants to be picked up, I'll start to again."

Cawti went to the bench and sat and watched as Norathar closed her eyes. She kept them closed for some time; occasionally her lips moved a little. Cawti could imagine what was going on—old acquaintances, some of them almost friends. Yes. Surprise, greetings, caution, evasions . . . "I'm going to be Empress someday. How much is it worth to you to have the Empress owe you a favor?" Maybe not quite so direct; but then again, Norathar wasn't big on subtlety, was she? There would be hesitation, and finally, maybe, a few pieces of information swimming in a sea of qualifiers like the bits of bread in a prisoner's broth. She remembered prisoner's broth. The memory wasn't pleasant. She missed Vlad's cooking, too, sometimes. As well as his nasty wit, and—no, no point in that.

Norathar walked up to her. "Two names. I don't know either of them, but my sources tell me it's probably one or the other. One is Rynend, who was given the job by the Council. The other is Shribal, who's been heard to make remarks about wanting to pull it off."

"I haven't heard of them either."

"Where should we start?"

"Rynend, I think."

Norathar nodded. "We have more leverage if it ties directly to the Council."

"Exactly. Where do we find him?"

"He works out of his home. On Greenway, in the Parapet."

"Of course," said Cawti. "What's the best way to play this?"

Norathar frowned, then said, "I think the best bet is just me. If I don't get anything, we'll both take on Shribal."

"This is a comfortable bench," said Cawti. "I'll wait here."

Norathar nodded, concentrated, and vanished with a quiet pop of displaced air.

This is a ... yet endowed with power ...

CHAPTER FOUR
TWO DAYS EARLIER, DATHAANI

The Jhereg spoke slowly, his voice as melodic as he
could make it, which wasn't very: *And it so happened that Barlen called together the gods that dwelt
in the Halls of Judgment, and said, Our enemy will
attack us anew. We must prepare ourselves. And so
each of the gods, in his own way, spoke of the
preparations he would make, whether in arms, or
magic, or strength of body. But then Mafenyi, the
artificer, said, I will make me a mighty device, that
in the hands of one who touches the powers, will
close whatever door our enemy may open to our
world.*

*Barlen spoke high praise for Mafenyi, and the oth-
ers of the gods did as well, and so Mafenyi went
forth, built the device, casting it into the form of a
tiassa, all of silver, small enough to fit into the hand,
yet endowed with power to close the world against
the enemy.*

And when it was complete, Mafenyi sent it forth

into the world, knowing it would be found when it was needed.

It wasn't about the money. Not really. To be sure, it never would have occurred to him to work for free, and the size of the payoff in this case pleased him immensely; but at heart, he wasn't motivated by money.

It was the job itself—the pleasure of arranging each detail, and then watching it all come together. He wondered if he had been a Yendi in some previous life. He'd had the thought before, and, the more he thought about it, the more convinced he was.

"Dathaani?"

He glanced up. "Oh, sorry; I was musing."

His guest said, "You stopped in the middle of the story."

Dathaani's guest was a young gentleman named Ched, of the House of the Hawk. Dathaani had invited him over for several reasons. First, Ched, despite his relative youth, had something of a reputation as a collector and popularizer of myths and legends. Second, Ched had a small gambling problem which had turned into a large debt. Third, Ched had expressed a willingness to engage in slight, insignificant dishonesty, provided no law was broken, to see this debt wiped away. Dathaani had bought up the debt, pleasing himself, Ched, and the author of the loan. Everybody won. Dathaani liked it when things worked out that way.

"Actually," he said, "that's pretty much it. Do you have it?"

"I have the gist of it. If you want me to be able to repeat it back, I'll need to hear it again."

"Presently. First, you need to know what to do with it."

"All right, I'm listening."

"There is an Athyra named Kosadr."

"Funny, that's the same name as the Court Wizard."

"What a coincidence. His favorite place to drink is a private club called Shim's. I've bought you a membership."

"All right. I can do this."

"Good."

"Funny, I've never come across that story before."

"If you want to touch it up a bit I'm good with that. Just so long as the key elements come across."

"The key elements being the silver tiassa, and what it does."

"Exactly."

"Actually," said his guest, "the story isn't bad."

"Thanks. Do this, and you owe no one anything."

"Good."

"Oh, and I assume I don't need to tell you to keep your mouth shut about it."

"No, no need for that at all."

Dathaani thought he might have detected a slight shudder running through the young Hawklord. If so, all to the good.

Some hours later, he sat in the same place, speaking to another guest; this one wore the gray and black of House Jhereg, and was, as Dathaani couldn't help but be aware, significantly more female.

"Right. Yes. I require necromancy."

"That is legal, provided it injures no one, and with a few other exceptions. What effect do you require?"

"The appearance of a gate about to open."

"The appearance? Not the gate?"

"Not the gate."

"Why ask me? Any—"

"It needs to appear as if it is the Jenoine." Then, "Come, Lady Cheoru. If you keep staring at me like that, I'll start to think you're ensorceling me."

"Appear as if the Jenoine are trying to break through?"

"Exactly. And it must be convincing."

"Are you aware of what will happen if I do that?"

"Oh yes," he said. "I am very much aware. There are certain devices the Empire uses to monitor such activity. The devices themselves are not guarded against—"

"And are you aware of what will happen to us if we get caught?"

"I don't believe I'll be caught. And if I am, you'll not be implicated, of course."

"I don't even know how to set a price for that. I'll need to think about it."

"Take as much time as you need."

"It is not impossible that the Enchantress of Dzur Mountain will interest herself. It's happened before."

"That's as may be."

Cheoru hesitated. "Have you a location in mind?"

He opened a map and indicated the marked spot.

"That is very close to the city," she said.

"Yes, it is."

"Very well, I trust you know your business. One thousand."

"I assume you'd prefer coin. Send someone by to pick it up."

"My man's name is Jessic. I'll let you know when I'm ready."

"I'd like two days' notice."

"Two days? This is a matter of hours. I can give you two days' notice whenever you wish."

"Now then."

"Very well."

Dathaani rose and bowed. "A pleasure, Lady Cheoru."

"Lord Dathaani."

Once she was gone, he carefully counted two hundred five-imperial coins into four bags of fifty each. As he did so, he discarded a few which showed sufficient wear to reduce their value. When finished, he set the bags aside, and studied his notes, making sure he hadn't missed anything. He continued until he heard a clap at the door, which he assumed, correctly, to be the messenger for the gold.

When the messenger had left, he put on his cloak, strapped on his sword, checked the dagger in his sleeve and the other in his boot; then he went out. He followed Westwind as it curved and twisted and turned into Spinners. After half a mile, as he came to the Parapet, he turned onto Greenway, with its flowering hedges marking the private homes of the almost wealthy. Number Eighty-eight was a dark green house of three stories, with an artificial stream surrounding a rock garden. To look at it, one might think it the home of an Iorich advocate, or a successful Jhegaala merchant.

Dathaani approached the door and pulled the clapper.

There was little that frightened Dathaani, and, if

you'll accept that being nervous is a different feeling than fright, there was even less that made him nervous. Meeting with Rynend was one of those.

He did his best to hide the nervousness, because it was humiliating; but Rynend could have him killed by just making the suggestion. And Rynend was the sort to do it if he got irritated. It was hard not to keep that in mind while having a conversation.

Rynend didn't have an office; like most of the higher-ups in the Organization, he operated out of his home. And like most higher-ups in any organization, he liked to make people wait. So Dathaani sat in the parlor and waited.

After ten minutes that felt like an hour, Rynend appeared with a bodyguard—a burly fellow who looked like his face had been carved out of the same marble as the floors. Rynend himself was small, elderly, and frail-looking. Dathaani rose and bowed; Rynend gestured that he should sit again, then sat down facing him.

Rynend looked at the bodyguard, who walked to the far end of the room; far enough that he was effectively out of earshot. Then the boss said, "Dathaani, you have something, or not?"

"I have something, my lord."

"Yeah? Is it good? Will it finish this business, or let me down?"

"I like the chances."

"You like the chances. Well, I don't like chances, I like sure things."

"Yes, my lord."

"So, do we have a sure thing?"

"No, my lord."

"No. See, that's not the answer I wanted. I wanted you to say, 'This Easterner will no longer pollute the world with his miserable, unclean presence.'"

"I understand, my lord. But, I don't know, it seems like it might be a bad idea to lie to you. To tell you something is certain when it isn't."

"You think that's a bad idea?"

"I do."

"You're right. You don't want to tell me something that isn't true, because then I'll be sad, and you don't want me to be sad."

"I understand, my l—"

"But if this worthless crumb gets away, then I'll be sad, too."

"Yes, my lord."

"So tell me what you need."

"Blades to do the finalizing, a sor—"

"What about you?"

"I do the set-up, my lord. I'm not such a reliable hand with a blade. Also, with enough effort, this can lead back to me. That could be bad for all of us, so I need to make it hard for anyone to find me. Put me near the body, that's more connection than we want."

"The body. I like the sound of that."

"Yes, my lord."

"All right. Blades. More than one?"

"We'll have surprise, certainly. But you know about his familiars?"

"How many do you want?"

"At least three."

"Three!"

"Yes, my lord."

"Can't get professionals; no one will work that way. I can find you muscle."

"Make it five, then."

"All right. What else?"

"A sorcerer to teleport the blades once we have the fix, and a note from you asking the Imperial representative to help get me what I want."

Rynend didn't look happy. "You need the representative?"

"I'm afraid so, my lord."

"Why?"

"We'll need someone close to the Orb to pull the location and transfer it to the sorcerer to do the teleport. It should be done right away; if we wait even half a minute, he might have moved, and then things don't go so smooth. We have to catch him flat."

"What if the Empress refuses?"

"Legally, she can't."

"You sure?"

"Yes, my lord."

"It sounds complicated."

"It is."

Rynend shook his head. "I don't like complicated."

Dathaani waited.

"All right," said Rynend. "You don't go near the rep. Tell me what you need, and when you need it, and I'll arrange it."

"Yes, my lord. I've met with someone from the Left Hand. Once I have the name—"

"Make sure whoever you find is able to appear at court."

Dathaani nodded.

"So, the set-up. You like it?"

"It was a tough problem, my lord, but I think I've solved it. As I said, I like our odds."

"But it's complicated."

"Yes, my lord."

"So, how are you getting him?"

"I've recruited help finding him."

"Help. From who?"

"The Empress."

After a moment, Rynend said, "You'd better explain. No, forget that. Don't explain. I don't want to know. You have a time and a place?"

"A place and a day; the time is iffy, but I'll have some warning before we get his location. And then we move instantly. The blades have to be ready."

"How much warning?"

"Between half an hour and an hour."

"All right," said Rynend. "I'll get you the blades, send them to you. You have a meeting place?"

Dathaani told him where to meet.

"All right. Next I want to hear, this problem is solved. You understand?"

"Yes, my lord."

"Anything else?"

Dathaani hesitated. "There is, my lord. You have to know, this is going to raise a stink. A big stink. If word gets out that the Organization is behind this, and we did it just to get this guy, they're going to come down on us hard. The Empire. I need to know you'll back me if this works."

"Back you how?"

"I'd be very sad if heat came down, and the Organization decided to use me for ice."

Rynend sat back in his chair and steepled his fingers.

"How bad will the heat be?"

"My lord, we are making it look as if there is about to be a major attack by Jenoine. They'll pull out everything they can: troops, sorcerers, everything. If things work the way I want, nothing will come of it. But if they find out, it'll be bad. Very bad."

"Okay, then. If you get this bastard, I'll protect you from any heat that comes down. You'll be a rich man, and I'll see to it you live to spend it. But if you miss him, you're on your own. Clear enough?"

"Yes, my lord. Very clear."

"And you're good with that?"

"I'm good with that."

"All right. Anything else?"

"No, my lord."

"You can find your own way out."

Dathaani stood, bowed, and found his own way out, the hairs on the back of his neck still standing up.

Relax, he told himself. *You'll either be rich, or you won't need to worry about it.*

Still and all, he really did like the odds.

CHAPTER FIVE
NORATHAR

The Dragon Heir was admitted to Rynend's home by a burly, narrow-eyed man who looked—and no doubt was—much more bodyguard than butler.

"I have business with Lord Rynend," she said.

"He isn't expecting you," stated the other.

"Show him this," she said, and handed over the ring with the mark of the Heir on it.

The bodyguard walked out to deliver the errand, just as another, cut from the same mold, though a little shorter and burlier, came in to take his place. Norathar had nothing to say to him; he evidently felt the same.

A short time later, the first returned along with Rynend himself, who could have been from the same family as his bodyguards, except that the cut of his clothes spoke of substantially greater wealth.

"What do you want?" he said, handing back her token.

She accepted it and put it away. "A few minutes of your time, if you can spare it."

"Concerning what?

"Imperial politics, conspiracies, saving your life and reputation."

He frowned and studied her. "I recognized the seal. But you look like a . . . who are you, anyway?"

"I'm called the Sword of the Jhereg." She couldn't help being pleased to see his eyes widen.

"Well," he said. "Come in."

She followed him into a room that could have belonged to a successful advocate: dark woodwork, small sculptures on ledges, cut-glass decanters, a very large desk, bookcases full of heavy-looking volumes. With the delicacy of an Issola, Rynend sat in front of the desk, rather than behind it, motioning Norathar to a stuffed chair facing it. There was a small table between them; he asked if she wanted wine, or perhaps an ice.

"I don't want to take up that much of your time," she said.

"All right then. I'm listening."

"Just to state the obvious, I'm not here to do you any favors. It's a case of my interest running with yours."

"What are we talking about?"

"The failed assassination attempt on Lord Taltos, and the catastrophe that will fall on your head when your assassin is found and the Empire traces it back to you."

There was not a flicker of response from him, unless his blank expression itself was a response;

Norathar was inclined to think it was. She let the silence build itself. Eventually Rynend said, "Not that I'm admitting anything, but—failed?"

Norathar forced herself not to smile. First try! "Five people showed up to attack Lord Taltos an hour ago. He wasn't there. Four of them are dead. None of them were especially good, by the way."

"What do you want?"

"First, let's be clear on your situation. The Empire is liable to find out what happened, and why. If—as I suspect—there really is no threat from the Jenoine, then think about all of the expense and disruption this has caused, and consider how they'll feel when they put it together."

"Are you threatening to go to the Empire?"

"No. I've no need to go to the Empire. They'll investigate and either learn about you, or they won't learn and will take it out on the Organization. Then what will your position be?"

Rynend smiled without humor. "You making an offer?"

"Yes. I keep your name out of it, of course. And I can't guarantee that the Empire will be satisfied with what I give them, but I think it's a good possibility."

"What are you going to give them?"

"The body of the guy who put it all together. I know it wasn't you. You don't work on that level."

"His body."

Norathar nodded.

"I see. And how will they know he's the guy who did it?"

I'm still working that out, she thought. "You'll have to trust me on that."

"Trust you."

Norathar nodded.

"Well, you have a good reputation. And I don't have much choice."

"I wasn't going to say that."

"No need. What do you want?"

"Who did it?"

"No, I mean: What is it you want for clearing this matter up for me?"

"Oh. That's personal. I have my own reasons; you owe me nothing."

He didn't even pause. "His name is Dathaani."

"How do I know he's the one?"

"You'll have to trust me."

Norathar frowned. "Give me something."

"I've nothing to give. Have someone talk to him, drop some hints and see how he reacts."

"It's a possibility."

"I got nothing else."

"All right. Where is he?"

"His home is on Garden, in the Cliffs. But he's more likely to be at an abandoned inn on Newalter and Slate. That's his rendezvous during the operation."

Norathar stood. "I know the place. All right. If everything works out, I won't be in touch."

Rynend rose and nodded. "Then I look forward to not hearing from you."

He escorted her to the door. She walked a hundred feet down the street and teleported.

Cawti was still waiting on the bench. Norathar approached her.

"What are you looking at?" said Cawti.

"Trying to decide if you're pale."

"Compared to whom?"

"Compared to how you look when you haven't lost blood."

"I'm fine."

"All right."

"Shall we take a coach?"

"Why not ride in comfort?"

Cawti took a step, then hesitated. "Norathar?"

"Hmmm?"

"Is this going to leave you vulnerable?"

"What do you mean?"

"Will it give the Jhereg leverage on you? They can threaten to tell what you've done——"

"They're smart enough to know what will happen if they threaten me."

Cawti nodded.

Norathar checked the time and said, "Sixteen minutes after the hour. One and six is seven."

Cawti nodded, and they went to the seventh coach in line, earning dirty looks from the first six coachmen. They climbed in; the poor coachman was so startled that he had been selected that he had no chance to open the door for them, and only barely remembered to close it. Norathar gave him the streets.

The coach shook as the coachman climbed into his seat; then he made the "yip-ha" of his profession, and the team of horses—Norathar had thought they looked tired—put the coach into motion.

Newalter and Slate, she thought. *I know the area. It's just over the Stone Bridge, near the old refinery. Not much Jhereg activity. Not much of anything, in fact.* She looked at Cawti, who was looking at her, probably thinking the same thing. Cawti's hands were in her lap, but a finger tapped the hilt of the dagger at her left hip.

It was a long ride; they settled in. Norathar faced forward, Cawti sat facing her. As they passed through Little Deathgate the coachman whistled, and the horses began to trot. Norathar chuckled, and noticed Cawti doing the same. *At least he didn't drive around it,* she thought.

"You know the area better than me," said Cawti. "When we arrive, what will we find?"

"Not much, anymore. There was a refinery there, years ago. It blew up."

"I remember hearing about that."

Norathar nodded. "No one lives there, few go there. The inn is called Antlers. I doubt it does any business, except for letting out the space to private parties once in a while."

"Dathaani," said Cawti.

Norathar nodded.

"You've heard of him?"

"The name sounds familiar, but I can't recall from where."

"We could take some time to learn about him," said Cawti.

"We could," said Norathar. "Except that we risk Her Majesty learning his name before we can act."

"I keep forgetting that you care about that now."

Norathar nodded, accepting the words at face value.

"So how do we play it?" asked her partner. "Make the body vanish? The Empire won't be able to learn anything if he just vanishes."

Norathar frowned. "I can't say I like it much. Usually, there's no one looking for your target until after the job. With this, lots of ways for things to go wrong."

"I know. What do you suggest?"

"You're the one with the ideas."

Cawti laughed a little. "My idea is to kill him. We'll worry about after, after."

Norathar sighed. "I'd object if I had a better idea." She hesitated. "There's also another issue: making sure it's the right guy."

"My," said Cawti. "That's a problem we've never addressed before. Better tell me about it."

Norathar related the conversation. Cawti listened, then was quiet for a while. "I don't know," she said at last.

"We could talk to him," said Norathar.

Cawti scowled.

"Let's think about it," she said.

Norathar nodded.

Cawti turned her head and watched Adrilankha roll past. After a moment, Norathar did the same.

Eventually they arrived. The coachman dismounted and assisted Norathar out the door; Cawti managed on her own. Norathar paid him and said, "Wait for us; we shouldn't be long."

He bowed and climbed up to his seat, looking as if he were prepared to wait indefinitely.

There were few structures still standing in the area—the rubble had been cleared from what had once been the petroleum refinery, but there remained an empty lot surrounded by a few houses that appeared deserted. The inn was easily identified—the sign appeared freshly painted. It was a tall, thin wooden structure, and Norathar wondered how it had survived the explosion.

They approached the building and Cawti said, "Shall I . . . ?"

"Yes."

Her partner walked around the side of the building. Norathar waited until she had disappeared around the corner, then approached the front door. Norathar always took the front.

"*Ready,*" said Cawti into her mind.

"*Go,*" Norathar said, and stepped through the door.

The sound of the door opening echoed loudly, so any thought of surprise was gone at once. "*Drawing,*" she said, and did so.

To her right was a stairway, to her left and ahead was a single, large room. A bar on the right ran from near the stairway to the far wall, which had a single door, which, as she watched, flung open to reveal her partner, a dagger in each hand.

There was no sign of a host—nor was there any sign of bottles behind the bar. The room was full of small, round tables, with chairs upended on them, as if to clear the floor for sweeping. After a long fraction of a second, she saw that one table was occupied, its chairs set upright. The figure was, it seemed, looking at her from under a hood. As she watched, he reached up and pulled the hood back, revealing a head full of curly brown hair, and bright, sharp eyes. He carefully set his hands on the table, and waited.

Norathar approached, aware of Cawti closing the distance as well. She stopped just a bit more than her sword's length away. The table was between them, but Cawti was behind him.

"You," he said, "are not who I was expecting."

Cawti looked at her; she mentally shrugged. "I imagine not."

"Mind if I ask who you are?"

"We're the ones who killed the assassins you sent after Lord Taltos."

"Oh," he said. He glanced behind him, seeing Cawti for the first time, then turned back to Norathar and said, "Who is the Lyorn?" Norathar saw Cawti's eyes widen, but her partner gave no hint that there was danger, so she kept her eyes on the target.

"Actually," said Whitecrest from behind Norathar's right shoulder, "I'm a Tiassa."

Norathar said, "You are Dathaani?"

"That's my name, yes."

Without turning, Norathar said, "Perhaps you should wait outside, Countess."

"I won't be a party to anything illegal."

"That," said Norathar patiently, "is why I suggested you wait outside."

"No," said the Countess. "I don't play those sorts of games."

From behind Dathaani, Cawti was expressionless; she was waiting for a signal, or to get an indication of what the play was.

Norathar wished she knew. "Why did you come, Countess?" she said.

"To speak to Dathaani. To find out if he really did what I think he did, for the reason I think he did it."

"You think he'll tell you?"

"You know, I'm sitting right here," said Dathaani.

"Very well," said the Countess. "Will you answer some questions?"

"Depends on the questions."

Cawti shifted, just a little—Norathar read it as a question: Shouldn't we just kill him and be done with it?

She barely shook her head, and waited.

"Is the Jenoine invasion real?" said the Countess.

"Perhaps," said Dathaani, "you could give me some reason why I should answer?"

Norathar cleared her throat. "I can. It didn't work. Four of the idiots—that is, the assassins—you sent after Lord Taltos are dead. If the Empire learns of your plan, and the Jhereg learns that the Empire has learned, what do you suppose will happen to you?"

Dathaani sat back in his chair. "I see your point."

"We can, if nothing else, offer you a cleaner death."

He nodded. "Yes, I suppose that's something." He sighed. "It's irritating. I thought I had everything worked out."

"I know the feeling," said Cawti dryly.

"So," said Norathar. "Care to answer her questions?"

He cleared his throat. "What was . . . I remember. No, it isn't real."

"How did you manage that?" said the Countess. "No, never mind. It isn't important now. Later, maybe. It was all just a set-up to kill Lord Taltos?"

Dathaani coughed. "If I admit that—"

"Don't be an idiot," said Norathar. "We are so beyond that."

Dathaani sighed again and nodded. "True. All right, yes. That's what it was about."

Whitecrest said, "Now what do we do, Highness?"

"This is your show, Countess. You tell us."

"We bring him back to the Palace and turn him over to the Guard, I think."

"What will happen to him?"

"I don't know the law. It may count as treason, in which case he'll be starred. Or it might simply be considered a nuisance on a grand scale, in which case a whipping will suffice. In either case, there won't be action taken against the Jhereg, for which he'll be held responsible."

"That's acceptable to me," said Norathar. "You?"

"I didn't think I had a choice," said Dathaani.

"You don't. I was asking my partner."

Dathaani chuckled grimly.

"We're done with the part I care about," said Cawti. "I'm indifferent toward the rest."

"I knew that," said Norathar. "But I had to ask."

Cawti nodded. Norathar noted, as she had before, that Cawti had the gift of perfect control of her muscles; when she moved her head, there was not a hint of movement of the point of either dagger. Still not turning her head, she said, "Very well, Countess. If you wish him arrested, then so be it."

"Good," said Whitecrest. "And you, Lord Dathaani. If you are arrested, will you make a full confession?"

"I will tell you everything but the names of the others who were involved," he said.

"And did the man who hired you know that you were going to create anarchy, panic, and disorder throughout the city by your method?"

"No," said Dathaani.

"Will you so testify under the Orb?"

"No," said Dathaani.

Daro was quiet for a moment; then she said, "I think that will do." Then she called loudly, "Come!" and Norathar, hearing the door open, turned her head and saw a pair of Dragonlords come into the room, both of them wearing the gold half-cloak of the Phoenix Guard.

When Norathar turned back, Dathaani was rising, his hands well clear of his body, palms out. He unbuckled his sword belt and put it on the table, then a pair of daggers followed it.

"Arrest that man," said Whitecrest. "I'm not sure of the exact charge, but a suitable one will be found."

The guards moved in and flanked Dathaani, one of them taking his arm above the elbow. They escorted him out the door.

Norathar said, "Astonishing that they just happened to be there, Countess."

Whitecrest smiled a little.

Cawti moved up to stand beside Norathar, sheathing her daggers. Norathar returned her sword to her scabbard. "How long have you known, Countess?"

"Known what, Your Highness?"

"That it was all an elaborate attack on Lord Taltos."

"Oh. When I saw your partner's reaction."

"What did that tell you?"

"That she knew something I didn't, is all. After that, it was a matter of paying attention and putting the pieces together."

"So then," said Norathar slowly, "you could have stopped the alarms days ago?"

"No. Until I found out who was behind it, I had no way of knowing if the Jhereg had created the threat, or were just using it."

"I see. How did you find Dathaani?"

"I was following you from outside the Palace, when you hired the coach."

"Oh," said Norathar.

She looked at Cawti, who shrugged. "We've been played."

"No," said Whitecrest. "I don't see it that way. That man," she gestured toward the door, "tried to play us all. We stopped him."

"It was," said Norathar, "an impressive move. Not something I'd have looked for. He thinks big. I respect that."

"Be certain to mention that at his trial," said Whitecrest.

"Can we keep this quiet? That is, see that it stops with him?"

"Yes," said Whitecrest. "It wasn't, in fact, the entire Jhereg behind it, was it?"

"No."

"Then if one or two others are getting away, it isn't the worst injustice the Empire has ever seen."

"No," said Cawti, "it isn't."

"Then we're done here, yes?"

"Yes."

"Please give my warmest regards to your son."

"Thank you. I shall."

Norathar bowed to Whitecrest. "It has been a pleasure."

"Thank you, Highness."

Whitecrest bowed to each of them in turn, then walked out the door.

"Are you going to tell Vlad?" said Norathar.

Cawti shook her head. "He doesn't need to know. What's important is that I know."

Norathar nodded. "I wish this place was open," she said. "I could use a drink."

"There's Kokra's place."

"Good idea."

"It's going to be odd drinking after a job without using the client's money."

"I'll put it in as part of my royal expenses, and charge it to the Empire. Just on principle."

"Good principle," said Cawti, and the two of them headed out to the waiting coach.

CONCEPTION
(An Interlude)

"I have an idea," said the goddess.

"Which one is it?" asked the god.

"Which one? You're saying I only have two ideas?"

"Two kinds. The kind that frighten me, and the kind that annoy me."

"Oh." She considered. "It might be both."

"Right, that kind. All right, let's hear it."

"I want a grandchild."

"That," said the god called Barlen, "isn't an idea. It's a desire."

"You figured that out on your own?" said Verra.

"You're adorable when you're sarcastic."

Verra sniffed.

"All right, so what's your plan to acquire one?"

"I was thinking I could get my grandchild to arrange it."

"Verra, if you are going to play with time again, I beg you to remember that there are laws about that."

"Why?"

"Why do we have the laws? If I recall, you were the one who first proposed them, when we started to understand—"

"Yes. Why?"

"You said something about paradox causing the utter destruction of all of time."

"You have a good memory."

"Unfortunately, I do."

"So then, why should I worry about it when no such risk applies?"

"And how can you be certain there is no such risk?"

"Because if I find my grandchild, then it clearly works, and there is no paradox."

Barlen stared at her. Eventually he said, "I don't even know how to begin to respond to that."

"Well, you might ask me how I intend to find my grandchild."

"All right. How do you intend to find your grandchild?"

"That will take some explanation."

"This is bound to be good," said Barlen.

Aliera lowered herself into a white chair in a white room. She picked up the white goblet from the white table and drank. The wine was red, which she was sure was intended as a joke.

"Hello, Aliera."

She turned her head. A chair that hadn't been there before was occupied.

"Hello, Mother."

"You don't seem excited to see me, dear."

"I don't yet know what scheme you need me for, Mother."

"Maybe I just want some family time."

"That seems unlikely."

"But it's true."

Aliera's eyes narrowed and she tilted her head. "Family time?"

"Yes. In a manner of speaking."

"Ah," said Aliera. "In exactly *what* manner of speaking?"

"Have you ever thought about having a child?"

"Not seriously. Eventually, when I meet someone worthy."

"You haven't met anyone worthy? Ever?"

"Not worthy to father a child with me. Well, once, I suppose. But—"

"Ah."

Aliera stared at her. "You do not mean that."

"Oh, but I do."

"Mother, this is meddling beyond all reason and propriety."

"Now, now. I'm just giving you the opportunity. Whether you take it is up to you."

"I can't believe you're serious about this."

"Of course you can."

"Aside from everything else, he's, well, *dead*."

"Trifles."

"Mother!"

"Care to take a walk with me? Oh, stop looking so suspicious."

"Is suspicion unreasonable?"

"Oh, no. It's entirely reasonable. And justified. I just don't like the look. Come."

Aliera rose without another word and followed the goddess into the suddenly appearing swirling mists that filled the room, and then her lungs, and then her mind, so she was no longer walking through mist, but she was mist, and she didn't move, but was pulled by the vacuum like a black funnel ahead of her, moving always forward, though Aliera knew that direction didn't mean what it felt like here.

As much to see if she could as for any other reason, she formed the thought, *Mother, where are we going?*

Through you, dear.

Through—I don't understand.

We are traveling through your essence, your past, what makes you who you are.

My genes?

Must you be so prosaic?

How are we traveling through my genes?

In large part, metaphorically. Physically, insofar as that means anything, we are adjacent to the Paths of the Dead.

Adjacent?

Close enough that I can play with time until I find—ah! There! It's a girl.

What—

I'm sorry, dear, I must cut off your senses for a moment; you two can't meet yet. I need to ask someone who doesn't exist for an impossible favor.

This is bound to be good, thought Aliera.

And so the goddess, outside of time, planted something like a thought in the mind of one who did not exist, thus to bring her into being. Gods can do that. They shouldn't, but they can.

This done, she called in a favor from one who, though not a goddess, held power that even the gods might fear; and had certain other skills as well.

"What is that?" said Tukko, staring at the paper spread out on the table.

"A rendering of Kieron's bower," said Sethra.

"Bower?"

"His home, if you will."

"In the Paths?"

"Yes."

"And you have this because . . . ?"

"We need to duplicate it."

"We?"

"The Necromancer and I."

"Why?"

Sethra gestured at the small silver object on the table. "To plant that under the bed."

Tukko started to ask why, but evidently thought better of it. He took the artifact, held it up, and studied it from every angle.

"Please be careful," said Sethra Lavode. "Delicacy is not your strength, and if something happens to it, I'll have to make an explanation I'd rather not."

"To whom?" said the other. "The Easterner? What can he do?"

"No, to Verra."

Tukko shrugged and set the item back on the table. "I don't fear the gods."

"It isn't about fear," said the Enchantress. "It's about trust."

"I don't trust the gods, either."

"I mean—"

"I know what you mean. I always know what you mean. What are you going to do with it?"

"Use it, then return it to Vlad."

Tukko snorted. "What will *he* do with it?"

"I've no idea. But it's his, at least for now."

"I suppose. What are you going to use it for?"

"Verra has asked for a favor."

"And in return?"

"A favor, not a bargain."

"I don't trust the gods."

"We share a common enemy," said Sethra.

Tukko didn't answer. Sethra stood up and took the silver tiassa from the table.

"That isn't much. What is all this supposed to accomplish, anyway?"

"Let me explain."

"This is bound to be good," said Tukko.

In the place between land and sea, between truth and legend, between the mundane and the divine—that is, in the place called the Paths of the Dead—there are four stone steps leading down to nothing. It's probably symbolic—most things are in those climes.

A few paces to the right of the stairway to nowhere is what looks like an impossible geologic occurrence: in a clear meadow there is a circle of obsidian, taller than a man, some fifteen feet in diameter, broken only by a three-foot opening facing to the west—insofar as "west" has any meaning there.

Of course, it only appears to be natural, it was fabricated to look natural, perhaps because its designer believed the products of nature to be more aesthetically pleasing than the works of Man. Men often believe nature to have a better artistic sense; nature has no opinion on the matter.

Within the circle is nothing except a low, wide bed. As we look, there are two people on the bed, lying on their backs in a tangle of blankets, arms, and legs.

"Do you know," said Aliera as she recovered her breath, "there are some who would call this incest."

"Not to my face," said Kieron.

"Nor to mine. But still—"

"How many generations separate us?"

"I've no idea. Hundreds."

"And do you remember me, from then?"

"No. I've heard about you, of course. I've read. But I don't remember. I'd like to." She frowned. "Well, perhaps, now, I wouldn't."

"The point is anyone who calls this incest is being an idiot. And in any case, I'm more interested in how you managed it."

"Managed what?"

"This place."

"Oh. The Necromancer fabricated it. She said something about correspondence."

"Who?"

"The Necromancer. A demon. I'm not sure from where. She created a place that matched yours then sent the one and pulled the other."

"So, where are we?"

"Right here," said Aliera, running her hand up Kieron's chest.

"I mean—"

"I know what you mean. I don't know. Does it matter? We can be together."

"It's just that I feel different."

"Different how?"

Kieron hesitated, then said, "Alive."

"Oh," said Aliera. "That, um, that isn't because of the place."

"What, then?"

"Let me explain," said Aliera.

"This is bound to be good," said the Father of the Empire.

SPECIAL
TASKS

*How an Easterner Was Discovered
Under Unusual Circumstances,
Causing Some Degree of Consternation
Among the Authorities*

It is well known among those who live to the north of the city of Adrilankha that as the great river makes its penultimate southward turn it creates pools, bars, eddies, and shoals. Moreover, as it makes this turn, it will often choose these pools, bars, eddies, and shoals as places to deposit any stray floating items it may have collected during its long journey from the far north. This flotsam may include an oar dropped by a boatman, a cake of soap dropped by a bather, a toy soldier dropped by a child, some spinnerweed flowers dropped by nature, or even, perhaps, a body.

The reader will, we trust, forgive the perhaps overly histrionic revelation of the particular object with which our attention is concerned. We hope, at any rate, that a life has not become such an unimportant thing as to render a small measure of drama inappropriate to the revelation of its end.

The body, we should say, was floating face upward,

and turning in a slow circle in a channel separated from the rest of the river by a short, barren sandbar. It was seen first by a Teckla who was driving an ox-cart toward Favintoe Market. This Teckla worked land that abutted the river a quarter of a mile from the sandbar; thus the Teckla, whose name proved to be Dyfon, passed by it every day. In the past, he had found an intricately carved doll, the tin cap of an ornate oil lamp, three feet of chreotha-web rope that he had thought at first was a pale yellow snake, a walking stick, and more than forty particularly interesting samples of driftwood, some of which he was able to sell. This, however, was his first body, and so he wasn't entirely certain what he should do. After some few moments of contemplation he decided to pull it to shore—his work with hogs and poultry having left him without any special distaste for handling the dead.

Dyfon waded a few steps into the shallow water, grabbed the nearest boot, and pulled. Then he frowned and remarked, "Well now, it seems this fellow is alive." The ox, we should add, had no immediate reaction to this statistic.

Having come to the conclusion that the fellow at his feet was a living rather than a dead man, Dyfon went on to make further inspections, followed by their attendant observations. "An Easterner, or I'll be planted," he said. "Complete with hair 'neath his nose. And looks to be bleeding as well."

Dyfon finished pulling the Easterner to the shore, then considered, not wishing to make a hasty decision which he might have cause to regret. The reader will of course understand that Dyfon had never before had the experience of pulling a body from the river, still less a living body, and an Easterner, and one that was bleeding; so for these reasons, it is our opinion that he may be forgiven a few moments of consideration.

At the end of this time, which was not, to be sure, as long as one might think, he came to a certain decision, and being a practical man as Teckla so often are, he at once put this decision into action. He sat down and removed his boots, and then his stockings—they being, as it happened, his second pair—and put these (that is to say, the stockings) over the two biggest wounds, the one being a slash low on the Easterner's side, the other a stab wound in the shoulder a scant few inches above the heart. He pushed the stockings, which, though not without holes, were of thick wool, as hard against the wounds as he could. Having done this in a workmanlike manner, he replaced his boots and set off with his ox to see if he could find help.

About two miles farther along, the road split, one side going directly to the market, the other leading toward the town of Junglebrook. This latter road, some distance before reaching the village we have just had the honor to mention, passed before a small travelers' rest where, more often than not, could be found whichever pair of Phoenix Guards was, on this day, responsible for this region. Insofar as Dyfon hoped to find just such a pair, he was not disappointed; they sat in the far corner of the tavern, the man nursing a stout, the woman sipping a porter, both of them obvious by the gold half-cloaks draped over the backs of their chairs.

After a brief moment spent gathering his nerve as if it were grains of sand to be pulled into a pile, he approached them and bowed so deeply that his forehead positively touched the floor. The man glanced at the woman, rather than Dyfon, and said, "Good Nill, I nearly think our dull patrol has become interesting."

"Well, Farind, and so do I. For not only would a Teckla never speak to us save under unusual circumstances—"

"Which conclusion I had also come to."

"—But, moreover, there is blood upon both of his sleeves."

"Blood which, you perceive, is not his own."

"Therefore, we are about to learn of a dead or injured person."

"Who is not a Teckla."

"Not a Teckla? More than not a Teckla; who is not human!"

"Ah, there you have me. How have you deduced this?"

"You wish me to tell you?"

"If you would, for I am always eager to gain experience in the art of deductive reasoning, so vital if I am to rise to higher rank in the Phoenix Guards."

"Well then, good Farind, it is this: As you have already concluded, were it animal blood, there would be nothing to tell. Were it a conflict among Teckla, they'd not have told us."

"Exactly."

"But if it were of any other House, he should be paralyzed with fear lest we accuse him of harming the noble, or failing to report it quickly enough, or lying, or any of the other thousand things Teckla fear us for." At this point, she turned to the Teckla, addressing him for the first time. "Is the Easterner still living?"

Dyfon was unable to speak, but did manage to nod, at which time the two Dragonlords rose. "Then guide us to him," said Farind. "For I find my partner's logic completely convincing."

Dyfon, in response to this, tried again to speak, but then merely bowed and turned away, looking over his shoulder to see that the two Phoenix Guards were following him. This they were doing, donning their uniform cloaks as they did so. Once outside, they retrieved their horses from the stable, had them saddled, and mounted with practiced ease. As they did this, Dyfon went to his cart.

"No," said the guardsman called Nill. "Leave that. It will slow us down."

"On the contrary," said Farind. "Bring it. It will make it easier to bring the body."

Dyfon opened his mouth, closed it, then did the same with his hands. Farind observed this and said, "You may give this to your master in lieu of the supplies you were unable to get; he should be sufficiently understanding." With this he tossed a silver coin to the Teckla, who dropped it and then recovered it.

"Thank you, my lord," he managed. Farind carefully noted the expenditure in a note-book he carried for the purpose, after which he nodded to Dyfon to indicate that it was time to go.

Dyfon began to lead the way, driving the ox at his usual steady pace. He wondered if the Easterner might have died while he was gone, or, to the left, have recovered and walked off. He hoped fervently, should either be the case, that he would not be held responsible by the two Dragonlords. From this we can conclude that a Teckla is no less capable of hope than anyone else; indeed, if there is any trait that is universal, it must be hope, or, rather, the capacity for hope. It may well be that even Easterners are possessed of this capability.

Dyfon guided them well, and, as it chanced, the Easterner was not only there, but still breathing. The two Dragonlords dismounted and gave him a cursory inspection. Nill glanced up and chuckled. "I'm sorry, my friends, but you will miss this meal." Dyfon, following her gaze, saw a pair of jhereg circling overhead and shuddered.

"Interesting," said Farind. "You perceive he carries a scabbard for a sword, and a dagger in his sleeve?"

"And charms about his neck."

"Shall we bring him to a physicker?"

"Let us see what else he carries. I suspect he may be of the House of the Jhereg, for else how would he dare carry a weapon openly?"

"And yet," said Farind, "he does not wear the colors."

"So I had observed."

"And then?"

"What is this?"

"An Imperial signet! An Easterner with an Imperial title!"

"Well," said Nill, "this is an enigma wrapped in, ah . . ."

"Another enigma?"

"Precisely."

"I suggest we bring him to headquarters. There they can decide if he should be given to the care of a physicker."

"And yet, should he die on the journey, and prove to be important in some way, then headquarters would be required to consider the expense of a revivification."

"Well, and if they are?"

"Should they then decide we were culpable, we might be charged for it."

"Ah, I should mislike that."

"As should I."

"And then?"

"Let us examine his wounds, and attempt to determine how quickly this decision ought to be made."

"Very well, I agree with this plan."

They made a quick examination and deduced that, thanks to the Teckla's stockings, the Easterner would most likely survive being moved. This decision made, they loaded him onto the oxcart, where he suffered through a bumpy ride with significantly less discomfort than he would have experienced had he been awake.

While it is the case that the headquarters of the Phoenix Guards was located in the Dragon Wing of the Palace, the reader should be aware that, when Farind and Nill spoke of headquarters, this was not the place to which they referred. Instead, on Old Quarry Road, not far from the market that had been Dyfon's original destination, was the North Central Guard Station, a two-story building of baked brick painted a particularly hideous shade of orange. It was to this station that our Dragonlords referred when they spoke of headquarters, and it was, therefore, to this station that the Easterner was accordingly brought.

Upon their arrival, a messenger was at once dispatched for a physicker. Nill and Farind asked Dyfon for his name and lord, which information Dyfon gave for the simple reason that he was too frightened not to; and they also took down what little information he had, after which they went in to see their ensign. Dyfon, for his part, returned to his task and his life. To our regret, we must now bid him farewell, as he no longer forms any part of the history we have taken upon ourselves to relate.

Upon presenting themselves to the ensign, whose name was Shirip, they saluted and, in the brief and business-like manner she required, they explained what had brought them back early from their patrol. The ensign listened until they explained about finding the signet in his purse, at which time her eyebrows rose and she made a noise which Farind and Nill interpreted as surprise.

"I believe," said the ensign after some consideration, "that you did the right thing. For an Imperial noble to be permitted to die would reflect poorly on our ability to protect our citizens. And yet—"

"Well?" said Nill.

"An Easterner with an Imperial title. It is exceptional. More than exceptional, in fact, it is unusual."

"And then?" said Farind. "Shall we question him when the physicker has finished?"

"No," said the ensign. "While I have no fear of battle, nor of crossing swords with anyone you might name, still do I confess that there are things I fear. Rather than risking giving offense to an Imperial lord by questioning him, or annoying my superior officers by letting him go, I will inform the Wing of what has happened, and await instructions."

Nill said, "If I may speak, Commander."

"Yes?"

"This seems wise to me, only—"

"Well?"

"What if he should wake up before we have heard from the Wing?"

"Oh, in that case—"

"Well?"

"As the Vallista say, we will burn that house when we enter it."

Farind frowned, as he was not, in fact, certain that the Vallista said this; but he and Nill comprehended her meaning, and at once nodded and said, "We understand, Ensign. Shall we then return to our duty?"

"Yes, you do that. I will see that word of this matter reaches the proper ears."

Nill and Farind bowed and took their leave. The ensign, true to her word, at once wrote out a message to what the guardsmen called the Wing, but was, in fact, the actual headquarters of the Phoenix Guards. She made the decision that the message was not of sufficient urgency to require psychic transmission, and so, upon completing the message, dispatched a messenger, who, thanks to possessing, first, a good pair of legs, and, second, the willingness to use them, less than half an hour later reached the Offices of the Captain of the Phoenix Guard in the Dragon Wing of the Palace.

Once there, he wasted no time in pleasantries, but put the message at once into the hand of Lord Raanev, the personal secretary to the captain (not to be confused with the captain's confidential servant, whom we shall meet presently). This worthy received the message with the greatest aplomb, glanced at it, and at once replied with a single word: "Interesting."

The messenger, who had heard this flavor of comment before from the worthy Dragonlord, bowed and said, "Yes, m'lord. Is there an answer?"

"Remain nigh," said Raanev. "I will pass the message along, and, well, we will learn if there is a reply."

"I shall not stray from this room," promised the messenger.

"And you will be right not to," agreed the secretary.

With this reassurance, the messenger took a seat and began to wait. Waiting, we should add, was something he was especially skilled at, having had some thirty or thirty-five years' practice since the time he had first received this employment. What his thoughts were, or what methods he might have had to combat ennui, we cannot tell; but for the purposes of this history, we should add, such information would not be useful, and we therefore have no need to take up the reader's valuable time with it.

Even as the messenger—whom we have chosen to leave nameless as an indication of his unimportance both to history in general and to our history in particular—was taking a seat, Raanev opened a door located in the back corner of his office, and, passing through the doorway, stood before his superior, who was none other than Khaavren of Castle Rock, with whom the reader may, perhaps, be familiar from our earlier histories. For the benefit of the reader who is, for lack of opportunity or for some other reason, unacquainted with these histories, we will say two words about Khaavren, who at this time was Captain of Her Majesty's Guard.

He was, then, well into his middle years, being somewhat more than eleven hundred years of age, and if he had lost some of his youthful flexibility, both in body and in spirit, he had gained in strength. His eyes were as sharp as ever and still glinted with the same quick intelligence; and if his mouth only rarely curved into the spontaneous smiles as before, his chin nevertheless showed the same determination. Beyond this, his wrist was as firm and supple as it ever was, and his ears, which had once been honored by winning the attention of an Emperor, had lost none of their cleverness.

Raanev placed himself before this worthy and bowed. "My captain," he said, "we have received word of an Easterner, found wounded near the river."

"Well?" said Khaavren, as if uncertain about how this intelligence could have anything to do with him.

"Moreover," said Raanev.

"Yes, moreover?"

"According to a signet upon his person, he holds an Imperial title."

"An Easterner with an Imperial title."

"A wounded Easterner with an Imperial title."

"Tell me, Raanev. Which seems to you more likely: an Easterner with an Imperial title, or an Easterner who has, for reasons of his own, stolen a signet?"

"Oh, it is obvious which is more likely, only—"

"Yes?"

"I have heard no report of such a signet being stolen."

Khaavren frowned, struck by the extreme justice of this observation. "Nor have I heard such a report," admitted the captain, "and you are right to point this out."

"I am pleased that my captain thinks so."

"Oh, I do. And not only that—"

"Yes, Captain?"

"I believe we should reflect on this situation."

"I have no argument to make with such reflection."

"But in order to reflect, more information is required."

"I agree with the captain that, when reflecting, having information upon which to reflect is often useful."

"Is the messenger still waiting?"

"He is, Captain."

"Then have him return to Ensign Shirip. Instruct her to investigate this Easterner, then report to me here."

From this, the reader may deduce that Khaavren, who had been wont to run out to learn what he could, now had others to do this work, and had such information as they acquired brought to him; whether this was a result of his increased responsibility, or increased age, we must leave to the reader to decide. Raanev, for his part, had no occasion to speculate, but merely carried out the orders of his superior officer.

The messenger, who had been waiting for just

such an occurrence, also carried out his orders; and did so with such effectiveness that in a short time Ensign Shirip had received the message with as much accuracy and precision as if she'd heard it from Khaavren's own lips. For her part, she understood that, when given an order by the captain, there was no question of joking, and so she at once carried out an inspection of the Easterner, and spoke at some length with the physicker attending him.

This done, she called for a coach and driver and, leaving a subordinate in charge, made her way to the Imperial Palace. Once there, she found the suite of the captain, where a servant named Borteliff, of whom we will learn more later, admitted her to Khaavren's private office.

Now this office was, first of all, spacious, as befit the Captain of the Phoenix Guards, who was, among other things, responsible for the safety of Her Majesty. In addition to the door by which first Raanev and now Shirip had entered, there were four others. One of these, in the far back, led via a short tunnel to the outside, and it was used by the captain for his own comings and goings. The one to the left (that is, Shirip's left as she entered) communicated with a large hallway that was the quickest way to reach the Iorich Wing (although the reader must understand that the quickest way was not, in point of fact, quick). A third door, next to the one in back, led to a wide, heavily guarded area where teleports were permitted both in and out, and, beyond that, to certain council chambers where the captain could meet privately with anyone with whom he wished to consult. The final door, on the right, led by as direct a route as possible to the throne room in the Imperial Wing.

In addition to the doors there was a small alcove where the captain might hang his hat and cloak and also his sword. The rest of the room was dominated by a large walnut desk—a desk that the captain kept clean by the simple expedient of making others do his paperwork whenever possible. In addition to the desk, there were five chairs arranged in a semi-circle in front of it. Each of these chairs was, we should add, quite comfortable, featuring arm-rests and cushions; because with his present elevated rank, he was now visited by those who deserved better treatment than was generally afforded even an officer of the guard. Khaavren's own chair was not unlike him: it was simple and without padding or ornament, firm, and gave the appearance of being entirely functional.

It was in this office, and, more precisely, in this chair that Khaavren sat and, with a nod, greeted Ensign Shirip.

"Captain," she said, saluting. "I have inspected the Easterner, as you ordered."

"And you were right to do so. Is he conscious?"

"Not yet, but the physicker is hopeful."

"How was he injured? By he, you understand," added Khaavren, who was always careful to avoid confusion, "I refer to the Easterner, not the physicker."

"I understand all the better, Captain, because the physicker is a she."

"Ah, then there can be no ambiguity."

"Exactly."

"So then you will tell me of his injuries?"

"I will do so this very instant."

"Excellent. I am listening."

"Four cuts and two stab wounds, Captain. All but one cut and one stab are shallow and insignificant. He is cut on the right shoulder and elbow, and the right leg above the knee, as well as a significant gash on the left side, just above the hip. There is a shallow puncture wound in the left shoulder, as well as a serious one low on his right chest, only just missing the lung."

"How many weapons caused the wounds?"

"Three."

"So, unless one of them fought with two weapons, there were at least four attackers."

"Four, Captain? And yet—"

Khaavren brushed it aside. "A tolerably skillful player. Other than his wounds, what did you observe?"

"He seems somewhat slight for one of his race. He has grown hair above his lip, but none on his chin. His cheekbones are high, like those of a Dzurlord. His ears are round, and close to his head. He has thick eyebrows and long lashes, and his chin has a crease, as if it were cut, but there is no scar. He does have a faint scar to the left of his nose and another beneath his right ear, and he is missing the fifth finger of his left hand."

Khaavren nodded. "Is his hair dark? That is to say, black?"

"It is, my lord," said Shirip.

"His brows are thick, his chin strong with no trace of point?"

"You have described him, Captain," said Shirip, with a raised brow.

The captain answered the question implied by the look: "I believe I know him."

"And then?" said the ensign.

"I must see him."

"But, does he in fact hold an Imperial title?"

Khaavren replied with a brusque nod, informing Shirip that, not only was her question answered in the affirmative, but, moreover, that the captain no longer wished to continue the conversation. Shirip understood both of the messages her superior officer did her the honor to convey, and so asked no more questions.

For his part, Khaavren at once made arrangements for a carriage to bring him to where the wounded Easterner was. We should note in passing that the Khaavren of two hundred years before would have ridden a horse rather than a carriage; but we should also note that the Khaavren of two hundred years before was younger; and younger, we should add, by the amount of two hundred years.

Thanks to the efficiency demanded by the good Tiassa of all of those whom he commanded, it was only moments before he was informed that carriage and driver were ready. With another of his expressive nods, he invited Shirip to accompany him in the conveyance.

They climbed into the coach, reaching it, as the reader will no doubt deduce, by the door which we have earlier had the honor to describe, and settled in for the brief ride. Khaavren, having no wish for conversation, initiated none. Shirip took this as a cue, and also remained silent for the duration.

After some little time, they arrived at the North Central Guard Station, where the coachman—a private soldier detailed for this duty because of his skill with horses—alighted and held the door for the captain and the ensign. Khaavren led the way into the station with the ease and command that came naturally to him. He at once went to the infirmary, politely clapping outside of the door. The reader should understand that even the Captain of the Phoenix Guards ought not to enter an infirmary before being assured that no one was in the midst of a delicate procedure; while interrupting a physicker in the midst of an operation is less hazardous than interrupting a sorcerer in the midst of a complex spell, it is not less discourteous.

On this occasion, rather than a call to enter, the door opened and the physicker emerged. She was an Athyra, of medium height and middle years, with what appeared to be a permanent crease in her brow, and a proud nose of the type usually associated with Hawklords. She closed the door softly behind her before bowing to Khaavren and saying, "I have been expecting you, my lord."

"Well, and here I am."

"No doubt, you wish to know of my patient's condition?"

"You have guessed the precise nature of my errand."

"Then I will tell you what you wish to know."

"And you will be right to do so."

"In the first place, you must know he has been badly wounded."

"That much I had already deduced."

"Moreover, I am unable to cast the usual spells to prevent mortification."

"How, unable?"

"Exactly."

"But, what prevents you?"

"I am uncertain. Yet my efforts have failed."

"Well, and then?"

The physicker frowned, the creases in her forehead deepening. "I have used older, more primitive methods of cleaning the wounds, and if these are successful, I would expect him to live."

"Is he awake?"

"Not as yet."

"Can you tell when he will regain consciousness?"

"No more than I can prevent mortification; that spell, too, fails."

Khaavren frowned. "Then I will wait here until—"

He was interrupted by a sound not unlike that the wind makes when passing through a hollow cavern—a sound which seemed to emanate from the other side of the door near which they stood. Without another word, the physicker opened the door and entered, Khaavren at her heels.

CHAPTER THE SECOND

*How the Captain Spoke
to the Easterner, and the
Easterner Received a Visit*

Inside was a high, thin bed, upon which lay the Easterner, covered by a sheet and a blanket. His eyes
were squeezed tightly shut, but opened as Khaavren
and the physicker approached. He looked at the
black silken scarf about her neck and whispered, "If
you have something for the pain, I would be not ungrateful."

"I'm sorry," she said. "My spells will not work on
you."

He closed his eyes again. "Opium?" he said.

The physicker frowned. "I am not familiar with
this term."

The Easterner appeared to sigh. "Of course you
are not," he said, putting something of a sarcastic
twang to his voice. His eyes then turned to the captain and he said, "To what do I owe the honor, my
good lord, of a visit from—" He stopped here,
coughed, winced, and then continued. "—such a high
official of Her Majesty's elite personal guard?" We

should add that, to judge from the tone, this question was also not devoid of a sarcastic, or at least an ironic, element.

Khaavren, for his part, ignored the tone, and merely responded to the words, saying, "It is of some concern to Her Majesty when an Imperial nobleman is found to be injured, and questions naturally arise."

"How," said the other, "then I am not under arrest?"

"Not at all, I assure you," said Khaavren coolly.

The Easterner squeezed his eyes shut again, then opened them once more. "I know you," he said. "You are Lord Khaavren, are you not? Brigadier of the Phoenix Guards?"

"Captain," said Khaavren, by way of both affirmation and correction, thus conveying the maximum amount of information in the fewest possible words; a custom of his, and one that this historian has, in fact, adopted for himself, holding efficiency of language to be a high virtue in all written works without exception.

"Captain of the Phoenix Guards," agreed the Easterner. "Brigadier of—"

"We'll not speak of that," said Khaavren.

"Very well."

"But if I might know your name, my lord?"

"Vladimir, Count of Szurke. If you wish for conversation with me—"

"I do, if you are able to talk."

"I will make the effort."

"Very well, then. We have met before, have we not?"

"Your memory is excellent, Captain. Although at that time, I was called by another name."

"Vladimir of Taltos, was it not?"

"If you will permit a small correction, there is no 'of.' It is a patronymic; a custom of my people." The Easterner, we perceive, did not follow the captain's maxim of efficiency in use of language, a fact we will endeavor not to hold against him.

"I understand," said Khaavren.

"What is it you wish to know?"

"What do I wish to know? Why, I wish to know what happened to you! You perceive, an attack on an Imperial nobleman is not a matter about which there can be any question of joking. I wish to know who attacked you, and what led to it."

"I understand."

"So then, if you would, tell me precisely what happened to you."

"I would be glad to do so, only—"

"Yes?"

"I have not the least idea in the world, I assure you."

"How, you don't know what happened to you?"

"I do not."

"What is it you remember?"

"I was walking north along the riverbank, and then I was here."

"And so, you do not know how you became injured?"

"I suspect I was set upon."

"Yes, that is my suspicion as well. And, if that is so—as seems almost certain—it is my duty to find the miscreants and see them brought before the justicers."

"Captain, I note you say, 'them.' "

"Well, and is it not a perfectly good word?"

"Oh, I have nothing whatever against the word, depending upon its use."

"Well then?"

"But to me, it seems to imply that there are more than one of these, as you call them, miscreants."

"Yes, that is true," said Khaavren, struck by the extreme justice of this observation.

The Easterner continued, "Do you, then, believe there were two or more?"

"I put the number at four or five," said Khaavren.

"So many? I am astonished that I survived such an attack."

"Well," said Khaavren laconically.

"If, as you say, you know nothing of this incident—"

"I do say that, and, what is more, I even repeat it."

"—then how is it you know the number of attackers?"

"From the number and the nature of your wounds, as well as certain rents in your clothing, which I took the liberty of inspecting."

"Ah. Well, in your place, I should have done the same."

"No doubt that is true."

"Speaking of my weapon—"

"The weapon that fits the scabbard was not found."

"But other weapons?"

"Your belongings are in the trunk under the bed."

"Very good."

"But, to return to the subject—"

"Yes, let us do so, by all means."

"You say that you have no memory of what befell you."

"None whatsoever. In fact, it would be good of you to tell me what you know."

"You wish to know that?"

"It concerns me greatly, I assure you."

"I can see that it would. Well, this is what happened, to the best of my belief: You were attacked, you defended yourself, and, as you were nearly overwhelmed, you threw yourself into the river to escape. You did manage to escape, but lost consciousness shortly thereafter, no doubt from the loss of blood, and the exertion, and perhaps the shock of the cold water."

"I see. What you tell me is most interesting, and I appreciate it very much. Only it seems odd that—"

"Yes, that?"

"That I survived immersion in the river, which is exceptionally wide and deep, as well as cold and fast."

"That is true, as far as it goes."

"Well?"

"But there are often places where portions of the river, as it were, meander off on their own, for one reason or another. These places are shallower, and slower, and narrower; perhaps even warmer, I could not say. It was in such a place that you were found."

"I comprehend. You have explained perfectly. Except—"

"Yes?"

"Why would I have been attacked?"

"Oh, as to that—"

"Well?"

"Perhaps they attempted to rob you."

"Ah, that is possible. The roads are not safe."

"We do what we can."

"I had not meant to imply criticism."

Khaavren bowed to indicate he was not offended, and continued. "As we both wish the same thing—that is, to determine exactly what happened to you, and who did it—there are, perhaps, ways of learning this."

"Oh, are there indeed? Tell me more, Captain, for you interest me extremely."

"There are sorceries that are sometimes able to enter the mind and recover lost memories."

"Ah, you say sorceries."

"Yes."

"Well—" The Easterner broke off, appearing to be in some confusion. After a moment, he said, "Yes, well, I am afraid sorcery will not, that is to say, it is impossible."

"Impossible?"

"It is, I assure you."

"And would still be impossible if you were to remove that amulet that is hanging about your neck?"

The Easterner's eyes widened somewhat, then he said, "You are observant, and have some skill at deduction."

"Well?"

"In any event, I will not remove the amulet; I require it for my safety."

"If I may ask, safety from what?"

"Ah, you wish to know that?"

"I do."

"Well, from any who would do me harm; and I nearly think there are those who would wish to do me harm."

"Oh, I do not deny that—indeed, we have very nearly proven it."

"That is my opinion as well."

"And yet, you have no opinion on who might have wished to harm you?"

"None whatsoever."

"That is remarkable."

"Well."

"It couldn't be the Jhereg?"

The Easterner returned Khaavren's bland look and said, "How the Jhereg? What have I to do with them?"

"In one sense, nothing anymore. In another, a great deal. For example, they would like you dead."

"You think so?"

"I am reliably informed of this."

"Well, I do not deny it."

"It is best you do not, I assure you."

"Yet I promise that whoever attacked me, my good Captain, it was not the Jhereg."

"You confuse me."

"That is not my intention."

"You pretend to know the attack was not carried out by the Jhereg."

"And if I do?"

"And yet you claim to have no memory of the attack. How is this possible?"

"How is it you know how many attacked me, when you weren't there?"

"A simple deduction from facts."

"Precisely. As is my conclusion that I was not attacked by the Jhereg."

"Ah, is that it? Then, what is this famous deduction?"

"Tell me yours, first."

Khaavren shrugged. "There were marks of three distinct weapons on you."

"And if there were?"

"You were not surprised, or you'd have been killed."

"Well, that makes sense."

"A man able to survive an attack by three individuals is certain to have dispatched at least one of them before that one was able to harm him."

"Your logic is admirable."

"My logic thanks you. Now, as to your deduction?"

"The Jhereg rarely employs gangs in such matters; one is sufficient, or two at the most. Moreover—"

"Yes?"

The Easterner smiled coldly. "It is not simply death they wish for me."

Khaavren, after a moment's thought, understood what he had been told, and was unable to repress a shudder. "Well," he said at last, "I am convinced."

"It is good that you are."

"But if you will permit another question."

"Yes?"

"If you are attempting to avoid the Jhereg—"

"So you have said."

"—why have you returned to Adrilankha?"

"In fact, I have not returned, but rather was on my way out after returning for a visit."

"A visit?"

"I have family here."

"Ah, I comprehend. I, too, have family, and it grieves me when I must be apart from them for any length of time."

"Yes. And so I return when I can."

"I would do the same."

"I am gratified that you understand."

Khaavren coughed. "Then let us move on to details."

"Yes, let us. I am always in favor of details."

"That is good. Then tell me this, if you would: Where were you, when you last remember?"

"Near the river, some nine or ten miles north of Profimyn."

Khaavren nodded. "And your reason for being there?"

"My lord?"

"I asked your reason—"

"I heard you, good Captain. But I do not understand why you do me the honor to ask this question."

"It is my duty," replied Khaavren laconically.

"Ah, your duty."

"Exactly."

"Well, I have nothing to say against duty."

"I am glad you do not."

"But I do not understand how your duty requires you to inquire into my personal affairs."

"How can you know if your personal affairs are not, in some way, related to the attack you suffered? These things can happen; I have seen it."

"I do not doubt you."

"And then?"

"My affairs are, nevertheless, personal."

"If you question my discretion—"

"Oh, not in the slightest!"

"And then?"

"Nevertheless, am I obligated to speak of matters important only to myself? It is unusual for the Empire to require this."

"Oh, it is not unusual at all, under the circumstances."

"Circumstances? What are these circumstances?"

"Why, the circumstances that you have been the victim of a crime. Surely you would like to see the perpetrators brought to justice, would you not?"

"Why, I care very little about it, I assure you."

"You astonish me."

"Do I?"

"Very much."

The Easterner shrugged his shoulders. "No doubt they had reasons having to do with social maladjustment and childhood neglect. And, after all, are not all crimes addressed in the Halls of Judgment? And if they are never brought there, well, that is a judgment itself, is it not?"

Khaavren studied the Easterner after this remarkable speech, as if unable to find the words with which to reply. At last he said, "You are very complacent, my lord."

"It is my nature," said the Easterner.

"I comprehend," said Khaavren, who was especially skilled at comprehension. "Nevertheless, you perceive how useful this intelligence would be to me in the performance of my duty."

"Ah, that word again!"

"Consider how Her Majesty would feel were she to know that, not only had Imperial counts been attacked on the highways, but her own personal guard had not even begun an investigation. Surely you perceive what sort of position you put me in."

"Now you appeal to my kindness."

"Well, have you any?"

"A little. But I try to be careful how I spend it."

"And do you not think this a worthy cause?"

"Oh, no doubt it is."

"Well then?"

The Easterner sighed. "If you truly wish to know—"

"I do, I assure you."

"I was taking a stroll up the river. I am very partial to the river, and often walk along the banks."

"A stroll?"

"Exactly."

"I understand. Now, you say you remember being ten miles north of Profimyn."

"That is correct."

"That puts you nearly twenty miles from where you were found."

"Does it? That is a long way."

"It seems unlikely that the river carried you twenty miles, wounded, and delivered you up alive."

"It seems unlikely to me as well, good Captain."

"And yet, you have no answer to this conundrum?"

"It grieves me to tell you that I have none at all."

"Then I shall have to discover one."

"Of course, I wish you all success."

"May I depend on your cooperation?"

"Entirely."

"I am gratified to hear it."

"And I trust you will keep me informed as to what you discover?"

"I will not fail to do so, my lord."

"How will you begin the investigation?"

"Ah, I must consider that. And as for you, my lord—"

"Yes?"

"Rest now, and trust your physicker."

Lord Szurke, as he was called, nodded briefly and closed his eyes again. Khaavren, for his part, made his way out of the room accompanied by the physicker.

After saluting the physicker, the captain took himself to the offices of Ensign Shirip, whom he found behind her desk. He motioned for her to remain seated, and himself sat in a chair opposite her. The ensign said nothing, but remained alert and attentive, ready to respond to whatever orders or questions the captain did her the honor to address to her.

Khaavren, for his part, wasted no time before bringing the conversation to the subject of his choosing. "We must see if we can learn what happened to the Easterner. It will be difficult, because he refuses to cooperate."

The ensign frowned. "That may be a clue itself."

"It is probable," agreed Khaavren.

"How shall I proceed in this investigation?"

"Send teams to Profimyn and learn what you can. If the Easterner was, in fact, there, someone will have noticed him. See who else was there."

"And if we turn up nothing, Captain?"

Khaavren shrugged. "We will see. For now, carry

out—" He broke off abruptly, as there was a clap outside the door.

"Who is there?" called the ensign, assuming, correctly, that it being her office, the interruption was her responsibility.

"Erbaad," came the answer. "With a message."

"Can it wait until the captain has finished his conversation with me?"

Erbaad, from the other side of the door, said, "I do not know, Ensign, because the message is for the captain."

Khaavren frowned, and nodded to the ensign, who called to the messenger to enter. When this messenger had entered and saluted, Khaavren said, "You have a message for me?"

"I give you my word on it."

"Then, you have something to tell me?"

"The captain has understood exactly; I have something to tell you."

"Very well, I am listening."

"This is it, then: there is a visitor."

"A visitor? Then, someone is here to see me?"

"Not you, Captain."

"Not me?"

"No, Captain. The Easterner."

"A visitor for the Easterner?"

"Precisely. I took the liberty of informing the visitor that it would require your permission, Captain, to see him."

"And you were right to do so," said Khaavren. Then, turning to the ensign, he said, "How long has the Easterner been here?"

"A few hours."

"And was anyone informed that he was here?"

"No one at all."

"And yet, he has a visitor."

"Exactly."

"This is worthy of remark." Then once more addressing Erbaad, he said, "Describe the visitor."

"She is an Issola, Captain, with a strikingly pretty face, marked by delicate brows beneath a high forehead, a sharp but attractive nose, sensuous lips, and a firm chin. Her hair is light, her complexion fair. She is slight of build, but strong; perhaps a little shorter than average at six and a half feet. Her fingers are long and elegant, with calluses that make me suspect she plays a musical instrument. She wears the green and white with leather coverings, as one dressed for travel, and from the scuffs on these leathers she is an accomplished horseman. Her blade is short and heavy, of a simple and functional kind that convinces me she knows its length."

"I see," said Khaavren, to whom a picture of the visitor appeared in his mind's eye as clearly as if he were looking at her. "What name does she give?"

"Lady Saruchka of Reflin."

"I do not know her. What does she wish?"

"She said nothing except to express her desire to see the Easterner."

"How did she refer to him?"

"As Lord Taltos."

"Taltos. Not Szurke. I see. Very well, take me to where she is."

"This way, Captain."

Khaavren accordingly followed her toward the

entry way, where the lady was waiting, just as described. She rose as Khaavren entered, and bowed with all the grace one would expect of an Issola. Khaavren, returning the bow, said, "Lady Saruchka of Reflin? I am Khaavren of Castle Rock."

"An honor as well as a pleasure, Lord Khaavren. Naturally, I have heard of you, and all you have done for the Empire."

"You are kind, my lady."

"Not at all."

"I am told you wish to visit the patient."

"If you please, Captain."

"May I ask the reason for the visit? I give you my word, I would not ask such an impertinent question did not my duty absolutely require it."

"Oh, I understand completely, good Captain, and I should have been astonished if you did not ask."

"You are most complaisant, my lady."

"I wish to see him because he is a friend, and I have heard he was injured, and thus I wish to assure myself regarding his health and comfort."

Khaavren hesitated, then said, "I apologize for the interrogation, my lady, but would you be good enough to tell me how it is you learned he had been injured?"

"Through a mutual friend. Captain, I understand that it is your duty to be inquisitive, yet this questioning seems, if you'll pardon me, extreme."

"I understand that it might seem so, my lady, but I assure you, there is a reason."

"Ah, a reason!"

"Exactly."

"And is this a reason of which, without betraying your duty, you might inform me? For I confess, this has made me as curious as a Hawklord."

"If you wish to know, I will tell you."

"I very much wish it."

"This is it, then: Count Szurke, or Lord Taltos, if you prefer, was not merely injured; he was attacked."

"Attacked!"

"Exactly. And it would be irresponsible of me to permit anyone to see him before assuring myself that, by doing so, I was not subjecting him to any danger."

"I understand completely, Captain, and, moreover, I compliment you on your attention to your duty."

"You are gracious, my lady."

"For my part, I will give my sword into your keeping, and, moreover, swear to you by my hopes of Deathgate that I mean no harm to Lord Taltos, but, on the contrary, desire nothing more than his swift recovery to full health."

As she spoke, she unbuckled her sword belt and placed it into Khaavren's hand. Khaavren, hearing her words, bowed and said, "My lady, that is more than sufficient. Come, I will escort you to his room."

When they reached the room, Khaavren gave a perfunctory clap, then opened the door and stepped back, bowing slightly to indicate the Issola should precede him. As she stepped into the room, Khaavren, whose sharp eyes missed nothing, carefully observed the expression that came over the Easterner's countenance, and the captain had no doubt that this expression was one of intense pleasure. Indeed, Count

Szurke, in spite of his weakness, smiled and attempted to sit up.

Lady Saruchka rushed to him as he collapsed back onto the bed, and Khaavren, close on her heels, heard the Easterner say, "Ah, my lady, you ought not to have come here."

"What nonsense you speak, to be sure." She then turned to the captain and said, "You now perceive that I am no threat to his welfare; may I request a few moments alone with him?"

Khaavren bowed and said, "I have no objection to this plan."

"You have my thanks, good Captain."

With this said, Khaavren bowed and left the room. After some consideration, he decided against listening at the door, and so instead he placed Lady Saruchka's weapon in Erbaad's hands with instructions that it was to be returned when the Issola left. This done, he instructed Ensign Shirip to have a horse prepared for him. Shirip neither made a comment nor asked a question, but simply did as ordered, with the result that in five minutes Khaavren was mounted and riding northward.

After an hour of riding, he found the place where the Easterner had washed up, and he spent some time studying the river, noticing the flow of the currents and the effect of the sandbar. He decided, as a result of this study, that it was more likely that the Easterner had entered the river on this, the west bank (which was, in point of fact, south), than that he had survived crossing the entire river. This was fortunate, as it would have been an hour's ride to the nearest bridge, and there was neither horse nor man ever born who could cross the river this close to its mouth.

Having come to this conclusion, he led his horse (a roan gelding of the Egyeslab breed) northward (actually westward) along the bank, his sharp eyes missing nothing. After a quarter of a mile, he stopped and, nodding to himself, tied up his horse and began a minute inspection of the ground. He was still engaged in this activity when night came on, making its gentle way across the muddy expanse of the river; but instead of stopping, he lit the lantern with which he had supplied himself before setting out, and continued.

Eventually he decided that he had learned all that he could, and so he extinguished the lantern, mounted his long-suffering horse, and rode back to the headquarters building where Shirip was still on duty, having determined that she would remain so until certain that the captain had no further need of her services.

In the event, it was well done, because conversation with her was exactly what Khaavren wished when he returned. He began this conversation himself, by saying, "Is there any change in our patient?"

"The physicker last inspected him three hours ago, shortly after the Issola left, and determined that he would almost certainly live."

"So much the better. I have made an inspection of the ground where the fight took place."

"And did you learn anything, Captain?"

"You mean, beyond confirming what we already suspected: that our Easterner lies like a Yendi? Yes, I have. Or, at any rate, I have formed certain conclusions, which I will test by speaking again with Count Szurke in hopes that he will either admit to the truth of what I tell him, or will, by some mannerism, betray himself if he lies in denial."

"May I do myself the honor of complimenting the captain on this plan?"

"Then, you think it a good one, Ensign? You perceive I ask your opinion."

"I do, for which compliment I thank you. Yes, it seems to me a good plan if you acquired reliable knowledge, and I am certain that you have."

"You will judge for yourself. I had suspected there were four or five attackers. In this, I was wrong."

"How, wrong?"

"In fact, the number was nine."

"Nine!"

"Yes, there were nine. It was easy to determine, as the ground was soft and, before the altercation began, all nine were lined up facing him, and he, with his back to the river, faced them. They remained this way for some time, no doubt having conversation, because the impression of his boots had time to settle deeply, and he stood as one will when having conversation, rather than assuming any sort of defensive position."

"And yet, nine!"

"There are reasons why he survived against nine opponents. That is to say, reasons beyond simply his skill, which is not inconsiderable."

"But, what reasons?"

"For one, he had help of some sort."

"Of some sort, Captain?"

"Not human."

"I do not understand."

"Nor do I, Ensign. Yet there were unmistakable signs that at least two of his attackers were engaged in some sort of combat nowhere near Count Szurke. And yet, there were no footprints near these two except their own. It is possible that he is a skilled illusionist, and so two of his opponents were engaged with phantoms. It is also possible he was able to summon or control birds, and used these against his enemies. There was no blood near either of these places, and yet a considerable number of leaves and twigs had been cut from the trees, as if the attackers were swinging their swords wildly over their heads."

"And yet, Captain, that still leaves seven."

"As I read the signs, one of them was removed from combat in the first instant after speech ended, by either a thrown knife or a sorcerous attack of some kind, because there are signs that one of those facing the Easterner fell to her knees and remained in that position for some time, after which she collapsed to the ground, where she remained, bleeding, until after the battle, when she was assisted from the field by two of her comrades."

"I see. But that still leaves six."

"One of whom was killed at the first pass. His body fell in such a position that it was in everyone's way for the rest of the battle, and there was so much blood lost that no one could have survived."

"So, then, there were five remaining. Still—"

"As I read the signs, he had wounded two of them almost at once. It is almost as if—"

"Yes, Captain?"

"As if he attacked them, rather than receiving the charge. But that is impossible because, ah, yes, I think I know what happened. For now, what is important is that, when it came to combat, it was three against one. Each of them wounded him at least once. They pressed him hard, back toward the river, until he was so severely wounded that he threw himself into it and chanced to luck, being unable to continue the contest."

Shirip nodded, able to see the fight as clearly as if she herself had been a witness to it. She said as much to Khaavren, who replied, "There is yet one more significant detail."

"And that is, my lord?"

"Something of a breeze came up after the fight. I cannot say long after, but there are leaves scattered here and there, covering many of the signs, but not stepped on."

"And this is of interest because?"

"At a spot very close to the river, there is a place where the impression remains in the ground of a thin sword, such as an Easterner might use. There are the prints of someone in small but expensive boots approaching it and leaving it. The boots stepped on some of the leaves that fell after the battle."

"And so?"

"Someone arrived after the fight, looked around, took the Easterner's weapon, and left."

"Ah, yes, I see that, Brigadier."

"I wonder if the Easterner knows who this might be?"

"Will you ask him?"

"Yes, and about other things, as well."

"It seems to me, Captain," she said, "that it will be strange indeed if you are unable to learn something from this Easterner when you confront him with the facts you have accumulated."

"Good then," said Khaavren, standing. "I will go and see him."

Having made this decision, Khaavren wasted no time putting it into action. He at once went to the patient's room, where, after clapping and receiving no response, he admitted himself. After no more than three minutes, he returned to Ensign Shirip and sat in front of her desk once more. "Well," he said. "Our patient has escaped."

Shirip rose to her feet, crying, "How escaped?"

"Perhaps it would be better to say that he left, as he was not a prisoner. And yet, he left by climbing out the window."

"How was he able to do so?"

"As to that, I cannot say. I saw no indication that he had assistance of any kind."

"But, Captain, what do we do?"

"Do? Why, nothing."

"How, nothing?"

Khaavren shrugged. "We have no legal grounds to hold him, and by escaping through the window he proved we have no medical grounds either."

"And yet, the case—"

"Ah, as to the case."

"Well?"

"Continue the interviews, learning as much as you

can. We will collect the information, and hold it against future need."

"Then, you think the matter is not ended?"

"I do not know what the matter actually is, Ensign. But, so far as it goes, no, I do not think it is ended. I believe that Count Szurke and I will have more to do with each other before the Empire becomes significantly older."

*How Khaavren Had a Confidential
Meeting with a Friend
Which Caused an Old Investigation
to Be Reopened, and How Khaavren
and Daro Enjoyed an Evening Out*

The reader will, we hope, forgive us if, before we continue, we say two words about the writing of history, as this will serve to explain why we made certain of the decisions we have made in describing the events we have taken it upon ourselves to relate.

The renowned musician and composer Lord Levhas has stated that music consists of the notes played and spaces between them, each of them being equally important. In the same way, the narration of history consists of what is told and what is omitted. History is as much of a science as physics, mathematics, or sorcery; the narration of history is as much of an art as music, psiprint, or sculpture. The art, then, consists in the selection of the events to be included and those to be excluded that will most effectively lay bare the scientific laws in operation.

The uneducated but alert reader will, at this point,

worry that the historian may, by the careful selection of events, attempt to "prove" a set of pre-conceived notions that do not, in fact, correspond to the truth. We cannot deny that this may happen, as those who are familiar with the "history" written by certain desert-born mystics can testify.

But in fact, this analysis, apparently so convincing, ignores a vital factor: the active brain of the reader. That is to say, should a supposed historian attempt to distort the meaning, significance, and causes of the events he describes, it seems to us this cannot help but reveal itself to the alert reader. The historian's awareness of this, in turn, cannot but serve to encourage the most scrupulous honesty and rigorous precision in his work.

We have taken the time to explain this because the reader cannot fail to notice that our narrative, initially flowing seamlessly from a Teckla to certain guards to an ensign and to Khaavren, will now abruptly move about in time. It is our opinion that a narrative that behaves in this manner ought to be required to explain itself, which it has now done: the discontinuity in time merely corresponds to the historian's choice to omit details he deems insignificant or distracting, instead focusing his and the reader's attention on matters of importance.

With our reader's permission, and, we hope, understanding, we must now, as promised, move forward in time, an action we take with full awareness of the suddenness of our temporal shift, yet confident that it is the best way to present to the reader the history we have undertaken to relate. It was, then, fully three months after the events described in the previous chapter that Khaavren, who, having been able to learn nothing of the injured Easterner and having thus given it no more thought, had the matter called to his mind. It came about this way:

Khaavren was in his office studying the most recent reports on the disposition and preparedness of those under his command when there came the sound of wood rattling with the particular timbre that indicated someone had pulled the clapper-rope outside of the door leading to the conference room. There were only a very few individuals who might ever enter by this door, and in the case of none of them was there any question of joking; therefore Khaavren at once called for the person to enter.

The door opened, and a figure came through the doorway. The figure, we should add, was hooded and cloaked in dark gray, and walked with a firm, even pace until, arriving before Khaavren's desk, it seated itself.

"Well," said Khaavren. "Although I have no doubt that pleasure has nothing to do with your visit to my office, nevertheless, I assure you that it is a pleasure to see you."

"I give you my word," said the other in a soft, almost musical voice, "my feelings are entirely the same."

"I am glad to hear it. While I would enjoy spending some time in conversation, I should imagine that you have come here with a particular purpose, and that of some urgency."

Khaavren observed the gleam of white teeth within the cowl, and the other said, "You think so?"

"It seems to usually be the case when you visit me, my friend."

"I do not deny it."

"And so?"

"Yes, there is a matter I would like to bring to your attention."

"Well, you have my attention, therefore this is a good time to bring a matter to it."

"So much the better. Do you recall that, three months ago, you investigated the beating of an Imperial count?"

"You must know, Pel, that I would not forget something like that after only three months."

"That is true; I merely wished to recall it to your mind."

"Well, you have done so. What then?"

"A new matter has come before us, and one that, I believe, ought to become a subject for the Special Tasks group."

"Ah, you think so? And Her Majesty?"

"Has not yet been informed. Whether to do so will be up to you after you have heard what I have to say."

"And this matter relates in some way to the attack on Count Szurke?"

"I will lay the matter before you, and you will judge."

"Very well."

"Do you have the reports on the investigation you ran?"

Khaavren tilted his head. "I think the more significant question is, do *you* have the reports on the investigation I ran?"

The other chuckled. "You know that I hear things."

"Yes, but it seems you also read things."

"Come, is it a problem?"

Khaavren shook his head. "We will not speak of it. Instead, tell me what you found significant in these reports."

"I noticed the same thing you did, my friend."

"You refer to an interview conducted in the village of Swells?"

"Precisely."

"Then, indeed, we noticed the same thing."

"Let us see. If you would, my friend, please read the appropriate section."

"Very well, if you wish." Khaavren rose and opened up a chest next to his desk, and from there removed a box labeled simply with the year and the word, "open." In this box he found a thick envelope wrapped in white ribbon, and from this, after some looking, he removed a particular folio. He sat down again, and, after some searching, read the following aloud: "'Question: Have you seen any Easterners in the last few days or weeks? Answer: Easterners, Your Lordship? No Easterners. Just Chreotha brewers, a few Orca, Dragonlords like yourselves, some Issola, a couple of traveling merchants—Jhegaala—and a Lyorn who was visiting his cousin. No Easterners, Your Lordship.'"

"Ah, was that the passage that caught your attention, Khaavren? I am astonished."

"Are you? But, if there was anything else significant, I confess that I missed it."

"Well, that is only fair, as I missed any significance in what you read."

"Well, I will explain what I noticed if you will tell me what I missed."

"That seems perfectly equitable, and I accept."

"Then I am listening."

"If you will turn back to the eleventh page—"

"You seem very well acquainted with this document, Pel."

"It is possible that I have seen it."

"Very well. There, I am now looking at the eleventh page."

"Do you see where your observant and well-trained guards describe purchasing six bottles of wine to loosen the tongues of those they wish to question?"

"Yes, I see it, and I even approve."

"In the margin, you perceive, they list the expense of these bottles."

"That is customary, Pel; for if they did not, they could not be reimbursed for this expense, but must pay for it out of their own pockets."

"Of course, it is a perfectly reasonable custom."

"Then what—ah. I see. I had not observed before, but that is an unreasonably low price for six bottles of Eprishka wine."

"Exactly."

"And yet, I do not perceive—"

"Come, Khaavren my friend. What do you know of the Eprishka wine?"

"I know that it is excessively sweet to my tongue, but is nevertheless a not-unpopular wine, grown and bottled in the Eprish region."

"That is correct, my friend. And permit me to say in passing that your palate agrees with mine. Do you know anything of how it is distributed?"

"Distributed? Why, I confess I never gave it a

thought. Presumably carters load barrels, or cases of bottles—"

"That isn't precisely what I mean by distribution, my friend."

"What then?"

"I mean that it is not sold to retailers, but only directly to inns, and in large quantity."

"So then?"

"In most cases—if you will pardon the unintentional play on words—an inn will only make this purchase if there is some sort of significant event to take place."

"So, then, if the bottles are being sold cheaply, it means a significant event was planned for, and did not take place."

"My dear Khaavren, your wits are as sharp as ever."

"Are they? So much the better. I need my wits to be at their sharpest whenever I speak with you. And yet, it seems, they are not sharp enough to see how this matter is of sufficient importance to gain your interest."

"In itself, it is little enough. But it caused me to wonder what sort of event might have been scheduled, and why it was canceled."

"You wondered that?"

"I did."

"Well, had I noticed the price, I would almost certainly have wondered as well."

"I do not doubt you."

"I would have more than wondered, Pel; I would have investigated."

"I am certain you would have."

"And, if I had investigated—"

"Yes? If?"

"What would I have discovered?"

"You would have learned that a bard was sched-uled to perform on the day after Count Szurke was beaten, and the performance was canceled on that very day."

"Interesting indeed."

"Even more interesting is the bard. Not a Teckla, as you would expect. But an Issola. Her name is—"

"Saruchka!"

"Exactly."

"And so, the beating of this Easterner led this Issola to cancel her performance."

"So it would seem."

"And yet, I do not see how this information, sig-nificant as it is, might turn the incident into a matter for the Special Tasks group."

"Patience, Khaavren. First, I must acquaint you with an item that did not pass across your desk. Some years ago—"

"Years!"

"Yes, Khaavren. This is an old matter that has just now taken on new dimensions."

"Very well, I apologize for interrupting. Some years ago?"

"Yes. Some years ago there was a request for Imperial reimbursement for a lost object from Lord Feorae."

"Feorae? County and city investigations?"

"The same."

"A request for reimbursement."

"Exactly. My staff—that is to say, certain friends

of mine keep a sharp eye out for unusual matters, even the most trivial, on the principle that the smallest incident may have larger implications."

"I agree with that principle, my friend."

"I am glad you do. And so, this request struck my friend as being out of the ordinary."

"I agree that it is unusual. If something is lost, well, one cannot generally ask the Empire to reimburse the cost, unless—"

"Yes?"

"Unless it was lost pursuant to Imperial matters. Is that not the law?"

"It is close, Khaavren. In fact, the law reads, lost *or failed of recovery* pursuant to approved discharge of Imperial duties."

"Ah, so then, it is the 'failed of recovery' that is significant?"

"Exactly."

"In other words, Pel, Feorae lost a possession, and he did not recover it because of Imperial duties."

"That is the claim."

"It is most unusual."

"That was my thought."

"Nevertheless, well, what of it?"

"Word has reached my ears—"

"Many words reach your ears, Pel! I sometimes wonder if you have been gifted with more ears than the customary two."

"If I have, Khaavren, I take my oath that the excess only exist metaphorically."

"I do not doubt you. But, you were saying?"

"Yes. Word has reached my ears that the object he wishes reimbursement for was stolen."

"Well, and was it so reported? That is, did he report this theft to himself, and cause himself to investigate it?"

"No, in fact, he did not."

"That is something else that is unusual."

"It is. And there is yet another matter of interest."

"With all of these matters of interest, it no longer startles me that you have become interested. What is this one?"

"The author of the request for reimbursement."

"The author of the request?"

"The author was what directed my attention to you in the first place."

"How me? I recall no such request."

"Not you, Khaavren."

"Then, who is this famous author?"

"None other than the Countess of Whitecrest."

"My wife?"

"Exactly."

"Well, the matter is simplicity itself; I shall ask her about it."

"And I am certain you will get an answer; the Countess's loyalty cannot be questioned."

"I am glad to hear you say that, Pel, for it is also my opinion. So now I perceive why you bring the matter to me, and you are right to do so, but I still do not comprehend how it has any connection with the beating of Count Szurke."

"Nor did I at first. But, you perceive, once my interest in the matter was aroused, I could not help but look further."

"Well, and did you wonder what was stolen?"

"That was my first question."

"And did you find an answer?"

"Nearly."

"Well?"

"It took several years, as the matter did not seem pressing, but, yes, eventually I did learn."

"Well, and what was stolen?"

"A silver tiassa."

Khaavren bounded to his feet. "What is it you tell me?"

"It is described as a tiny sculpture of a tiassa, all of silver, with sapphires for eyes."

"This is . . . when did he request reimbursement?"

"Half a year after the uproar of a supposed Jenoine invasion that never occurred, during which, as you recall, the Court Wizard was furiously looking for—"

"A silver tiassa!"

"Exactly."

Khaavren sat down again.

"You may as well remain standing," said his friend.

"How, there is more?"

"Yes, for once I learned this, I could not resist attempting further investigation."

"I know you so well in that!"

"I was curious about two things especially. One, who stole it? And, two, how did Feorae acquire it in the first place?"

"And did you learn the answer to the first question?"

"No, but I learned the answer to the second."

"Ah! How did you discover it?"

"In the simplest possible way. After assuring him that this was a matter of first importance to the Empire, well—"

"Well?"

"I asked him."

"Ah, that was cleverly done, Pel."

"Was it not?"

"And so, how did he acquire it?"

"The details are murky, and it involves some quasi-legal activity that I would prefer not to discuss with you, my friend. But in the end, the trail leads to none other than your friend, the Count of Szurke."

"Indeed!"

"So it would seem."

"Well. Does he have the silver tiassa now?"

The other shrugged. "I do not know."

"We should attempt to find it."

"I agree."

"And I should have a conversation with Lord Feorae."

"Ah, as to that—"

"Well?"

"You may do so if you wish, but I have learned all there is to learn from him."

Khaavren nodded. "Very well, then. This job of tracing the tiassa, how do I convince Her Majesty that it is suitable for the Tasks group?"

"I am certain you can be persuasive, Khaavren."

Khaavren made a sound of disgust. "And I am certain you have suggestions that would be helpful."

"Perhaps I do."

"Well?"

"You might point out to her that this involves an attack on an Imperial nobleman, which is something she cannot be pleased about."

"That is true."

"And, moreover, it has to do with the false Jenoine invasion, which I know is a subject upon which she has strong feelings."

Khaavren nodded. "That will help."

"I am always pleased to be of assistance."

Khaavren stood. "I will go now."

"If you don't mind, I shall await you here."

"Certainly," said Khaavren, smiling. "That will make it easier for you to look through my files."

"Now my friend, have you ever known me to do anything so obvious?"

"Never." Khaavren stood and strode to the door. "Which is exactly what makes it subtle."

An hour later he returned, to find his friend still sitting in the same place. Khaavren sat behind his desk and said, "How much can you tell me?"

There was, for the moment, a gleam of teeth from within the cowl. "How much do you imagine I can tell you, my friend?"

"Oh, you know I have no imagination."

"You have Her Majesty's approval of the mission?"

"Yes, I managed to convince her. She is still angry over the false Jenoine invasion, and is perfectly aware that the matter goes deeper than the man who was punished for it."

The cowl nodded. "As I'd have expected," came the soft voice.

"The Special Tasks group will investigate to see if

there is a connection between this mysterious silver tiassa and the attack on Count Szurke."

"Precisely."

"Pel? Why am I only now being informed?"

"I was conducting my own investigation, until today."

"What happened today to change your mind?"

"I saw the connection between the two investigations."

Khaavren studied his friend for a moment, wondering, as he always did with the Yendi, what he hadn't been told. He said, "Well, I will certainly look into the matter."

"I am confident you will find whatever there is to be found."

Khaavren sighed. "Very well, then. But of course, with so little to go on, I can promise nothing."

"I believe we understand each other. I do not expect promises or guarantees."

Khaavren smiled. "At any rate, you understand me, and that is sufficient."

When his friend had left, Khaavren settled back to consider his next move. The file concerning the investigation into the attack on Count Szurke was still before him; he therefore took a few minutes to refresh his mind on the details. After this time had passed, he put the file down and rang the bell for his confidential servant—not to be confused with his private secretary.

The individual, then, who responded to this bell was a man whom we have already met briefly—that is, the individual who went by the name of Borteliff. Physically, there was nothing unusual about him: he had the round face and stocky build of the House of the Teckla; his nose was short and snubbed, his mouth rather thin and pinched. Now this worthy had been employed by the Empire—that is to say, by Khaavren—for several years. Khaavren had discovered him while on a mission in the duchy of Tildhome, where the Teckla had been employed as a procurator for a textile manufacturer. Borteliff, a Teckla of middle years, had so impressed the captain with his organizational abilities and discretion, and above all his reticence, that he had at once offered him a new post, a post which the procurator had accepted with all the more alacrity as Khaavren's mission had resulted in the destruction of his previous employment.

Many of those who worked with or near Borteliff believed he was mute. In fact, he was capable of speech; it is merely that he had discovered many years before that, as a servant, the less he spoke, the more he was valued. He therefore developed the habit of saying little. Having adopted this laudable custom, he then found that the less he spoke, the better he was able to listen, and the better he listened, the more precisely he could carry out the tasks entrusted to him. This, quite naturally, increased his value to his employer still further; and thus, the less he spoke, the more he was valued, and the less he spoke; with the result that, at the time of this history, he'd scarcely uttered a word in a year.

In addition to his laconicity, the worthy Borteliff had many other virtues: he was precise, careful, had a remarkable head for details, and was disposed to obey orders at once and without question. The reader will not be astonished to learn that, with this list of qualifications, Khaavren not only depended on this servant, but considered him invaluable.

Borteliff, then, appeared at once upon hearing the bell, and presented himself before the captain with a slight bow, which he used to indicate that he was prepared to receive any instructions with which he might be honored.

Khaavren, unusual though this may be in a Tiassa, considered each word to be a precious commodity, and he thus hoarded them as the proprietor of a counting-house hoards his coins and notes. On this occasion, he doled out the following: "Attempt to learn the present and recent whereabouts of a bard named Saruchka, House of the Issola. Inform the Countess that I will sup at home. Any information arriving is to be forwarded to me there. Take this file and have copies made, and see that each member of the Tasks group has one. They are to be informed that the group will meet to-morrow at the tenth hour. That is all."

Borteliff bowed to indicate that he understood, and turned and set about his errands.

With complete confidence in the Teckla, Khaavren gave no more thought to the tasks he had assigned this worthy; instead he simply returned home, where his sword and cloak were taken by Cyl, an elderly servant who had been with the Manor since before the Interregnum, and who, by this time, understood the complex relationships between Imperial service, county service, and family life better than did any of the others who lived there, particularly including the Countess and Lord Khaavren. Accordingly, as he relieved the captain of the aforementioned burdens, he said, "The Countess is on the Terrace."

"Thank you, Cyl," said Khaavren, and brought himself to one of the two terraces that had been built to provide a view of the ocean-sea; one of them was frequently used by the Countess to see to Imperial business on fine days; the other was referred to by all as the breakfast terrace, for the reason that it was most often used for outdoor repasts on fine mornings.

Khaavren found her at once, and she looked up from her work and greeted him with that smile that, as the captain had said more than once, would lighten up a dark room. "My lord," she said, extending a hand, "you are home early. How delightful!"

He kissed her hand and took a chair beside her. "Yes, madam, to make up for what I fear will be a long day to-morrow, and perhaps more long days after."

"Ah, is there excitement at the Palace?"

"Two old investigations have come together, and thus must be renewed. Apropos, you may know something of one of them."

"Ah, indeed? You know I am eager to be of help in your work, as you are always helpful in mine. What does it concern that I may know something of?"

"It concerns Lord Feorae, a silver tiassa, and the matter of the false Jenoine invasion of some years ago—which invasion, as you know, was never thoroughly understood by Her Majesty."

"Ah, yes," said the Countess. "I may, indeed, have information on that matter."

"Information that you never gave me before, madam?"

"Ah, my lord, do I hear a hint of reproach in your voice?"

"Merely curiosity, madam. It seems unlike you to withhold information that could be useful in my work."

"The circumstances were unusual."

"But you will explain them?"

"Certainly, and this very moment, if you wish."

"I would be very pleased to hear this explanation."

"Then I will tell you."

"I am listening."

"You know that the supposed invasion was merely a plot by the Jhereg."

"Yes, madam, I am not unacquainted with this circumstance."

"Do you know the object of this plot?"

"That was never revealed."

"Yes, my lord. Because to reveal it would have led to unfortunate circumstances for the Empire."

"How unfortunate?"

"Her Majesty would have been forced to take official notice, and this, in turn, would have required legal, and possibly violent, attacks on the Jhereg, and the Jhereg would, of course, have responded. Her Majesty thought it best, after having foiled their intentions and executed the perpetrator, to let the matter lie. Lord Feorae cooperated by not reporting the theft of his sculpture, and I filled out the forms to see he was, at least, reimbursed for it."

"It was Her Majesty's decision not to press the investigation further?"

"It was."

"Very well. What was the plot intended to accomplish?"

"The assassination of a certain Lord Taltos."

"Taltos! Count Szurke?"

"The same."

"I had not been aware of how badly the Jhereg wants this Easterner."

"Nor was I, my lord."

"How was this plot to work?"

"The intention was to trick Her Majesty into locating this Easterner, at which time Jhereg assassins would kill him."

"And how is Feorae involved?"

"By chance, he held the object that the Jhereg were using as a pretext to convince Her Majesty to locate Lord Taltos."

"The silver tiassa."

"Exactly."

"What became of the object?"

"As to that, I do not know. It was stolen from Feorae, and evidence left pointing to Lord Taltos. But it is clear that the Easterner did not, in fact, steal it. And so it is unknown what in fact became of it."

"I see."

"It may also prove useful to know that Lord Taltos is married."

"Ah, is he?"

"That is, he was. His estranged wife lives in South Adrilankha, and still cares sufficiently for him to take great risks in order to save him."

"That is good to know."

"My lord, I'm sorry that I didn't inform you of this before. Her Majesty—"

"I understand completely, madam. I would have done the same, had Her Majesty made the request of me." He kissed her hand again, and smiled.

"Thank you, my lord. What will you do now?"

"To begin, I will attempt to locate the silver tiassa. It is possible that whoever has it will prove to be the key to this matter."

"I hope so indeed, my lord."

"But first—"

"Yes? First?"

"First, madam, I plan to spend a relaxing evening with my adored wife."

"Permit me to say, my lord, that I am in entire agreement with this plan."

"If you wish, we can even venture out-of-doors. Might an evening of music be to your taste?"

"My lord knows how I love music."

"As do I. There is always an entertainer at the Fingers."

"That would be lovely. But is it not the case that there is a performance tonight at the Adrilankha Concert Hall?"

"That is true, madam; and yet I know that you prefer social to compositional music."

"I enjoy both, my lord, as do you, though I'm aware of your preference for the latter. Yet—"

"Well?"

"I believe that, today, the notion of dressing in all the finery Noli can find, and even doing my nails and my jewelry, would be a particular treat."

Khaavren smiled. "And I will dress as the Count of Whitecrest, with a blue silk cloak and a feathered cap, and you will be on my arm, and I will be the envy of all. And when I have had my fill of that pleasure—"

"Yes? What then?"

"Why, then we will pass within and treat our senses to Jengi's 'Symphony of the Northern Sea,' conducted by Jengi himself."

"I can think of nothing more pleasurable."

"Nor can I conceive of a better way to relax before diving into a task that, I assure you, will have me as busy as I have been in some little time."

"Let us not think of that now!"

"With this I agree."

"But is there time?"

"The concert does not begin until the ninth hour. An hour to dress, an hour for a leisurely drive, a few minutes for a late supper at the Boiled Hen, and we will still have time to mingle."

"Then it is a plan!"

This plan, unlike those of a military nature, in the event worked out exactly as intended. They arrived at the concert hall and entered, smiling and speaking with casual acquaintances. Khaavren, of course, noticed with great pleasure the glances, open or covert, cast on the Countess, who, according to her custom, wore Lyorn red in the form of a low-cut gown with a long train, bunched sleeves, and no shortage of lace. Her jewelry, diamond ear-rings and a ruby brooch, completed the outfit. These external features, however, paled in comparison to her wit and charm, which were on full display to anyone who joined what quickly became a large group that formed around them awaiting the bell that signaled the concert was to begin.

The bell sounded, and the massive doors were opened by servants in the blue and gold livery affected by the hall. Khaavren, Daro, the Lord Mayor, and her husband all went to the box reserved for them, relaxing into the plush velvet seats while a servant hurried to see to any refreshments they wished. Below them, the orchestra was spread out, awaiting the lowering of the lights and the arrival of the conductor.

"Do you know," said Khaavren, "I had never before remarked upon the number of nobles who make up the orchestra. To be sure, most of the performers are of the merchants classes—Chreotha and Jhegaala—but I see a Tiassa in the horn section, and another playing the organophone; and I am certain that there are two Issola in the string section, another among the singers, and yet a fourth playing percussion."

The Lord Mayor's husband, a Hawklord named Cellith, said, "You are very observant, my lord. And it is true; Issola especially are often called to a musical life. Compositional music only, of course."

"Why only compositional music?"

"Because social music would be beneath the dignity of an Issola; none of them would consider such a life, and, to be sure, the House would be outraged."

"Well," said Khaavren. "That would normally be interesting information. In fact, there is only one circumstance which keeps it from being of interest."

"And what is that circumstance, my lord?" asked Cellith.

"That I have promised not to think about work until tomorrow," said Khaavren.

Daro pressed his hand as he made this enigmatic remark, and, just at that moment, the house lights dimmed as the conductor entered, and, as nothing else that happened that evening has any bearing on our history, we will say no more about it.

Chapter the Fourth

*How Khaavren Met with the
Special Tasks Group, and a
Matter That Has, Perhaps, Been
Puzzling the Reader
Is Finally Explained*

The next day, Khaavren arrived at the ninth hour and rang the bell for Borteliff, who indicated with the merest inclination of his head that the captain's instructions had been carried out.

"Then, a search has begun for the bard, Saruchka?"

Borteliff nodded.

"Has any trace of her yet been found?"

Borteliff gave a negative indication. Khaavren accepted this, dismissed Borteliff, and made certain that there was nothing that required his immediate attention. This being established, Khaavren checked the time, then went through the door that, yesterday, his friend had entered from. He followed it until at last he reached the special conference room that had been set aside for his use. Taking a position at the head of the long table, he awaited the arrival of the Special Tasks group.

Khaavren had been waiting less than five minutes when the door at the far end opened, and in came a Dragonlord with short hair and light eyebrows. Without a word, she walked to the second chair from the right on the far end, and sat down. As she was sitting, another entered, this one a Dzurlord who wore a silver band about his forehead, setting off the black of his hair; he took a seat next to the Dragonlord. Another Dragonlord arrived at about this time—an older man with a barrel chest and powerful arms; he sat next to Khaavren. Next came a man, hooded, in the colors of the Athyra; he sat on the other side of the first Dragonlord to have arrived. Last to arrive, directly on the heels of the hooded man, was yet another of the House of the Dragon, this the youngest of them, a woman who seemed to have hardly reached her four hundredth year, and who still had the clear eye and bright smile of youth. She sat at the far end of the table, at which time Khaavren said, "That is all of us; the others are away on missions."

They nodded, and awaited his further words. As it falls out that they are waiting, we cannot see any harm in saying two words about the individuals whom we have mentioned, as some of them will play no insignificant role in the remainder of our history.

The short-haired Dragonlord was called Timmer. She had been born into the impoverished nobility, which similarity with Khaavren gave him a certain sympathy with her. Upon leaving home, she had joined Combrack's mercenary army, and had there risen to sergeant. She sustained an injury from a poorly aimed spell at Cook's Bluff, and so was in hospital when the army, as is well known, went missing in the Gevlin Pass. Without employment, she joined the Phoenix Guards for, as she thought, temporary duty. However, she discovered she had a talent for investigations—in particular for learning more from witnesses than the witnesses were aware that they knew. When Khaavren became aware that this talent extended to supervising investigators, the captain—that is to say, the brigadier—enlisted her in the Special Tasks group. She had, therefore, two commanders: both of them Khaavren.

The Dzurlord was called Dinaand. He had studied sorcery under Brestin, who had also trained Kosadr, who was, at present, the Court Wizard. While Kosadr studied arcana associated with the Orb, with a further specialty in defenses against the Jenoine, Dinaand became fascinated with the sorceries of identity and location. This was unusual for a Dzurlord—they being more the sort of studies favored by Hawklords, while a Dzur will generally prefer to specialize in the offensive and, occasionally, defensive uses of magic. When Khaavren learned that there was a Dzurlord with these skills, he—after his usual close investigation into the individual's background—at once offered him a position which would permit him to put his training into practice; an offer that was accepted at once.

The man in the cowl who appeared to be an Athyra was, as the reader has no doubt realized, none other than Khaavren's friend Pel, a Yendi. As prime minister, he was not actually a member of the group, but attended as a representative of Her Majesty, and, of course, to keep himself informed.

The older Dragonlord was called Cialdi, and, though he looked old, he was, in fact, older. He had achieved the post of Superintendent of Investigations for the Adrilankha Police as far back as the Interregnum. After the Interregnum, he had come so near to identifying and gathering sufficient evidence to convict the mysterious Blue Fox that Piro, the Viscount of Adrilankha, had recommended Cialdi to Piro's father, who was, as the reader is no doubt aware, Khaavren. Cialdi was an expert on Jhereg operations, having taken the lead in bringing down Lord Hiyechin's palm-steel operation, as well as having discovered the means whereby stolen jewelry was being smuggled out of the city. Cialdi, then, worked for both Khaavren and Piro (as well as reporting to the Lord Mayor of Adrilankha, and the Chief City Constable). It should be added that, as no conclusive evidence had been found, the matter of the Blue Fox was never mentioned by any of them (except, occasionally, the Chief City Constable, who remained utterly oblivious to what the others, and, of course, the reader, all knew). Cialdi was perfectly aware of the general contempt in which police were held, and cared not at all unless it was mentioned to him in an offensive manner; he was also renowned as a duelist.

The last individual was also a Dragonlord; she was called Palaniss. She had come to Khaavren's attention as a concealed operative during the coal-tax rebellion, when she had acquired significant information by disguising herself as a Lyorn and insinuating herself into the confidence of Lady Vilnai. Later, she directed a covert operation against the Duke of Loghram. While, strictly speaking, the operation failed, it succeeded in that it led to the discovery of Loghram's spy network within the Palace; and, in any case, Khaavren was sufficiently impressed by Palaniss's thoroughness and professionalism that he offered her a position in Special Tasks. We should add that Palaniss was not wealthy, and so the stipend was not unwelcome. But even more than this was her passion for all matters relating to military intelligence, and as this position promised her opportunities to practice her art, as she called it, she did not hesitate before agreeing.

These were the five people, then—three Dragonlords, a Dzurlord, and a Yendi—who turned their eyes to their chief, Khaavren, to await his words.

He said, "There is an Easterner named Vladimir Taltos, Count of Szurke. He holds an Imperial title. Before that, he was a Jhereg, and is now being hunted by that House for criminal activity that ran counter to their preferred criminal activity. Last month he was set upon and attacked, but not by Jhereg. He survived the attack, and, for reasons of his own, will not cooperate with the investigation into it."

Khaavren looked at the five faces assembled there. "Three months ago, I had an ensign send out teams to learn what could be learned in the general area where the attack took place. The results of the investigation were sent to you yesterday. I will now read you an interview in which I noticed something interesting." He then gave the date and location at which the interview took place and at once proceeded to

read them text—not a sound was heard save for
Khaavren's voice as he did so; everyone in the room
giving him the complete attention he was due.

When he had finished, he put down the papers
and said, as he usually did at this point in an investigation, "Has anyone an observation to make?"

For a moment, no one spoke; then the Dragonlord who had entered last cleared her throat.
"Brigadier—"

"Yes, Palaniss?"

"I, for one, do not see what observation one might
make."

"You see nothing unusual there?"

"Nothing, Captain."

Khaavren picked up the papers again, and reread
a certain passage: "'Question: Have you seen any
Easterners in the last few days or weeks? Answer:
Easterners, Your Lordship? No Easterners. Just
Chreotha brewers, a few Orca, Dragonlords like
yourselves, some Issola, a couple of traveling
merchants—Jhegaala—and a Lyorn who was visiting
his cousin. No Easterners, Your Lordship.'"

Having finished reading, Khaavren said, "Well?"

Palaniss said, "I am afraid, Brigadier, that I fail to
see what is of interest there."

"Do you? We were lucky enough to get a catalog
of strangers passing through—you'll note that this is
from a Teckla who works at a public market, and so
sees everyone passing through. Apropos, I must
make a note to commend the guardsmen for thinking to interview him. So then, let us look at these
strangers one by one."

"Very well, Brigadier, I agree with this."

"The last thing he mentions is a Lyorn, visiting his cousin."

"Yes, my lord? But the Baron of that region is a Lyorn, as is mentioned on page thirty-nine, and why should he not have a cousin?"

"You are correct, Palaniss. Let us pass on. What of the Chreotha brewers?"

"There are two public houses there, my lord; it would seem reasonable that brewers should come by from time to time."

"Once again, I see no flaws in your reasoning."

"I am gratified that you do not."

"So then, what of the traveling Jhegaala merchants?"

"The brigadier must be aware that there is no small number of such merchants, each with his wagon or cart, drawn by horse or mule, traveling and trading among the small villages."

"I am very much aware of this. So then, that is not out of the ordinary?"

"Not the least in the world."

"I agree. What of the Dragonlords, dressed like guardsmen, as he says?"

"But, my lord, you know that different pairs of guards are assigned to pass through the towns from time to time, and see that all is well, and listen to complaints."

"I know that very well."

"So then, there is nothing odd in that."

"With this, I agree. What, then, of the Issola?"

"The Issola?"

"Some Issola. I say again, *some* Issola. Some unknown number of nobles of the House of the Issola. Are there any Issola holdings in the region?"

"None, Lord Khaavren."

"Well, and then?" He looked around the room.

No one spoke except Timmer, who said, "Well, I agree. It is unusual."

"Does anyone disagree?"

There was the shaking of heads all around the table. The older Dragonlord said, "I admit, it is unusual; but is it significant?"

"Ah, as to that."

"Well?"

"What is your opinion, Cialdi?"

"I am uncertain, Brigadier."

"Anyone else?"

The young Dragonlord said, "I, too, fail to see anything in the report you have done us the honor to read to us that may have bearing on the attack on the Easterner."

"Perhaps there is no bearing, Palaniss. But it is something unusual that has happened in the area we are investigating. Therefore, I wish to know more about it. Also, another matter has been brought to my attention." Khaavren summarized what Pel had observed about the wine, and the discovery the Yendi had made. As the reader already knows of this, nothing can be gained by merely repeating it, and so the historian has therefore chosen to omit it save by reference. When this summary was finished, and his listeners were considering the significance of what they had heard, Khaavren said, "Also, I have been reliably informed that another matter has a direct bearing on this case, and may prove important to unlocking it."

"And what matter is that?" said the others.

"It concerns," said Khaavren, "the theft of a small sculpture of a tiassa, all in silver, from the collection of Lord Feorae. The theft was carried out as part of a Jhereg scheme aimed against the same Lord Szurke whose attack we have been discussing. That is the connection between them, and so we will be investigating both matters."

There were general nods from around the table, and the Dzurlord said, "Brigadier?"

Khaavren nodded to him, saying, "Yes, Dinaand?"

"How is it you wish us to proceed, in order to learn more about it?"

"I have directed some of my forces to finding Lady Saruchka. Our main effort will be an attempt to find the silver tiassa. As to how we will go about that, has anyone any suggestions?"

Dinaand said, "I know of no way to locate it using sorcery unless it were to be in our possession long enough to plant a trace spell on it; and if it were in our possession, well, we would not need to locate it."

"That is true, Dinaand," said Khaavren, struck by the extreme justice of this observation. "So, then?"

"Perhaps," said Timmer, "we could send our own teams back to that area and see if there is more to learn. While this will not net us the artifact, it may provide useful information."

Khaavren nodded. "That is a good plan. See to it."

"As for finding the tiassa," said Palaniss.

"Yes?"

"It seems to me that the Jhereg who was behind the false invasion was executed."

"Your memory does you credit," said Khaavren, "for that is exactly what happened. And then?"

"I wonder," said Palaniss, "if a thorough search was ever made of his residence."

"Ah, that is an excellent thought," said Khaavren. "Look into it."

"I will not fail to do so, Brigadier," said the Dragonlord.

"Are there other suggestions?" said Khaavren, looking around the room.

There were none.

"Very well," said Khaavren. "You will all, of course, stay in touch with me. Let us be about Her Majesty's work."

With that, Khaavren rose, as did all of the others except Timmer, who said, "Your pardon, Brigadier."

Khaavren stopped. "Yes, Timmer?"

"May I speak with you privately?"

Khaavren sat down and nodded.

One by one, the others filed out of the door through which they had arrived. Pel hesitated, as if he wanted to stay, but in the end he just shrugged and followed the others.

"Well then," said Khaavren. "What is it?"

"I know this Easterner, my lord. Count Szurke, as he is called."

"How, you know him?"

She nodded. "Does the brigadier recall the Fyres matter?"

"When Loftis was killed. I cannot forget it. He was involved?"

"He was."

"How deeply involved?"

"Very deeply."

Khaavren's face hardened. "Loftis's killer was never found."

"No, my lord. He was not the killer. In fact, he avenged Loftis."

"His name appears in none of the reports, Ensign."

She met his eyes. "I am aware of that, my lord."

Khaavren grunted. He knew very well that, with the sort of inquiries the Special Tasks group was assigned, a certain amount of discretion was necessary. "Was he helpful?"

"Extremely, though it must be added, for his own reasons."

Khaavren nodded. "What can you tell me about him?"

"He is, or at least was, an assassin."

Khaavren's nostrils flared, but he gave no other sign of emotion. "What else?"

"He had the charge of a boy, human, Teckla, under a hundred."

"Charge?"

"He took responsibility for him. From what I learned, heard, and deduced, Szurke felt responsible for something that happened to the boy."

"I see. What else?"

"He keeps his bargains."

"You claim he is honorable?"

"For an Easterner, yes."

Khaavren nodded. "Very well. What else?"

"He is a known associate of Kiera the Thief."

"Ah, is he! That brings to mind the stolen silver tiassa."

Timmer shook her head. "That wasn't her work."

"How, you are certain?"

Timmer nodded. "I looked into it. It was sloppy, and signs were left."

"False signs, were they not?"

"Nevertheless, Kiera would have left none. She especially would not have left signs pointing to Szurke, as they are friends."

Khaavren nodded, accepting her judgment, and said, "What else?"

"I saw from your report that you speculate he might have had arcane or mundane assistance in the fight."

"Yes, that is true."

"I can tell you the nature of that assistance."

"Ah, can you? I hope, then, that you will do so."

"He practices the Eastern magical arts, by which means he has two Jhereg—that is, if the brigadier will forgive me, two of the animals—who watch over him, and assist him in various ways."

"What ways?"

"When I saw him, they were often perched on his shoulders, or else flying about watching, and, I have no doubt, magically reporting to him what they saw."

"This is most remarkable, Ensign. Are you certain?"

"I am."

Khaavren nodded. "This Easterner is formidable, for one of his race."

"With this, I agree, my lord Brigadier."

"Is there more?"

"That is all, my lord."

"If you think of anything else pertaining to this Easterner, or this mission, tell me at once."

"I will not fail to do so."

Timmer rose, bowed, and took her leave; Khaavren returned to his office. He sat behind his desk. Borteliff, who was engaged in placing folders in a file cabinet, looked at him. "Well," said Khaavren. "We seem to have landed ourselves a thorny problem."

Borteliff, who would not even permit himself a grunt of agreement, bobbed his head slightly. Khaavren nodded back and returned to other matters.

A few hours later he was still at his desk, the remains of a bowl of soup and a few crusts of bread in front of him when he was informed that Palaniss wished to see him. He directed the Dragonlord be admitted at once.

"Brigadier," he said.

"Palaniss, you have something to tell me."

"I have indeed."

"Well, if you have found the silver tiassa, do not delay, for I wish to know at once."

"Alas, we did not find the artifact."

"So much the worse!"

"However—"

"Ah! Ah! You found something, then?"

"It would be strange if I did not, for it was a small place, and I made certain to miss nothing."

"Was it, then, unoccupied?"

"Oh, no; a Chreotha family had moved in. I had them wait in the street until I was finished."

"Ah, very good. So then, what did you find?"

"In the floor of the master bedroom was a concealed hole, as one might use to hide valuables."

"I see. And what was in it?"

"Nothing."

"Nothing?"

"Nothing, except—"

"Well?"

"Except a piece of velvet, as if to provide a resting place for something delicate."

"That is very significant. And did you inspect the velvet?"

"With the greatest care."

"And what did you learn?"

"That something had, indeed, been laid on it, and it looked very much as if it could be a small, sculpted tiassa."

"So then, it was there!"

"That is my conclusion, Brigadier."

"That was well done, Palaniss."

"You are kind to say so, Brigadier."

"Now the question is, what became of it?"

"He could have removed it."

"Unlikely. He was arrested, you recall, before the operation was completed."

"That is true."

"Could the Chreotha family have taken it?"

"No, Brigadier. They had installed a safe, and their valuables were in there. If they knew of the concealed hole, they would have used it, as it was better protection than the safe."

"You looked in the safe?"

"Of course."

Khaavren nodded. "So, then, it was taken after the Jhereg, Dathaani, was arrested."

"By whom?"

"That is the question."

"And can you answer it?"

"Perhaps I can, by asking another question."

"If you have a question, well, I am listening."

"This is it, then: Who else, besides Dathaani, knew Dathaani had the silver tiassa?"

"The thief he hired to steal it for him?"

"Yes, that is true. Who else?"

"No one."

"No one?"

"Oh, yes—there was some talk of the Countess being aided by a pair of Jhereg, was there not?"

"There was."

"We must find out who these Jhereg are."

"That is useless, for I already know."

"How, you know?"

"Yes, I was given this information."

"And does the brigadier wish to share this information?"

"One of them, I will not say. There are certain matters of high politics involved."

"Very well, I accept that. And the other?"

"A certain Easterner who, it happens, is or was married to the Count of Szurke."

"Ah, ah."

"You perceive, Palaniss, that it all fits together."

"Indeed it does, Brigadier. So either this Easterner woman—"

"Cawti."

"—has it, or she has disposed of it, very likely to her husband."

"Who is, from your report, on the run from the Jhereg."

"Exactly."

Palaniss frowned. "I do not yet see how the Jhereg fits in."

"Nor do I. We will discover this."

"Yes, Brigadier. What are my orders?"

"Are you able to gain the confidence of an Easterner?"

The Dragonlord hesitated. "I do not know. It is not something I have ever attempted."

"Attempt it now. See if you can confirm that she took the artifact, and learn what she did with it. Remember that she is an Easterner. Flatter her by treating her with courtesy as if she were human—they cannot resist that."

"As you say, Brigadier."

With this, Khaavren dismissed her and silently considered what he had learned. After a brief period of thought—Khaavren, as we know, wasted thoughts no more than he wasted words—he concluded that he could come to no conclusions until he received more information than he at present possessed, and he accordingly put the matter out of his mind.

Some time later, he received a report from Timmer, but it was only that they had begun their investigation. This news, while welcome, did nothing to give Khaavren additional material with which to construct theories or test conjectures.

He worked well into the night, supervising the investigators (which he could do, thanks to the remarkable powers of the Orb, without actually being present), and when he was finally overcome by sleep, lay down on a cot in his office.

Borteliff woke him early the next morning with klava, a warm, moist towel, and the summary, prepared by his staff during the night, of any incidents of which the captain ought to be aware. He sipped the one, used the other, then quickly perused the third. As there was nothing in this latter that required immediate attention (some hints of trouble among longshoremen, the particularly gruesome murder of a wealthy Orca), he turned his attention once more to the strange matter of Count Szurke and the silver tiassa.

Within the hour, messengers began to deliver reports of investigations; these Khaavren read them as they appeared, making notations in the margins whenever anything caught his interest, such as symbols indicating more inquiry required, or pay particular attention, or see if this alibi can be sustained. He searched for patterns, and for unusual activity of any sort; particularly following the efforts to learn who the mysterious Issola nobles were.

In the middle of the afternoon, Palaniss returned, begging permission to report. Khaavren had her admitted at once, being anxious to hear what she had learned.

"Well, well, Palaniss," he said. "To judge by the expression on your countenance, you have not met with complete success."

"I'm sorry to say, Brigadier, that you are entirely correct."

"Ah, so much the worse."

"If you wish, I will tell you about it."

"That is exactly what I wish. Come, sit down. That is better. Were you able to find the Easterner?"

"Oh, yes; I found her. There was no difficulty in that."

"And was she willing to speak with you?"

"Yes, she was willing, although—"

"Yes?"

"She seemed cold, even unfriendly."

"That is odd."

"Yes, it seems strange, and even, upon reflection, ungrateful."

"Very true, Palaniss. Did you endeavor to follow my advice?"

"I did, Brigadier, and, I'm sorry to say, she was intransigent."

"Intransigent?"

"Exactly."

"Yet, you flattered her?"

"I treated her with all deference."

"It is unusual. More than unusual, it is strange."

"I couldn't agree more, Brigadier."

"So, then, she refused to tell you anything?"

"She pretended she had never heard of the artifact."

"Impossible!"

"I agree."

"Did you get any hint of deception?"

"Ah, as to that, it is possible."

"Possible?"

"She held her face immobile and kept her eyes on mine, as humans will often do when they do not wish to give away their feelings; it often means deception. I do not know what this means among Easterners."

"Nor do I. It is dangerous to make assumptions—"

"That is true, Brigadier. You have often said that when you assume, you are thinking like a fish.[*]"

"It is true that I have said that, and I am glad you remember. Nevertheless, we may, in this case, use as a working hypothesis that she knows more than she is saying on the matter."

"I am entirely in agreement," said Palaniss. "So, then, what is the next step?"

"Let us reflect."

"Oh, I am entirely in favor of reflecting."

"Good, then."

"But—"

"Yes?"

"Upon what should we reflect?"

"Ah, you ask that?"

"I do, and, if necessary, I even ask it again."

"Well, I wish to reflect upon this: If our assumption is correct, and this Easterner did take the artifact from the home of Dathaani—"

"Yes, if she did?"

"Then what might she have done with it?"

"Ah, yes. I must say, Brigadier, that that is a good subject upon which to reflect."

"I am gratified that you think so, Palaniss."

"So, then, I am now reflecting."

---

[*] In the Northwestern language, the word "assume" consists of syllables that, when broken apart, are not dissimilar to the sound for "fish" followed by the symbols that form the word "thought."

"As am I."

After some few moments of silent reflection, Khaavren said, "It is possible that she has it concealed in her home."

"Yes, that is possible."

"Or she may have given it to someone else."

"What of selling it?"

Khaavren frowned. "If it is made of solid silver, it is not without value, and yet—"

"Well?"

"Something tells me that, whatever her reasons for acquiring it, it was not for its monetary value."

"I know you too well, Brigadier, to mistrust your instincts."

"So, then, who might she have given it to?"

"She has a son, Brigadier."

"Ah, has she? Well, that is certainly a possibility."

"And then, of course, we must not forget her estranged husband, Count Szurke."

"In fact, Palaniss, it was toward him that my thoughts were tending."

"You think she gave it to him?"

"It is not impossible."

The Dragonlord nodded. "It certainly seems to be a possibility, perhaps even a likelihood."

"But then, if it is true, you perceive our situation?"

"I am not certain I understand what the brigadier does me the honor to tell me."

"Why, we are searching for the silver tiassa, are we not?"

"That is true."

"Well, if it is in the possession of Count Szurke,

that gains us nothing, as we have no way of finding him."

"Ah, that is true. So, in fact, this intelligence does us little good."

"That is my judgment, Palaniss. Nevertheless, I may be beginning to see the start of a pattern here."

"A pattern? Can you describe it?"

"Not yet," said Khaavren, frowning. "I must reflect."

"I will point out, in case you have forgotten, that the Jhereg are after Count Szurke."

Khaavren shook his head. "This is not the Jhereg. There is no direction, no goal. These are events that are occurring without a mind guiding them. There are many elements, many goals, many tracks. That is to say, we are seeing the result of a clash of intentions, not the working out of a plan."

"I see. But then, what must we do?"

Khaavren's eyes widened slightly. "Why, that was very well said, Palaniss."

"How, was it?"

"I assure you, it was."

"I am glad of that, Brigadier, only—"

"Yes?"

"I am uncertain what I said."

"Why, you asked what we must do."

"That is true."

"Yes, it is the answer."

"I confess myself puzzled, Brigadier."

"How, are you?"

"I give you my word, I am."

"That is all right, I have been puzzled at times."

"I am relieved to hear it."

"Shall I explain?"

"I would be pleased if you did."

"This is it, then: There are, as we have said, too many tracks and elements and directions to see how they fit together."

"And so?"

"And so we will not see how they fit together, rather we will bring them together. I believe that the best way to learn about the relationships among these people is simply to put them in the same place, and see what they do. That is to say, we are done with reflecting. It is time to act."

*How Khaavren Became Involved
with the Entertainment Industry,
and Her Majesty Permitted
the Captain, That Is to Say,
the Brigadier, to
Ask Her Certain Questions*

The first thing Khaavren did after dismissing Palaniss was to send for Dinaand, the Dzurlord, who arrived within five minutes, proving that he was always ready to respond to the brigadier's wishes, and that he was one of those with a keystone that permitted teleportation within the Imperial Palace. He entered, bowed, and, in response to Khaavren's gesture, sat.

"You summoned me, Brigadier? I presume, then, that there is sorcery to be contemplated?"

"In fact," said Khaavren, "it is not your skill in sorcery that I require on this occasion, but rather your knowledge in other areas."

"Other areas? To which other areas does the brigadier refer?"

"Music, good Dinaand."

The Dzurlord's eyes widened a little, then he smiled.

"I sometimes forget, Brigadier, how thoroughly you have studied those of us with whom you work."

"And so?"

"It is true that I spent some years as a musician, and any knowledge I happen to have acquired is at your disposal."

Khaavren knew, in fact, that the Dzurlord had been successful as an itinerant singer of medium quality and an outstanding player of the fretted vi'cello for a good score of years, and might be doing so yet had a drunk patron not been loudly disrespectful at one of his performances, the results of which had put an end to the patron's life and Dinaand's career. The brigadier, naturally, made no mention of this circumstance. Instead he said, "What made you decide to play a certain place, and not another?"

Dinaan laughed. "Why, money, of course."

"Is that all?"

"Well, not all, but certainly it was important. You perceive, I had no access to any of my family funds, and so if I wasn't paid, I didn't eat, whereas if I was paid well, I ate well."

"Yes, that is perfectly clear. But what were some of the other factors?"

The Dzurlord frowned. "It mattered if the room sounded good, and was clean. And, of course, the chance to play with particular musicians I admired was worth a great deal."

"How, was it?"

"Oh, of course! You must understand, for a musician to play with other musicians who excite and challenge him, why that is a special sort of joy. I had the honor to play with the harpist Liscreta once; a memory I shall always treasure. And on another occasion—"

"I understand, Dinaand. What is it that makes another musician desirable to play with?"

The Dzurlord frowned. "Well, he must be at least as skilled as one's self, preferably a little more skilled, so one feels challenged. And one must share similar tastes—Brigadier?"

"Yes, my friend?"

"Perhaps if you were to tell me what you are attempting to discover, I could be of more help?"

"Well, that is true."

"And so?"

"I will tell you."

"I am listening."

"This is it, then: I am setting a trap for a musician."

"Ah! A trap!"

"Yes."

"For?"

"Lady Saruchka."

"Ah, of course. I performed with her once. She is well known. Her House nearly exiled her, and her family all but disowned her."

"For playing music?"

"For playing *social* music."

"Ah, yes. Compositional music would be acceptable."

"Some in my House feel the same way," said the Dzurlord.

"And you played social music despite that?"

"Not in the least, Brigadier. Because of it."

"Ah, of course."

"So then, you wish to bring Lady Saruchka to you."

"You have understood me exactly."

Dinaand fell silent for a moment; then he said, "Yes, it shouldn't be too difficult. I know Lord Ramon represents her. We can find a good hall—say the Owl's Feet. Then we offer her Adham on lant and Dav-Hoel on fiddle, or, if they are not available, others of similar skill. From what I know of Lady Saruchka, she won't be able to resist." He frowned. "If it were me, I certainly wouldn't be able to."

"Good," said Khaavren. "How long is needed?"

"It can be set up in days, if Ramon can reach her and everyone else agrees. A good month for publicity."

"Do we need the month?"

"If it is to seem real, yes."

Khaavren sighed. "Very well."

"Shall I start working on it? That is to say, shall I visit Lord Ramon and have him put it together?"

"You are on good terms with him?"

"As good terms as it is possible to be with a musician's representative. He will be receptive to the plan, because he will see money in it. Of course, it will require us to lay down the capital for renting the hall, and to guarantee payment for the musicians."

Khaavren nodded. "You will have the authorization for the funds."

"And so?"

"Yes. The sooner begun, the sooner finished."

"Very well, Brigadier."

Dinaand took his leave, and Khaavren sat back in his chair, closed his eyes, and considered matters. He realized that he had done everything he could for the present toward solving the problem. It must be said that the brave Tiassa, though capable of exercising great patience, felt frustration when a plan was in motion but there was nothing to do but wait. Yet he had the strength to put this aside and resume his duties; after five minutes, he opened his eyes, sat up, and did so.

Over the next week, Khaavren, for the most part, busied himself with the day-to-day tasks of being Captain of the Phoenix Guards, a post with no shortage of duties. While he never let the matter of the silver tiassa get far from his thoughts, he was able to distract himself with his routine.

Every few days he would receive a report from Dinaand, describing his progress. Khaavren gave these reports the same exacting attention he gave to all reports. In the first week he learned, therefore, that matters were progressing: the hall had been secured, the other musicians had agreed, and a date had been set pending the approval of Lady Saruchka. It was at this time that he received word that Her Majesty wished to see him; as he had certain matters to discuss with the Empress, he agreed to see her in the Blue Room at once.

Being the captain, he did not require an escort—or rather, he escorted himself into the Imperial presence. He noted with the experience of an old courtier that the Orb was a pleasant light shade of green. Her Majesty (whom Khaavren noticed after the automatic observation of the Orb) was seated, wearing an informal gown of Phoenix gold.

Khaavren bowed and silently awaited his sovereign's orders.

"Well, thank you for seeing me so quickly."

"Your Majesty knows I am entirely devoted to her service."

"That is true, for you have proved it often enough."

"Your Majesty is kind to notice."

"I more than notice, I wished to especially commend your loyalty, Captain."

Khaavren bowed. "I repeat my observations on Your Majesty's kindness; but I am certain that is not all you wished to say to me."

"On the contrary, that is all I wished to say to you, Captain."

"How, that is all?"

"Entirely, Captain."

"And yet—"

"However."

"Ah, there is a however."

"Indeed there is. While I have no more to say to my captain, there are certain matters to discuss with my brigadier of the Special Tasks group."

"Well, I understand. Your Majesty must understand that between the two posts, I am sometimes confused about whose service is requested."

"I understand completely."

"I am glad Your Majesty does. So, then, how can I—that is, the brigadier of the Special Tasks group—be of service?"

"It concerns this investigation into the attack on Count Szurke."

"Your Majesty knows I am conducting an investigation."

"Yes, but it has come to my attention that this investigation has spilled over into other areas."

"Other areas, Majesty?"

"I refer to the false Jenoine invasion, which I have no doubt you recall."

"Oh, there is no question that I remember it."

"And then, Brigadier? Are these investigations running together?"

"So it would seem, Majesty."

"Well. Then I should imagine you would have questions to ask me."

"In fact, Your Majesty is perspicacious."

"Very well. That is why I wished to see you, so you could ask these questions."

"That falls out better than I had expected, Majesty, as I had hoped to bring this subject up after Your Majesty's business was complete."

"Well, you see, there is no need to wait."

"So much the better."

"Ask, then, Brigadier."

"Very well, Majesty. My first question is simple."

"It is?"

"Who was behind the false invasion?"

"Brigadier, you know who arranged it."

"Yes, Majesty. But who hired him to do it?"

"Ah, that. We never found out."

"Your pardon, Majesty, but—was an effort made to do so?"

The Empress shook her head. "No. If I had wished this to be discovered, you are the one I'd have asked—in one of your posts or the other."

Khaavren nodded as if that very thought had occurred to him. He hesitated, then said, "Your Majesty, why?"

Zerika sighed. "The Prime Minister and the Dragon

Heir appealed to me. They pointed out what it would do to the Empire if a full attack on the Jhereg were to be launched; and nothing short of such an attack would have discovered anything."

"I see," said Khaavren.

"You see," repeated Her Majesty. "But do you comprehend?"

Khaavren tilted his head. "If Your Majesty is asking if I approve, I would not do myself the honor to judge Your Majesty's decisions."

The Empress laughed—a genuine laugh, we should add, as opposed to the laugh of one intending to make a point. "I believe that you are being disingenuous, either with me or with yourself."

Khaavren started to speak, stopped, then permitted himself a smile. "Your Majesty may be right."

"So, then?"

"In this case, Majesty, I do not presume to pass judgment. I am not unaware that sometimes justice must be sacrificed to expediency."

"But you don't like it, do you, Captain?"

Khaavren stiffened. "I had thought Your Majesty was speaking to the brigadier."

Zerika laughed. "Well taken. What other questions do you have?"

"The artifact—the mysterious silver tiassa. Has Your Majesty learned any more concerning it?"

"Nothing but the rumors we heard at the time— rumors I am personally convinced were fabricated."

Khaavren nodded. "I do myself the honor to share this opinion with Your Majesty."

"That is good. What is your next question?"

Khaavren cleared his throat. "Is Your Majesty prepared for the risk that, by discovering what happened to Szurke, and tracing the silver tiassa, information will come to light that could have consequences, and require action?"

"I answered that when I gave you leave to have Special Tasks pursue the matter, Brigadier. What I wish to avoid is indiscriminate violence among the Houses. Should we learn of an individual—or several individuals—who are responsible for a crime, well, that is a different matter, is it not?"

"I do myself the honor to be in complete accord with Your Majesty."

"So much the better. What is your next question?"

"That is all, Majesty."

"How, all?"

"I can think of no others."

"You startle me."

"Do I? That is not my intention."

"Nevertheless, I expected more questions."

"Would Your Majesty condescend to tell me what questions you expected?"

"I had expected, Brigadier, that you would ask why you were never told of these things."

"Your Majesty expected that?"

"I did."

"Such a question might hint of reproach."

"It might."

Khaavren shrugged. "Majesty, it may be that the captain can be offended when it appears his sovereign does not trust him; but the brigadier knows very well that some matters must be kept between Empress and Orb—an expression I use literally in this case."

"I am answered. But do you not also wish to know if I expressed a wish to Madam the Countess that she not speak of this matter, even to you?"

Khaavren made no effort to conceal how startled he was by this question. "Your Majesty, I have no need to ask that; the Countess already told me of it."

"Ah. Well, I understand. So, there is no more you wish to ask?"

"Nothing else, Majesty. And permit me to say that I am grateful for your kindness in permitting me to put these questions."

"My lord Khaavren."

"Majesty?"

"I cannot go into detail, but Count Szurke—that is to say, Lord Taltos—performed a great service for the Empire at the time of the latest difficulties with Elde Island. In doing so, he made a bitter enemy of the Jhereg. There is nothing I can do about that. But recently he was beaten, and it is obviously not the Jhereg. There is something behind this, and it is big. I want it to be found, and the Empire protected."

"And Szurke?"

"If you can protect him as well, I would be gratified."

"I understand, Majesty. Only—"

"Yes?"

"Suppose it is not big?"

"What do you say?"

"Majesty, I am beginning to suspect that this entire matter is small, trivial, unimportant."

"If true, so much the better!"

"And?"

"Then it would be good if Szurke were protected anyway."

"Your Majesty, everything is now perfectly clear to me."

"Very good, Brigadier. That will be all, then."

Khaavren bowed deeply and took his leave of the Empress. He returned to his offices, where he caused bread and cheese and wine to be brought to him. He ate slowly as he considered what he had learned.

"Well," he said at last, speaking to the empty room, "it doesn't matter. It is Her Majesty's wish; it is therefore, to me, a command. If it weren't, I'd be holding the wrong position. Or, rather, the wrong two positions."

This settled, he put what, for another, would have been a moral dilemma out of his mind and continued with his duties.

The next day, Dinaand reported that Lady Saruchka had accepted the engagement. Khaavren replied, confirming (for the third time) the time, date, and location when the bard had promised to appear.

"That is good," observed Khaavren to himself. "Now we know where it will happen, and when it will happen. All we do not know is *what* will happen."

That night, he spent an evening quietly at home with the Countess, playing quoins-of-four, and later reading together; the Countess preferring re-tellings of folktales, while Khaavren spent time with his favorite poets of antiquity; occasionally they would read each other a passage or stanza.

At one point, the Countess said, "My lord, I know this mood you are in—a little smile that tugs at the corners of your mouth, and sometimes your eye narrows as if choosing to do so for its own reasons."

Khaavren looked up from his book and said, smiling, "Well, and what do you conclude from these statistics?"

"That you have solved a mystery, or finished the preparations for an operation, or both."

"The preparations are complete; the mystery is still to be solved."

"I have no doubt you will solve it."

"Your confidence inspires me, madam."

"So much the better."

"It will take another week to see the end of the matter, but to-morrow everything will be arranged."

"And you will achieve results."

"And be glad to have them, for this matter causes me some confusion."

"I look forward to hearing the answers, my lord."

"And I, madam," said Khaavren, "look forward to explaining them."

With that, by mutual consent, they returned to their books.

By two minutes after the ninth hour of the next morning, Pel arrived at Khaavren's office, and was admitted at once. Khaavren motioned him to sit, which he did. Pel said, "Would you be kind enough to tell me your plan for next Marketday?"

"If you wish to know, I will gladly tell you."

"Good, I am listening."

"This is it, then: I will arrive three hours before the time the musicians are expected to start, and take up a position at a wheelwright's across the street from the Owl's Feet. There I will be able to watch whoever arrives."

"And then?"

"And then, once everyone is gathered, I will go in."

"Once you are inside, what will you do?"

"I will confront those from whom I wish to get answers."

"Just you?"

"Who else is needed?"

"But, you say, confront them?"

"Yes. And, with everyone there, it will be strange if I cannot learn who is doing what, and why."

"And once you have learned?"

"I will take whatever action seems appropriate."

Pel shook his head. "This is not what I had expected, my friend."

Khaavren shrugged. "When we last spoke, it is not what I had expected either."

"And so?"

"What do you want, Pel?"

"Whatever is best for the Empire, of course."

Khaavren laughed. "I forget sometimes that you are without ambition, my lord the Prime Minister."

"I have had ambition, Khaavren, as you well know. But I have found that, having gratified it, my goal now must be to prove myself worthy of the position to which my ambition led me."

"My friend, you have never had to justify yourself to me, and we have strayed from the topic of our conversation."

"Not in the least, Khaavren."

"How, we have not?"

Pel sighed. "No, for this matter concerns the good of the Empire."

"My dear Pel, if there was something you had wished me to do, you ought to have told me what it was, then I could have done it."

"Not to do, my friend. To discover."

"It seems to me that we ought to discover what is going on, once all of those concerned are brought together."

"You think so?"

"The Horse! I hope so!"

"And yet—"

"Pel, what did you want to learn that you didn't tell me about before?"

The Yendi sighed. "There are times that I regret—but I suppose there is no point in complaining, is there?"

"None that I can see."

"My old friend, are you laughing at me?"

"Without malice, good Pel."

"I accept that, then."

"May I do myself the honor to repeat my question? What did you want to learn that you didn't tell me about?"

"Khaavren, I know that you remember the false Jenoine invasion."

"Of course."

"And, no doubt, you remember the real one of a few years before, by the Lesser Sea."

"I was not there."

"No, but someone else was."

"Sethra Lavode."

"Well, yes. But that is not who I meant."

"The Warlord?"

"She was also there, and yet—"

"Pel, do not make me guess."

"Count Szurke."

"What do you tell me?"

"I tell you that this Szurke—Lord Taltos the Jhereg—was first present at the Lesser Sea when the Jenoine attempted to break through, and then was the object of a false invasion a few years ago. And now he appears once more. I want to know what this Easterner is doing, and why he is doing it. I want to know his plans and intentions. He cannot be arrested, because he has made a friend of Her Majesty. But he is a mystery, and this disturbs me."

"And so you wished me to find out—?"

"Everything about him."

"And you didn't ask me because—?"

"Her Majesty would not have approved of the investigation, your duty would have required you to inform her, and you, my friend, have the unfortunate habit of carrying out your duty."

"It is true, I have acquired that habit."

"And so?"

"Well, I understand."

"I am gratified that you do."

"Moreover—"

"Yes?"

"I give you my word that if I learn anything of interest to you, I will not hesitate to inform you, and that I will even make what effort I can to discover as much as possible about this Easterner and his intentions."

"Thank you, Khaavren. The Empire thanks you."

"Oh, the Empire is not in the habit of thanking anyone, save now and again through one who represents it; but I will accept your gratitude with pleasure."

"You have it as a gift."

"And one I will treasure, I assure you."

Pel rose, bowed, and took his leave. Khaavren remained where he was for a moment, lost in old recollections. Then, with a shake of his head and a smile, he returned to his duties.

CHAPTER THE SIXTH

*How Events Unfolded at the
Sign of the Owl's Feet*

Khaavren, who had planned to arrive three hours early on that Marketday, was, in fact, at his post five hours before the appointed time. The post, in this case, was full of wood, wood-working equipment, and the distinctive smell of wood and the various oils and potions used to treat it—a smell which brought back pleasant associations for Khaavren from when, as a child, he had spent time with his father's carpenter, a pleasant, older Chreotha who was full of stories and was marvelously skilled with his hands.

Khaavren exchanged a few words with the wheelwright, a young Jhegaala full of new ideas that were, perhaps, not as interesting to Khaavren as they would have been to another wheelwright. Fortunately, the brigadier was not in a hurry on this occasion; he was perfectly willing to make sounds associated with interest until, at length, he was able to work the conversation around to those matters of more interest to himself—to wit, how, for a few coins, the proprietor would be willing to let Khaavren remain quietly in his shop. The proprietor, though disappointed at losing what he had hoped would be a customer, found solace in the coins. Khaavren carefully noted the expense in his note-book, and set about his task.

It was a warm day, with the enclouding so thin that shadows could be seen spreading out from buildings and walking in lockstep with passers-by. Khaavren leaned against the doorway, folded his arms, and settled in to wait. From this position, he watched the coming and going of the patrons of the Owl's Feet. He made the guess that there were more than twenty patrons there. This was not surprising, as the Owl's Feet dated back to before the Interregnum, and was known far and wide as a place with good food, better wine, and still better music. It was a two-story stone structure, marked by a sign showing the head of an owl above the feet of this bird; why it came to be called the Owl's Feet rather than the Owl's Head was something no one knew.

As Khaavren continued to watch, a group of eight arrived together, all of them in the green and white of the House of the Issola.

"Ah," said Khaavren, and permitted himself a small smile. "Her Majesty will be disappointed, and, most likely, so will Pel." This observation made, he checked to make certain his sword was loose in his scabbard, folded his arms, and resumed his vigil.

He recognized Lady Saruchka with no trouble when she arrived, some three-quarters of an hour before she was scheduled to play, which Khaavren had expected, Dinaand having told him that musicians customarily arrived early in order to prepare themselves and their instruments. At nearly the same time, two others arrived whom Khaavren guessed to be musicians, as they both carried cases that might contain instruments. Khaavren looked at them closely, because he was not unaware that these could be Jhereg, and the cases could conceal weapons. As he watched them, however, he decided that they were no more than they appeared to be.

In point of fact, an unexpected appearance by the Jhereg was his greatest worry. But Khaavren had been a Phoenix Guard too long to be easily deceived by a disguised Jhereg, and so he watched and studied. Khaavren's other worry was that he would miss the arrival of Count Szurke, should the Easterner choose to disguise himself, or to arrive by some unexpected route. In the event, he need not have worried—Khaavren recognized him at once, in the same nondescript leather garments he had affected earlier, with a light brown cloak that revealed the hilt of a sword. Szurke walked up to the door as if he had no reason in the world not to, paused, turned, nodded to Khaavren, then opened the door and entered.

How did he know I was here? was Khaavren's first thought. *Why did he want me to know he knew?* was his second. He remembered, then, what Timmer had told him about the Easterner using a pair of Jhereg to spy for him, which, he concluded, might answer the first question.

There was no point in waiting further, both because everyone had arrived, and because the musicians were scheduled to begin performing in only a very few minutes, and Khaavren knew that, however unlikely, it was possible the musicians could begin near to the time when they said they would. Khaavren waited patiently while a mule-drawn cart filled with firewood passed by, then quickly crossed the street and entered the Owl's Feet.

Khaavren waited by the door while his eyes adjusted to the dimness of the inn after the brightness of the street. The bar ran along the far end of the room; across from it, to Khaavren's left, was a small stage area raised about half a foot higher than the floor; no doubt where the performers would place themselves so they could be seen over a press of bodies and heard over a rumble of conversation. There were doors at each end of the bar, one, Khaavren knew, leading to a storage area, the other to a hallway with private rooms, and thence to another door to the outside.

When his eyes had adjusted, he glanced over the rest of the room. The Issola were all seated close to the stage, four each at two tables. They were seated in front of and beside the tables; none behind them—that is to say, they were all in good position to rise and draw in the shortest possible time. At that point, he realized that Count Szurke was, to all appearances, nowhere in the room.

Khaavren mentally shrugged. He had no doubt the Easterner would appear soon enough. It was now past the time when the musicians had been scheduled to begin, and the audience was becoming restless; it was simply a matter of waiting. He leaned against the wall near the door and waited.

Adham and Dav-Hoel were the first up; Adham

stepping onto the stage with a twirl of his lant over his head; Dav-Hoel merely stepping up, moving to the back of the stage, and fixing his gaze on the far end of the room.

Then, holding a reed-pipe, Lady Saruchka emerged, dressed in narrow pants of green and a tight-fitting white blouse. She smiled warmly at the audience as she stepped onto the stage.

And it was at this moment that the eight Issola all stood, as one, reaching for their weapons.

Khaavren wasn't certain where he came from, but, somehow, the Easterner, Count Szurke, was standing in front of the stage. A light-weight sword was in his hand, and two Jhereg were on his shoulders.

It seemed to Khaavren that it might be a reenactment, as it were, of the fight by the river.

The Issola charged.

The pair of Jhereg leapt from Szurke's shoulders, flying into the faces of two of them.

There was a flash as something left the Easterner's left hand, and one of the Issola stopped, staring down at a knife that had somehow appeared in his chest.

After that, however, it no longer resembled the battle by the river; Khaavren placed himself to the Easterner's left, his sword out and ready.

It is possible Szurke would have made some observation about this remarkable event, but, in fact, he had no time; Issola, though not, perhaps, as inclined to violence as certain others, are known to not waste time when the moment for action arises. These eight certainly did not.

That the reader may have a clear understanding of

events as they unfolded, it is absolutely necessary, at this time, to say two words about the positions of the significant individuals. (We use the qualifier "significant" to make it clear to the reader that we will not, at this time, be describing the position or action of the host or of those accidental patrons who do not figure in the calisthenics about to take place.)

So, then, as we look, the instant after the Easterner has thrown his knife, we see two of the Issola being chased about the room by Jhereg, in a scene reminiscent of some of the lower-class bawdies available for four coppers on Verendu Lane. With one of the Issola concerned—quite reasonably in the opinion of this historian—with the knife that had penetrated a full three inches into his chest, this left five Issola who were charging Count Szurke.

Or so they thought. In fact, they were facing not only Szurke, but also Khaavren, who, drawing his sword, placed himself in a guard position beside the Easterner.

Khaavren, as was his custom on such occasions, feinted toward one long enough to interfere with her attack, so that he could concentrate on the other. This opponent was an exceptionally tall woman who wielded an especially long sword to add to this advantage. Khaavren, therefore, took a step forward as he parried her attack, after which he disengaged with lightning speed and, still moving in, passed his sword through her body, leaving her stretched out full length upon the floor.

Meanwhile, the Easterner had taken a peculiar stance in which only his side appeared as a target. He emerged with another small throwing knife, though exactly where on his person it had been concealed was impossible to say, and, with a flick of his wrist, sent it underhanded in the direction of one of his enemies. Although the weapon had been thrown too weakly to do any damage, and even failed to arrive at its target point-first, it nevertheless caused him to duck, which permitted Szurke to address himself to his other opponents. He took a step backward, then, much as Khaavren had, feinted toward one while in fact concentrating on the other. This man was in the process of making a lunge at the Easterner's body—a lunge that would have had murderous effect if Szurke had remained where he was; however, not wishing to feel several inches of steel enter his vitals, he stepped lightly and quickly to the side, after which he delivered three very fast cuts with his thin blade to his opponent's sword arm, with the result that the Issola's weapon fell from his nerveless hand.

The three remaining Issola recovered their guard positions, as, in fact, did Khaavren. The two Jhereg, as if by command, returned to the Easterner's shoulders; the Issola they had been chasing took positions next to their comrades, also in guard positions. Szurke, for his part, not only did not assume a guard position, but, on the contrary, ignored his opponents entirely. Instead, he coolly turned toward the stage, bowed, and said, "My apologies for the delay in the beginning of your performance. I give you my word, I look forward to hearing your music once this little matter is disposed of."

No one spoke. In fact, there was no sound at all, save soft, constant cursing from the Issola whose arm and hand the Easterner had cut and the moans from the one Khaavren had wounded.

Khaavren, never removing his eyes from his opponents, said, "My dear Count, it is a pleasure to see you again."

"Well," said the Easterner.

"You left so quickly before that I feared the hospitality displeased you."

"In fact," said the other, "the klava left something to be desired."

"Indeed? I am concerned to hear it."

"It tasted as if it had been made with hot coffee, when, of course, the coffee must be made cold, then heated, then run through the filter."

"I had not been aware of this circumstance," said Khaavren. "And I thank you for bringing it to my attention."

"You are welcome," said Szurke laconically. "My lord Captain—or should I say Brigadier?"

"Captain," said Khaavren.

"Very good, then. My lord Captain, what should we do with these, ah, miscreants?"

"Miscreants?" said Khaavren.

"Brawlers in public places."

Khaavren chuckled. "I admit, the notion of arresting them on this charge appeals to my humor. It is less humorous, but more reasonable, to arrest them on a charge of attacking an officer of the Phoenix Guard; a charge, by the way, for which the punishment is death. However—" He paused here and looked at the four Issola who remained in guard position, weapons out. To judge by the expression on their countenances, the statistic recited by Khaavren had no effect on them whatsoever. "However," he continued, "for now, I should prefer to understand something of what this is all about." He paused, turned his head toward the stage, and said, "Lady Saruchka, might I trouble you to step forward?"

Now, the reader must understand that Lady Saruchka was not only an Issola, but, moreover, a performer; hence it should come as no surprise to the reader that her reply, when it came, was delivered in a calm, even voice with no hint of agitation. "I will do so, my lord, but I should prefer to have a sword in my hand. Alas, I left mine in the pacing room."

"But, my lady, if you had the sword, upon whom would you turn it?"

"Why, upon them, my lord. That is to say, my mother's brother, his son, his daughter, and her husband."

"As I had suspected," murmured Khaavren.

The Easterner, who was close enough to Khaavren to hear, said, "As I had suspected you suspected."

"Well," said Khaavren. "Would you care to explain matters to me?"

"It is not my place to do so. Perhaps Lady Saruchka would, if you asked."

The bard, hearing this, said, "Do you think I should, Vlad?"

"If you wish, Sara. It is entirely your decision."

"Perhaps I will, then."

As she finished speaking, she had placed herself next to Khaavren, and, holding her reed-pipe as if it were a weapon, she stared at the five Issola. "Or," she added, "you could ask them. Hearing their opinion cannot fail to be amusing."

Khaavren shrugged and, addressing the Issola whose arm had been wounded, said, "Would you care to offer an explanation?"

The Issola, who was ignoring the blood that continued to fall from his arm, said coolly, "My lord, what is it you wish to know?"

"In the first place, your name."

"I am Dury."

"Thank you, Lord Dury. Now, if you would be so kind as to explain, why did you attack this Easterner?"

"Why, what else could we do when he has dishonored our House and our family? You perceive, my lord, one cannot challenge an Easterner to a duel."

"Oh, I understand that well enough."

As this exchange took place, Khaavren observed a glance exchanged between the Easterner and the bard.

Khaavren cleared his throat. "Please forgive the brusqueness of an old soldier," he said. "But I will to be clear about this. The Easterner and the bard are lovers, are they not?"

"Yes," said Dury, at the same time the Easterner and the bard said, "No."

"But," added Szurke, "I would very much like to be."

"And I," added Saruchka, "am very nearly ready to consider it, out of annoyance if for no other reason."

"How, you are not?" said Dury.

"I answered the captain, my lord uncle," said Saruchka. "Had you asked, I would have declined to answer. With this in mind, I am certain you can understand my reluctance to give reassurances."

"And yet," said Dury, on whose face a certain degree of consternation was now visible, "it has seemed to me that the two of you have been seen together, and have met secretly, and—"

"Good my lord uncle," said Saruchka, "if our meetings were secret, well, then we did not want them known. If we did not want them known, what would make you think I will now explain them?"

"For my part," said Szurke, "I would be curious to hear the explanation from our brave captain."

"From me?" said Khaavren.

"Why not?"

"You believe I arrived already understanding the circumstances that led us all here?"

"You pretend you do not?" asked the Easterner with a smile.

"Well, perhaps I have certain guesses."

"I would admire to hear them."

"Shall I tell you, then?"

"If you would. You perceive, we are all listening."

"Then, if you insist—"

"To be sure, I do."

"—I will explain."

"Well?"

"This is it, then: The Lady Saruchka, who had already earned the ire of her family by playing social music, gave the appearance of having—how may I say this? 'Taken up' is I believe the expression, with an Easterner. That, in the event, they were wrong did not stop them from attempting to deliver a beating to the upstart Easterner. The Easterner, unaware of the reason behind the attack, or, indeed, the nature of it, assumed his life was in danger and reacted accordingly. This led to the death of—who, exactly?"

"My brother, Amlun," said Dury.

"Amlun is dead?" said the bard.

"Yes," said Dury.

"I'm sorry to hear it," said Saruchka. "Vlad, that wasn't nice."

"Sorry," said the Easterner.

"What remains to be answered," said Khaavren, "is, if you two were not romantically involved, just what were you doing together?"

"That is a good question," agreed Szurke.

"I'm glad you think so," said Khaavren.

"Another good question is, whatever became of the mysterious artifact called the silver tiassa?"

"What is that?" asked Dury.

"I had expected that you wouldn't know," said Khaavren.

"Well, I am pleased to meet your expectations, but what is it?"

"No, no," said Khaavren. "It is not for you to ask questions. It is for you to answer them, at least until I have decided what to do with you."

"It is up to you, of course, but may I suggest that finding us a physicker might not be unreasonable?"

"Cha," said Khaavren. "None of you are hurt badly."

"As you say," said Dury.

Khaavren, then, turned to Lady Saruchka and said, "What is your opinion, my lady? Should I arrest them?"

She laughed. "Aside from the amusement value, no. I imagine they are sufficiently chastised by having been defeated, twice, by an Easterner."

Dury kept his eyes facing straight ahead, and

made no response; but it is undeniable that his face reddened somewhat.

"Very well, my lady. I will do as you say. Naturally, the Empire has no interest in matters within your family, or between you and your House."

"I am pleased to hear it, my lord Captain."

Khaavren then turned to Dury, bowed, and said, "You may go."

For an instant, the Issola looked as if he might say something; then it looked as if he wished to do something; but in the end he simply made a deep courtesy and, enlisting the help of the others, assisted the wounded out the door.

When they had left, Khaavren turned toward Saruchka and said, "Now, then. Will you tell me of the silver tiassa?"

"I confess myself astonished, Captain, that you know so much of what has transpired, and yet have no guess about this artifact for which you have been looking for so long."

"But, how do you know we've been looking for it?"

"Vlad told me."

Khaavren turned his eyes to the Easterner, who said, "I could not imagine the Empire being so concerned about the health of one poor Easterner—Imperial title or none—as to devote this much effort to the search."

"And you reached this conclusion when, my lord?"

"When the concert was announced. It was obvious that it was only scheduled in order to bring us all together."

"And yet, you came anyway?"

"You perceive, Captain, that I am hardly going to pass up an opportunity to see Sara."

"Indeed? Then, the Lord Dury was not entirely wrong."

"Oh, he was perfectly right, if my wishes were the only consideration. But perfectly wrong when Lady Saruchka's wishes are taken into account."

"That is not necessarily true, Lord Taltos," said Sara with a smirk.

The Easterner coughed, and appeared to be uncertain about where he was looking. One of the Jhereg on his shoulders began to bob its head up and down furiously, almost as if it were laughing. Khaavren, other than a certain disgust at what was being implied, had little interest in the matter. He said, "In any case, it was not dalliance that brought the two of you together two months ago, nor that caused the lady to retrieve your sword—which sword, I perceive, she has returned to you."

"She was kind enough to do so," said the Easterner, who appeared to have recovered somewhat, although his face was now as red as Dury's had been.

"So then," said Khaavren. "The questions remain— what is the nature of the association between you, and where is the silver tiassa?"

"As to the last," said Saruchka, "I can tell you that it is where it is needed."

"The answer," said Khaavren, "is not satisfactory."

"I am concerned to hear it," said Saruchka.

"As am I," said Szurke.

"You must understand," said Khaavren, in whom a certain heat was beginning to rise, "that the Empire has invested no small amount of time and effort in this matter."

"Why?" said the Easterner.

"What do you ask me?"

"Why? What is the importance or significance of this object to the Empire?"

"As to that—"

"Well?"

"It is not my place to say."

"That is right," said Szurke. "Only—"

"Yes?"

"Then it is not my place to answer your questions."

"I understand, my lord. But if you do not—"

"Yes, if I do not?"

"I shall be forced to continue my inquiries."

"Well."

"And it is not impossible that these inquiries will involve finding you in order to ask you more questions."

"Well."

"And if I must hunt you, I can make no guarantee that others who might be looking for you will not also discover where you are."

"Ah. I see." A smile tugged at the corners of the Easterner's mouth. "You make a strong argument, Captain."

"And then?"

"You seem determined to discover what was behind all of this."

"And if I am?"

"It seems odd."

"And why would it seem odd?"

"Because you already know."

"You think so?"

"I am convinced of it."

"What makes you think so?"

"Because you are brigadier of the Special Tasks group."

"And if I am?"

"You could not have become involved in this without investigating me. I make no doubt that you know nearly as much about me as the Jhereg."

"I do not deny what you say."

"Ensign Timmer works for you."

"And if she does?"

"She would have told you what she knows as well. With all of this information, and with a mind like yours, you cannot have failed to discover the answer."

"That is possible," said Khaavren. "Nevertheless, I would prefer to hear it from you."

"If you wish," said Szurke. "The boy has it."

Khaavren nodded. "As I had thought."

"So then, what will you tell Her Majesty?"

"Yes. I am considering that very question. Tell me, do you know what it does?"

"I do not actually *know*, my lord. I have suspicions."

"And those are?"

"My lord, to be inspired, well, that is to find the moment when the conscious mind comes together with parts that are unconscious. Is that not true?"

"You speak in generalities."

"And if I do?"

"I prefer specifics."

The Easterner shook his head. "I've already said enough. Too much."

"You're afraid I'll attempt to take it?"

"If Her Majesty orders you—"

"I doubt she would do that."

"In any case, I have said all I intend to say on the subject."

Khaavren bowed slightly to signify that he understood. "Then I have no more business here," he said.

"Then I will bid you farewell, Captain, for I do have business here."

"Ah, have you?"

"Indeed. I am going to listen to music."

With that, Szurke sat down in the nearest chair. Lady Saruchka, smiling at him, turned and stepped back onto the stage, where the other musicians had been waiting patiently as unimportant matters such as life and death were settled.

Khaavren turned his back on the Easterner and the bard and took himself back onto the streets of Adrilankha, where his duty lay.

EPILOGUE

We met outdoors, beneath a low grass-covered hill. There were a few pillartrees here and there around us, but mostly we were in the open. We sat on the grass and said our various hellos in our various ways.

"How are you feeling?" said Sara.

"I don't know," said the boy. "Better, I think."

"You're sounding better," I said. "A lot better. Do you still have dreams?"

He nodded. "Not as often, though." He looked down at the object in his hand. "How does it work?"

"I don't exactly know," I said. "A god made it, that's all I can tell you."

"I don't either," said Sara. "I'm curious, though. Maybe when you don't need it anymore, I'll borrow it for a while and see what I can figure out."

I shrugged. "For now, if it helps—"

"*Someone's coming, Boss. A rider, just behind the hill.*"

I stood up. My hand went to Lady Teldra's hilt, but I didn't draw.

"What is it, Vlad?" Sara was standing, too, her hand on her weapon.

"I don't know."

"Just one? No effort at concealment?"

"Just one. Colors of the Tiassa. Oh, it's—"

"Of course it is. I should have guessed."

"Oh," said Sara, as he appeared over the top of the hill. "I should have guessed."

Lord Khaavren dismounted when he reached us, wrapped the reins around his hand, and bowed.

"What a pleasant surprise," I told him.

"I've no doubt," he said dryly. "Lady Saruchka, a pleasure to see you again. And what's your name, boy?"

Savn looked fearfully at him, but didn't speak.

"His name is Savn," I said. "And if you call him boy again, I'll—"

"You'll what?"

I smiled. "Ask you not to. How did you find us?"

"You remember Ensign Timmer, of course."

"She followed me?"

"Don't be absurd. She followed the bard."

Sara turned to me. "I could be a danger to you, if the Jhereg—"

"Life is full of danger."

"Right, Boss. And you're—"

"Shut up, Loiosh."

Khaavren said, "Is the artifact helping him?"

"Seems to be," I said. "How did you put it together?"

"From Timmer."

"I should have killed her while I had the chance."

"That would have been a mistake."

"I suppose. Why did you follow me here?"

"To find out if my guesses were right."

"And they are."

"Yes."

"How satisfying that must be."

"Yes. It will provide endless hours of pleasure contemplating it in my old age."

"My lord Khaavren, are you being sarcastic?"

"I have a dispensation from Her Majesty."

I couldn't help but laugh, which made me feel like he'd scored a point. "Well, then. You've found what you wanted, now—"

"May I see it?" I looked at Sara, who looked at Savn, then back at me. She shrugged.

"All right," I said. "Savn, show Lord Khaavren the tiassa."

The boy held it out. Khaavren stood over him, then knelt and studied it close-up. "It really is quite remarkable," he said at last.

"Yes," I said.

"What exactly does it do?"

"We don't exactly know. But I'm starting to suspect that it has its own plans."

"It went through everything just because it wanted to get to this Teckla boy?"

I shrugged. "Any point in a process looks like the process was leading up to it if that's as far as you've gotten."

"Pardon?"

"I said, any point . . . never mind. No, I don't think that was its goal. I don't know its goal. I'm just starting to suspect it has one."

"But, what does it *do*?"

"You're asking me?"

"Yes."

"All right." I considered. "As far as I can tell—just guessing—it unites the conscious mind with the unconscious. Sometimes, and in some ways, and under some conditions."

He frowned, studied the tiassa some more, then stood. "This is beyond the knowledge of a simple soldier."

"I'll be sure not to talk about it to a simple soldier, should I meet one."

"My lord Szurke, are you trying to antagonize me?"

"I'm not sure. Probably."

"I am not unaware of what you did for my son. Are you unaware of what my wife did for you?"

That stopped me. After what seemed like a long time, I said, "What are you talking about?"

He shrugged. "Ask your wife." Then he said, "Well. You've had that all along?" He drew and stepped back. "Use it, then, if you're going to."

I stared at Lady Teldra, not entirely sure how she had come into my hand.

"Vlad," said Sara.

I shook my head, took a deep breath, let it out, and re-sheathed Lady Teldra. "I don't know what—"

"Think nothing of it," said Khaavren, returning his sword to his sheath. "I shouldn't have been so abrupt; my apologies."

"What do you mean about asking my wife?"

"What I said. I'm sorry, Lord Szurke. It wouldn't be right for me to say any more than that."

I felt a hand on my arm, and Sara was standing next to me. I looked at Savn; he was pale and his eyes were wide.

"Let's all sit down," I said, and set the example.

Sara sat on the grass next to me, with that breathtaking grace; Savn was still sitting. The Tiassa said, "Not me. I've found out what I needed; I'll leave you in peace."

"What did you find out?" I said.

"I'll have to get back to you on that," he said.

Then he mounted his horse, turned, and rode away. I turned my attention back to Savn. I took Sara's hand, and she didn't pull it away.

TOR

Voted

**#1 Science Fiction Publisher
More Than 25 Years in a Row**

by the *Locus* Readers' Poll

———•———

Please join us at the website below
for more information about this
author and other science fiction,
fantasy, and horror selections, and to
sign up for our monthly newsletter!

TOR

www.tor-forge.com